CLEMENTINE
AND
DANNY
SAVE THE WORLD
(and each other)

CLEMENTINE
AND
DANNY
SAVE THE WORLD

(and each other)

LIVIA BLACKBURNE

Quill Tree Books
An Imprint of HarperCollinsPublishers

Quill Tree Books is an imprint of HarperCollins Publishers.

Clementine and Danny Save the World (and Each Other)
Copyright © 2023 by HarperCollins Publishers
All rights reserved. Printed in the United States of America.
No part of this book may be used or reproduced in any manner whatsoever
without written permission except in the case of brief quotations embodied
in critical articles and reviews. For information address HarperCollins
Children's Books, a division of HarperCollins Publishers, 195 Broadway,
New York, NY 10007.
www.epicreads.com

Library of Congress Control Number: 2022951830
ISBN 978-0-06-322989-1

Typography by Kathy H. Lam
23 24 25 26 27 LBC 5 4 3 2 1

First Edition

TO DIASPORA COMMUNITIES
AROUND THE WORLD
AND THOSE WHO INVEST IN THEM

CHAPTER ONE

CLEMENTINE

I LIKE TO MATCH DIFFERENT VARIETIES OF TEA TO different parts of my creative process.

Chrysanthemum is for brainstorming. For effervescent flights of fancy and flowery, optimistic tendrils of thought. Green tea is early-morning focus, for those times you wake up with an idea that won't wait, and so you pull on a sweater over your pajamas and type as fast as you can before the inspiration leaves you. Oolong is for productive afternoons. You have your idea, but your energy's flagging, and you need that shot of mellow warmth to pull you through. And Pu'er—rich, aged Pu'er—isn't for working at all. It's for relaxing, sipping memories, and steeping in friendship.

Right now, it's an oolong type of afternoon. I'm alone with my laptop in a cozy café corner, sipping a piping-hot mug. These leaves are on their third steep now, and their flavor has sweetened and become fruitier. Really, this tea's some of the best I've tasted, and I drink a lot of tea these days, probably more than my parents need to know about. An occupational hazard of tea blogging, I guess, but this stuff is supposed to be good for you, right? Maybe forty-year-old me will thank eighteen-year-old me for all the antioxidants I'm currently packing into my system.

Auntie Chen, the laobanniang, arranges this and that behind the counter. She catches me watching and smiles.

"How's the tea?" she asks in Cantonese-accented Mandarin.

"Hen hao!" I suppress a cringe at the sound of my voice. My accent is bad enough to make a panda cry. As 1.5-generation immigrants who came over in their early teens, my parents did their dutiful best to pass on their mother tongue to me. But Chinese school was always so early on Saturday mornings, and frankly, my parents' English is so good that I simply didn't need to work that hard at my Chinese. So here I am now, an eighteen-year-old Chinese American whose Mandarin sounds like lines spoken by the token white people who show up in old Chinese dramas. You know, the suave but linguistically imperfect white guy who tries to steal the heroine from her upstanding Chinese boyfriend.

I make up for my cultural inadequacy with a winning smile, and Auntie Chen's eyes crinkle in response. Better a customer with bad Chinese than no customers at all, I guess. Sadly, the latter scenario isn't all that unlikely around here. I look around at the empty tables, the door with the bell that's rung only once since I came in. The only other person here is a college student with muddy-blond hair and an Adam's apple that bobs in time to the indie rock coming out of his AirPods.

It's too bad this café doesn't get more business, because the pork chop here is always perfectly crispy, the oolong is fantastic, and Auntie Chen is so sweet. But I get it. The furniture is old, and the menu is scattered across three walls on bright pink paper with minimal English translation. And the continuous loop of old Chinese ballads from the even more ancient sound system can be trying even for those of us with grandparents who adore that stuff. I like it here, but the average customer looking for an accessible meal will probably find other places to go.

Anyways, I'm writing a tea review this afternoon, but not of this place's selection. I'm far too self-conscious to write a review while I'm at the restaurant itself, so I usually take notes and go somewhere else for the actual drafting. I tap my keyboard lightly and scroll to the top of what I've written.

Coming to Zucun Dimsum Palace is like visiting your Asian grandparents for afternoon tea. Antique furniture and wall hangings exude an old Chinatown charm. Service is also old-school. Don't expect hipster baristas or unicorn foam art on your latte. The auntie taking your order is just as likely to scold you on your choice of beverage as she is to approve of it. If you want something refilled or cleared away, gird your loins and be ready to make aggressive eye contact. Those who've perfected their tractor-beam gaze will be richly rewarded.

Is the tea worth it? In a word, yes. The Pu'er, directly imported from China, is well aged and fruity, of a quality that's hard to find even in Chinatown. And the pots of steamy, fragrant chrysanthemum are sure to stir up fond dim sum memories.

Zucun is a good dim sum shop that serves fantastic tea. But here's the thing. It's the 21st century, and competition from chain stores is fierce. Shops can't really survive on good tea, or even fantastic tea, anymore. Tragically we see this reality in the decreased numbers at most of these old-school establishments. It may be time to embrace the future, and I have a few suggestions.

1. Ambience. First impressions matter, and customers want a peaceful retreat, not their grandmother's cluttered living room. Yes, it's ultimately about the food, but it wouldn't hurt to decorate a little. Maybe swap out decorations that are too old to know what an animated GIF is? Fixing up the chinglish menus would go a long way as well.

2. Advertising. Social media is free, easy, and entertaining. These days, you don't have to go far to sniff out a café that's built a strong online following off its fun, fragrant content. Leveraging social media to turn your customers into community is what keeps them coming back.

3. Experiment with new offerings. Tradition is important, but there's nothing wrong with a little selective innovation. Why not try some iced tea? Or funky fusion snacks? Expand your selection, expand your customer base.

All in all, I have every confidence that mom-and-pop shops can survive and thrive in the 21st century. They just need to adapt.

I feel sheepish as I finish. Even though I'm not writing about this restaurant I'm currently in, I might as well be, and it feels like I'm talking about Auntie Chen behind her back. After one last proofread, I hit publish and close my laptop.

"Finished working?" Adam's Apple Guy has taken out his earbuds. The bass notes from his indie rock sound tinny against the backdrop of Chinese ballads.

I groan and twist the kinks from my back. "Finally."

"Are you Chinese?" He scans my face as if *Beijing* might be tattooed in fine print on my forehead.

It's never a great sign when a strange white guy starts a conversation by asking your ethnicity, but I give him the benefit of the doubt. Maybe he's genuinely curious. "My parents are from Taiwan. I was born here."

"Ah." His face lights up. "My last girlfriend was Korean." Uh-oh.

Maybe he doesn't see the spikes extending out of my skin, 'cause he keeps on talking. "Yeah, she was beautiful. Long black hair down to her waist. Dudes used to walk into walls when she passed by. And she had big eyes for an Asian chick. Double eyelids, like you. She swore she didn't get plastic surgery, but I was never too sure. I bet yours are natural, though, right?"

Ew.

Unbelievably, the guy's looking at me as if he expects me to be flattered. Instead, he gets the full force of my death glare.

He falters. "So, uh . . . What are you writing?"

I yank my laptop case shut. "A blog post."

Bless his heart, he keeps talking. "What's it about?"

"Men who exotify Asian women, and the sexual inadequacies motivating their racist fetishes."

I don't wait to see whether my words percolate into his brain. Instead, I throw my backpack over my shoulder, say bye to Auntie Chen, and duck out the door. Through the window, I see the guy put his earbuds back in, and I'm relieved he doesn't come out. With one last look over my shoulder, I start off toward home.

If anything can cheer me up, it's walking home in the late afternoon when Chinatown's streets fill up. It's a cool Southern California evening, good for washing off slimy encounters. I pass by a tourist group snapping pictures of the Chinatown Gate and a toddler throwing a tantrum under a bank with swooping old-China-style roofs. As I pass a bakery, its automatic door slides open and the smell of freshly baked egg tarts wafts out. I'm a block from my house when my phone buzzes. Reflexively, I glance at the notification.

Nikegirl117 has posted a comment on Zucun . . .

The screen name puts a smile on my face. Adenike's my assistant editor at the paper, and she's always one of the first to comment. By the time I wave to the doorman of my apartment building and take the elevator up to our fourth-floor condo, my phone's buzzed several more times.

Mom's home already, having swapped her journalist power suit for yoga pants and a tank top. Her black hair is tied back in a hair clip, and she's tossing Chinese sausage into our ancient Tatung rice cooker.

Rice cooker meal. Must be on deadline.

"Hi, sweetie," she says, juggling her attention between her phone, a fistful of baby bok choy, and me. "How was your day?"

"Not bad. How's your investigation?"

"I finally pinned down a former staffer for an off-the-record interview. It was quite enlightening."

Mom's been digging into a City Hall corruption case for the past few months. She's written for the *Jasper City Times* since I was born, but in the years since my sister, Claudia, left for college and I got old enough to navigate our neighborhood by myself, Mom's been on fire, churning out one groundbreaking piece after the next.

"Where's Dad?"

"Downtown concert hall."

Right, the Jasper City Philharmonic is unveiling their new concert series tonight. He'll be out late.

Anyone who's seen my mom's Pulitzer or my dad's Entertainment Journalism Awards isn't surprised at all to learn that I'm editor in chief of our school paper. I guess I didn't fall very far from the tree. It's a lot to live up to, though. When your mom's exposing corrupt politicians every week, and your dad's on a first-name basis with Yo-Yo Ma, it's hard to feel like your center spread about whether your school mascot could beat Iron Man in a cage fight is worthwhile journalism. (I wrote that one after losing a bet with the sports editor, and it got the biggest reaction out of all my articles last year. By far.)

My phone buzzes again. This time, the notification delivers a jolt of adrenaline.

Bobaboy888 has left a comment on . . .

I'd never admit it, but the mere sight of Bobaboy's handle makes my hair stand on end. I wonder what his complaint will be this time. Am I hopelessly out of touch? A tool of corporate America? Or perhaps I simply have trash taste in tea. I'm already going back through my blog post, trying to figure out what he'll nitpick this time.

"Does that sound all right with you?" asks Mom.

I snap out of my mental stress party. "Sorry, I was distracted. What did you say?"

Mom rolls her eyes and waves me toward my room. "Go on. Get it out of your system. No phone at dinnertime, though."

I smile sheepishly. "Thanks." The good thing about having parents who are on their phones 24/7 is that they can't really give you grief about being on yours.

My bedroom is small, but after eighteen years I've got it exactly the way I like it. My bed's in the corner, with periwinkle sheets neatly tucked in. Opposite it is my desk, with space for my laptop, a pencil holder with multicolored gel pens and one prized fountain pen, plus a blue retro desk lamp. My window looks out onto the Cantonese seafood restaurant across the street. When I'm bored, I watch the waiters fishing lobsters out of the window tanks. One time, a crab slipped its rubber band handcuffs and pinched the waitress on the thumb. I swear I could hear her scream through my window. The whole thing inspired an investigative series on the hidden perils of summer jobs.

I carefully plug in my laptop and take out my bullet journal. For tonight, I have calculus homework and outlining for an English paper. Shouldn't take too long, but I won't be able to concentrate on it unless I drop by my blog first. At least, that's what I tell myself.

So I sign on. The dashboard that greets me already has new comments spilling past the bottom of my monitor. I hold my breath and do a quick scan down the side. All friendly names on this screen. Always better to start in friendly territory.

First comment is from Nikegirl117.

Nikegirl117 (4:45pm): Insightful and intelligent as ever. And you're so right about Chinatown decorations. Just move past the seventies, can we? By the way, can't wait till you see my new magnum opus.

I grin at my screen. By "magnum opus," Adenike probably means she's finished the feature article on nontraditional pets that she pitched last week. I type a quick reply.

Hibiscus (5:32pm): Love you Nikegirl! <3 and I can't wait to see it too!

A few other regulars have commented. Chrysanthemum-Dreams shares a recipe for iced tea. TapiocaQueen once again finds a way to dunk on Starbucks without actually saying Starbucks. I type quick, friendly replies to each of them. It takes a lot of time to respond to everyone, but it helps build the blog community in a time when everyone's moving on to the newest social network. In the next thread, CantoCheese and TPopStar are arguing about the TeaTok meme where baristas blow the steam off a cup of tea to the accompaniment of "I'm Too Sexy." I leave a laughing face.

That's it for this screen. Bobaboy's comment can't be too much farther down. My stomach tightens in anticipation. Sure enough, his screen name pops into view with the next press of the page down button. Well, I can't avoid him forever.

I take a deep breath and read.

CHAPTER TWO

DANNY

AUNTIE LIN IS WAITING FOR HER WINNING TILE. I can tell because she has this way of tensing up and pretending to be relaxed at the same time. Every couple minutes, she starts tapping her finger on the table, only to catch herself and stop again.

Auntie Lin doesn't have all that many tells. She's about as serious a mahjong player as they come—the kind that doesn't even sort the tiles in front of her on the off chance her opponents might gain some intel from position alone. She's the type of player who doesn't do small talk except between rounds, and she gets grumpy if anything changes the winds of luck. One time, when I was seven, Uncle Howng had me sub in for him while he went to the bathroom. I'm sure he expected to lose that hand. I mean, I was seven. But the mahjong gods must have been bored that day, because I won a huge jackpot. Auntie Lin was so pissed that for an entire week, she chased me away from the mahjong table any time I got close. Apparently I was "ruining her luck." I couldn't get too upset, though, because she still squeezed candy into my palm every day before she left—the nougat wrapped in rice paper that she knew I loved.

All this is to say, I've been watching Auntie Lin play for a long time, and I know for a fact that she's about to win big.

Finally, she cackles, using her ruler to flip her mahjong tiles flat on the table. "Hu le," she crows while the others howl in protest.

"Again?" asks Uncle Tony.

Auntie Lin dusts off her sleeves. The gemstone rings on her fingers glint like her eyes. "If you don't want a serious game, don't come to play."

As they tear everything down and mix the tiles, I rush in with my tray and a new pot of tea, refilling everyone's cups and clearing a plate of watermelon-seed shells.

"Thank you, Danny!" says Auntie Lin, patting my arm. My eardrums, calloused from years of hanging around old Chinese folks, stand strong against her considerable volume. Auntie Lin always talks as if she's addressing the entire room. "You're always so attentive."

I never really know what to do when Asian elders praise you. The correct response probably involves falling to the floor and listing out all my faults one after the other until I've left no doubt in anyone's mind that I'm the least deserving recipient of praise that has ever groveled on this piece of earth. But then I'd spill the tea, so I just bow my head with an awkward smile.

"Danny Mok is such a nice boy," Auntie Esther chimes in.

Whereas Auntie Lin is loud and brash, the refined, silver-haired Auntie Esther reminds me of a Chinese Julie Andrews. She even has that old-world accent. "Tell me, do have a special lady yet?"

For a brief moment, I wonder if the real Julie Andrews would use the term "special lady." And then I wonder if I can avoid answering the question by pulling my head inside my apron. When I look up, I see all four uncles and aunties blinking curiously at me like a flock of septuagenarian seagulls.

"No," I mumble, feeling my face flush red. "No girlfriend."

"No girlfriend?" By the outrage in Auntie Lin's voice, you'd think I just told her that Szechuan hot pot was superior to Cantonese seafood. "But you're such a handsome boy!" She pinches my bicep—ouch. "And so strong!"

Okay, time for an exit strategy. "It's just that I'm so busy, Auntie Lin." When her eyes narrow skeptically, I add the clincher. "They give us so much homework these days."

"Ah!" Uncle Tony, who'd been cracking watermelon seeds on his still-good back teeth, raises his finger like Einstein discovering a new formula. "This boy has his head on right. Get your grades up. Get a job. Make lots of money. And then all the girls will come."

Growing up at Fragrant Leaves has bestowed me with the ability to exit quickly while holding a tray stacked high with dirty dishes. I make full use of that superpower now.

Once safely behind the counter, I duck through the door to the kitchen and unload the dishes into the sink. Other than the mahjong players, our only other customers are two older businessmen slowly nursing a pot of jasmine over an intense discussion of quarterly reports. I think I have time to hang out in back for a little bit.

Dad's in the office. His chair faces away from the door, so I can only see the spreadsheet on his computer screen and the gleam of his bald spot. He has his hand on the mouse, but he's not moving it or typing.

"Hey Dad, I'm going to do some homework, okay?"

Dad doesn't move. I think I might have heard a grunt in reply, but it's hard to tell over the clink of mahjong tiles in the next room. It's what I usually get from him these days, though he wasn't always like this. I remember, when I was younger, how he'd make his rounds in the dining room, chatting up the regulars. I could pinpoint where he was by following the raucous laughs that erupted around him. But time passed. The neighborhood changed. Our regulars started moving out as their rents increased, and we weren't fancy enough for the people who replaced them. We cut down our staff, and it seemed that with our shrinking customer base, Dad shrank too. He used to be the big-ideas guy in the family. He'd make all these charts, spreadsheets, and plans for where he wanted the restaurant to be in five years or ten. Nowadays, he still spends all his time looking at spreadsheets, but it just puts him into a funk.

I try again. "Hey Dad, do you think you could check on the customers in a bit?"

No answer. I guess I'll just keep an eye on the clock.

The tea shop's kitchen has an eight-burner stove, an ancient dishwasher that clinks at three different pitches, multiple pantry shelves, and two giant hot-water dispensers. Between all the industrial-strength equipment, my mom managed to squeeze one tiny table for kindergarten me to work on my letter worksheets. Over the years, the table's been infused with an ever-present cloud of tea essence and steam, which on good days makes me nostalgic, and on bad days makes me want to give it a good scrubbing. Nowadays, its wood veneer has faded spots from where my elbows have rested over a dozen years, and my ancient computer tower sits underneath. It's not the most comfortable study nook, but I make do. Once, after my twelfth birthday, I gathered up the courage to ask my parents if I could go home after school instead of hanging out at the restaurant. The "no" I received was resounding enough that I never asked again.

I plop down in my chair. I have a history paper due tomorrow on the role of trade in Western imperialism. You'd think I'd be interested, since there's a lot of tea involved, but I kind of drifted off during the lectures. I wonder if I can make myself seem smarter by waxing eloquent about the Silk Road. Or is that from a different time period?

As my computer boots up, I scroll through some time-wasting websites on my phone. There are a few new posts on the Jasper City Chinatown subcity on Linktropolis, a site where people post their favorite links and news for discussion. I'm scrolling past some mouthwatering pictures of street-vendor-grandma food when I glimpse a link to *Babble Tea*'s newest post. Hibiscus is one of the few remaining tea bloggers in this age of social media, and she's always saying the most out of touch things. What else can you expect, I guess, from someone who un-ironically calls herself Hibiscus? My finger hovers over the link. I can't stand her, but unfortunately, hate-reading cringeworthy blog posts is my kryptonite.

The website loads. As always, there's a faux artsy photo of a pot of tea surrounded by fake flowers and candles. She's put on some kind of filter so that the entire image looks overexposed and whitewashed.

Whitewashing. One of her main talents.

Hibiscus posts on general Chinatown issues, but her mainstay is reviewing local teahouses. I always tense up when I see a new review, because I never know if it's going to be about us. She did review us once, way back in the day, and proclaimed that we needed to update our background music. (Cue eye roll.) Maybe that'll be our one and only brush with Hibiscus's hot takes, but she does do repeat visits. Granted, I'd take a moldy orange's opinion as more authoritative than hers, but her audience is pretty big these days, and it'd be annoying to be skewered in front of so many people.

I skim the review. It's classic Hibiscus—pretending to respect culture and tradition while basically throwing it all under the bus, asking mom-and-pop shops to turn into avant-garde influencers and hashtag their way into the twenty-first century. As if being #blessed would really do anything for our bottom line.

My fingers twitch with the urge to type something back, but it's been a while since I checked on the customers. I take a quick glance toward the door. Well, maybe I have time for a quick reply. Okay, how to say this?

Serious question, Hibiscus: Do you even live in the real world, or are you some kind of AI-generated blogbot? I'd kind of assumed that a computer program would take better photos, but I'm really beginning to wonder.

I can't believe you hang your community-building hopes on social media, as if a bunch of unemployed influencers with matching goatees are going to turn us into some kind of fifties sitcom paradise. Do you really want our community spaces to become Instagram destinations where people snap humblebrag selfies before running off to the next pop-up museum? Real community isn't about fancy filters. It's about people who come together over decades, building ties and living life together. You can't get that through #afternoontea.

And really, iced tea at a Chinese tea shop? How about we come up with a mocha iced oolong cinnamon latte, just for you?

I read my comment over a few times, trying to think of more ingredients to add to that latte. But then the back door opens and Mom comes in, angling herself sideways to fit through with all the bags she's carrying. She's in full Asian-mom getup—loose-fitting flea market blouse and cropped pants, trusty errand-running visor with extra-long sun-blocking brim.

She says a few words to Dad through the office door. I don't hear a response, and a flash of worry crosses Mom's face. I wonder if that's how I looked when I tried to talk to Dad earlier. The flash disappears quickly, though. Over the past few years, as Dad slowed down, Mom sped up, moving from one thing to the next as if she might outrun whatever it is that drained Dad. She's always on her feet, even when eating. Which reminds me, I didn't see her favorite lunch plate in the dirty or newly washed dish pile today, which means she probably skipped lunch.

Mom dumps her bags by the cabinets before taking off her visor. "Danny! How's school?"

"Okay," I say.

Mom is looking through the door, checking to see if everybody's cups are full. Then she glances at the dishes piled in the sink. "Aiya!"

"I'll do them," I say.

Mom waves her hand, switching to rapid-fire Cantonese. "No, no. Do your homework. I'll do them after I go pick up the—" She looks at the clock on the wall and smacks her forehead. "Five thirty already? When does DHL close? They left us a slip that said they couldn't deliver a package. I have to go get it before it gets rerouted back to China. It's probably that specialty Pu'er we've been expecting." She hesitates, looking between the sink and the dining room. A few strands of her shoulder-length hair stick up from when she yanked off her visor. "Put the yogurt drinks in the fridge. I'll be right—"

I push my chair back. "I'll get the package. You stay here. Auntie Lin says she's been missing you."

One of Mom's grocery bags falls over, and she reaches over to straighten it only to have it fall over as soon as she lets go. "No, no, you have homework."

"I don't have that much tonight. I was just wasting time online anyways." Well, that second part is true, at least. But from the looks of Mom, she really needs a few minutes off. And to be honest, I'd much rather run to DHL than analyze the finer points of maritime trade.

"Are you sure?" She has that look she gets when she's torn between what needs to get done and what she thinks a good Chinese mom should do. I know she feels guilty about stopping my violin lessons a while back and not being able to send me to programming camp or whatever she thinks the cool kids are doing these days. One reason I try so hard to keep my grades up is so they don't feel like they need to get me a tutor.

"It's okay, Mom. I can do it. Really." I give my blog comment one last glance and press submit. Then I take the DHL slip from her.

Mom's sigh seems to melt out of her body. "Thank you, Danny, you are a good son."

I guess imperialism will have to wait.

CHAPTER THREE

CLEMENTINE

OUR NEWSPAPER EDITORIAL BOARD MEETINGS ARE on Thursdays, fifteen minutes after school lets out. Whenever my last-period class ends early, I like to run off campus and grab a snack for the crew. Everybody's hungry by then, and people think better when their blood sugar's up.

There's a boba place a block from our school with the best spicy, melt-in-your-mouth basil popcorn chicken known to humanity. It's the kind of place where you need nose plugs in order to safely pass by, because otherwise the siren smell of basil beckons at your nostrils, and the next thing you know, you're back out on the street corner with an empty wallet, grease stains on your shirt, and half a chicken in your shell-shocked stomach. But you'll be happy. Blissfully happy, so perhaps it's not a disaster if you leave your nose plugs at home.

It's a testament to my love for the newspaper staff that I sneak only a handful of pieces on the walk back to campus. Oily, peppery goodness wafts into the newspaper office as soon as I open the door. There's a smattering of people already there.

Wei, our opinion editor, turns around from what looks like a cat video on his computer screen. "Basil fried chicken? Clementine only brings the good stuff when she's really planning on cracking the whip."

I wade in, calling out like a hot dog vendor at a ball game. "Grease your stomach, grease your brain cells!"

Our business manager, Nadia, springs off the couch and grabs a handful of chicken off the top of my bag. It's gotta be sizzling hot, but you can't tell by the way she stuffs it into her mouth. "Goddess, I'm hungry." She sinks back into the couch and closes her eyes in basil-scented bliss. "My lard-coated brain cells are yours to command."

The newspaper office is the perfect blend of haphazard and organized. We have a large room under a staircase in the corner of the main school building, which means that meetings during the school day are accompanied by the thump of shoes going up and down the stairs. There are computer desks along two walls, a giant whiteboard on another, a table in the center that fits exactly four large pizza boxes if you cut off the tops, and a couch that some editor from years past brought in off the street. On a layout night two years ago, Nadia's predecessor swore she saw a bedbug crawl out from between the cushions. And in a way that only makes sense in the middle of a late-night, caffeine-infused deadline rush, the news staff spent the entire next hour wrapping every portion of the couch in a roll of industrial-strength Saran wrap that someone found in the closet. It's been a rather squeaky couch since then, although the plastic is great for preventing food stains.

I sneak a look at my email as more people file in. Not much new, just a newsletter from the *Jasper City Times* and a coupon from the corner doughnut store. The notification for Bobaboy's comment from yesterday is still there, and I swipe to delete it, perhaps with a little more violence than necessary. His latest comment was a real charmer. I didn't answer right away because I wanted to think through my response first. With Bobaboy, you don't want to shoot before your ammunition's fully developed.

A text pops up from Adenike asking whether she should pick up snacks. I text back a photo of the chicken and get a thumbs-up and heart emoji in reply.

The rest of the editorial staff files in: Felicia, the art director, sporting her newest mismatched ensemble of thrift store finds; Josh, the news editor, playing air drums to whatever he's streaming through in his earbuds; Bhramara, the features editor, lugging a backpack that's twice her body weight. They scatter around the room.

Finally, Adenike walks in, rounding out the crew. She's still sporting newly braided hair from her trip to Nigeria this past summer, covered today with a mustard-yellow head wrap that contrasts with her black leggings and blouse. She sniffs the air and makes a beeline for the snacks, snatching up the small bag of basil fried tofu reserved for her and retreating with it to perch on the armrest of the couch. She offers a piece of tofu to Nadia, who makes a gagging noise. Adenike shrugs and pops it in her mouth.

I take my place by the whiteboard. "All right, everyone. We need to flesh out our plans for our next big center spread. I think we've decided on 'Celebrating Chinatown'?"

Heads bob around me. I've been pushing this one for a while. And though it might not get as much initial enthusiasm as an Avengers cage fight, I think it's worth doing. Our school is right next to Chinatown, and a good 30 percent of our students are Chinese. The neighborhood plays an integral role in shaping our school culture and identity, and it's important to explore and acknowledge that.

"So we probably have room for three articles, more or less, on the spread. Give me ideas."

A thoughtful energy settles over the room. It's one of my favorite things about this crew, how everyone can shift from the distractions of the day and jump right into making this paper as good as we can get it. We're not a bunch of résumé padders. While a fair number of those do show up in the newspaper's greater ranks, the people in this room are here because they believe in the power of the written word.

Wei twirls his pen from one hand to the other. "Restaurant listings?" he throws out.

"Like a dim sum guide?" asks Felicia. Felicia may look like a mild-mannered artiste, but she can scarf down shrimp dumplings like a boa constrictor in a nest of baby chicks. She's given serious thought to becoming a competitive eater.

"Yeah," says Wei. "We could do a whole bunch of mini-reviews, like that one blog. The one with the big words and overexposed pictures." He waves his hand as if trying to scare the site's name out of the air.

"*Babble Tea*?" asks Bhramara.

"Yes, that one!"

Adenike smirks, though she has the good sense to limit eye contact with me to one quick glance. She's the only person in this room who knows I run that blog, and I prefer to keep it that way. It's just easier to be anonymous when you write something so hyperlocal.

Also, my photos are not overexposed. They're bright and airy. There's a difference.

Speaking of my blog, I suddenly get another idea for rebutting Bobaboy: he's totally caricaturing Instagram communities with his talk of influencers and goatees. It's like he doesn't know that real people, and yes, even Asian people, use social media too. Social media doesn't have to be superficial, and there are plenty of examples of internet communities influencing and building real-life ones. I get the overwhelming urge to jot these points down, but pulling out my bullet journal right now would raise a few eyebrows. Instead, I write "Restaurant reviews" on the whiteboard.

"Anything else?"

"What about a report on the changing population? I always find it fascinating how the demographics of Chinatown have evolved over the years," says Nadia. As business manager, she doesn't even have to be at these meetings, but she likes them, and she always has the best ideas.

"I like the thought of that."

More ideas pop out. A photo spread of landmarks. Interviewing the local Chinese dance troupe. A historical timeline of the neighborhood. Favorite places to people watch.

Josh tilts back in his office chair. "Maybe we can run an exposé on that Kale Corp takeover."

Everybody looks at him, and he widens his eyes in a mock deer-in-headlights expression. With his full beard, he reminds me of one of those goofy magnetic faces that kids cover with iron filings to make eyebrows and facial hair. Pretty impressive for a high schooler.

"Kale Corp takeover?" I ask.

"Yeah," he says. "I heard a rumor that they wanted to buy that strip mall on First and Hudson."

"The one with the tea shop and the grocery store?" asks Felicia, fiddling with her beaded glasses chain.

"Yeah. They want to put their own store in."

I attempt to twirl the dry-erase marker on my fingers like Wei, only to narrowly avoid painting my knuckles blue. "You think they're really going to do that?" Kale Corp does have a reputation of taking over the world, but landing in the heart of Chinatown seems a bit much even for them.

"Just what I heard on the grapevine." Josh's dad is a lobbyist at city council, so he does get better grapevine access than most.

This time I do pull out my bullet journal. "Do you mind

seeing if you can find out more about that?" I ask, jotting down a note. "I'll look into it too." This rumor bothers me more than it should. Maybe it's just the visual of a giant Kale Corp sign over one of my favorite sections of the neighborhood.

I step back from the whiteboard. "Anyways, this is a good list. I think we have enough for Bhramara and me to meet separately and hash out the specifics."

Bhramara's high ponytail bounces with her enthusiastic thumbs-up.

I look at my watch. "And we finished on time. Good job, crew."

There's a smattering of cheers. As everybody picks up their bags to go, I succumb to temptation and start jotting down notes for my response to Bobaboy.

Adenike sidles up to me. "That is not a newspaper face. That's a 'someone is wrong on the internet' face."

I give her a sidelong glance while shifting my body to cover my page. "You ever consider working for the CIA?"

"If Russian spies were as easy to read as you are, the Cold War would have ended in two weeks."

Adenike's actually a ridiculously good investigative reporter. Even my mom was impressed by her article about the school board's budget cuts last year. It follows, of course, that Nike's parents have their heart set on her becoming a doctor.

I jot down my last few bullet points. Why is Bobaboy so uptight about iced tea? I mean, his name is Bobaboy, for heaven's sake.

"Bobaboy?" Adenike asks.

"The one and only."

She tucks a stray braid underneath her headscarf. "I don't know why you don't just block him. It would greatly improve your quality of life."

I shrug, sticking my journal deep into my book bag. "My blog wouldn't be much of a forum for conversation if I blocked everyone who disagreed with me."

"You wouldn't have to block everyone who disagrees with you. Only the trolls working out their childhood insecurities in your comments section." Adenike's eyes widen. "Is that a white hair?" She pinches something on top of my head.

I grab a fistful of hair. "Really?"

She slaps her thigh. "You're the most gullible journalist I've ever met."

I scowl at her as we file out of the room. "Seriously, it runs in my family. My sister found a few strands last year and she's still in college."

We step out into the sunshine. "Well, my dear Clementine," says Adenike, giving me an extra-obnoxious hug to counteract my scowl, "I assure you that your locks are still youthfully black. Can't guarantee for how long, though, if you keep it up with Bobaboy."

With that, she heads off toward her bus, and I turn toward home. Adenike's not the only person who's asked me why I don't ban Bobaboy. I mean, it's not like my blog's full of yes-men—plenty of people raise opposing viewpoints or critiques.

But Bobaboy's the only one who posts antagonistic comments on a regular basis.

To be honest, there's another reason I don't block Bobaboy, though it might have outlived its life span by now. Two years ago, this racist commenter went on a rampage on my blog. He was offended that *Babble Tea* celebrated Chinatown, and he ranted on and on about how Asians were invading the country, taking education and jobs away from white people, and how places like Chinatown were horrible because people there didn't even bother to learn English. It got really ugly. At one point, he said that the only good place for me was a massage parlor.

To my surprise, it was Bobaboy who came the most strongly and quickly to my defense. He called out the racism and hypocrisy right away, pointing out that it was pretty rich to criticize Asian immigrants for obtaining legitimate employment and speaking their heritage language when the complainer in question benefited from the literal violence and genocide perpetrated by his own ancestors. Not only did Bobaboy make great logical arguments, he also managed to do it in this really sarcastic way that completely put the guy in his place. (The one and only time I've appreciated Bobaboy's sarcasm.) He even DM'd me afterward to ask if I was okay. I probably still have that message buried in my in-box, provided I haven't psychically disintegrated it with the sheer heat of my annoyance at him since then.

Which is to say, three days after that episode, Bobaboy went back to his trademark complaining and arguing and hasn't stopped since. It's been years now, and I flip-flop on what to think of that whole encounter. On good days, I take it as evidence that he's a decent guy at heart, even if we disagree about . . . well, everything. On bad days, I wonder if the whole thing was a setup to guilt me into never blocking him. If it's the latter, it's apparently worked, because I still haven't been able to press that button.

My hair blows across my face, and one strand looks almost blond. I grab at it and stare. Nope, just a trick of the light.

CHAPTER FOUR

DANNY

BRYAN FALLS AGAINST THE NEIGHBORING LOCKER as I'm packing my backpack for home. The clang of impact echoes down the hallway, but his faux-hawk stays impressively still.

"Korean barbecue tonight? Jess, Nate, and Meiling are coming."

I sort through the books on my locker shelf. Do I need my math book? No, not today, but I do need physics. "What time?"

"Six-ish."

It's been a long time since I've had Korean, and I'm salivating at the mere thought. But man, I'm exhausted after staying up late to write my paper. In my concluding paragraph, I caught myself referring to Holland as "the Dutchese."

"I'll pass this time."

You know that emoji where one eye gets big, one eye gets small, and the mouth goes completely flat? That's what Bryan's face does. He'd be the perfect mascot for the Universal Emoji Consortium or whatever secret society controls these things.

"Dude, you work too hard. Jess was saying how she hasn't seen you since the summer."

"You sure that's not 'cause she's been staring into Nate's eyes the whole time?" Ever since the two of them started dating, they've pretty much existed in their own universe. I'm surprised they're deigning to hang out with the rest of the crew tonight.

"Ha. Fair enough."

Bryan pushes off the lockers as I shoulder my bag. We've been walking home from school together since first grade, when we discovered we both had Spider-Man backpacks. By now, waiting for each other after the last bell is just something we do. No superhero backpacks these days, though. Bryan's moved on to a closeted-but-not-as-secret-as-he-thinks obsession with Little Lin, the newest Taiwanese pop ingenue, an obsession he feeds between pickup basketball games and *Grand Theft Auto* marathons.

"Seriously, though," says Bryan as we wait at a traffic light, "you need to get out more."

"I will. It's just a busy stretch right now with the shop."

He's heard that enough times that he just grunts. "I'll eat some extra kimchi in your honor," he says, peeling off toward his house with a salute.

I'd be lying if I said I didn't envy Bryan's life. I've never been able to go home after school and chill on the couch. It's always back to the restaurant, check what needs to be done. . . .

It wasn't so bad back in the day when we still had employees, a waitstaff, and more money in general. I spent a lot of time at Fragrant Leaves, but I also had my own hobbies and social life. In elementary school, I was pretty good at violin. I mean, all beginning violinists start out sounding like strangled cats, but I got out of the dying feline stage quickly enough that my teacher began talking about entering competitions in a few years. I was into it too, totally fascinated by the idea that I could move horsehairs over a wire and somehow end up with music. My mom didn't even have to bribe me to practice. Or, at least, she only had to bribe me once a week or so.

But then things changed at Fragrant Leaves. Between restaurant work and schoolwork, I had less time and energy for practice. My teacher never said anything outright, but she stopped mentioning those competitions. And then money started running tight. . . .

I wouldn't say my parents made me quit violin. It was just a part of my life that slowly died out. Dissipated, like the steam that comes out of our teapots.

In retrospect, I'd say violin lessons were the last time I felt I could have something that was truly mine. Since then, the restaurant's always loomed in the background. Wanna hang out with friends? See how many people are in the dining room first. New movie out? Check the dirty dish pile. I try not to resent it. It is what it is. But I do wonder, sometimes, if Bryan realizes how good he has it.

A few blocks later, I come through the door of our shop. None of the regulars are in. There's just one family in the corner poring over a *Lonely Planet* guide, so I slip into the kitchen. The first thing I notice is that the office door is closed. That never happens. My dad's a big believer in air circulation.

"Mom? Dad?"

The dishwasher gurgles as it finishes a cycle. The refill light on one of the hot-water dispensers is on. Is anyone watching the shop at all? I go back to the office and check under the door. The light's definitely on, and I hear muffled voices. I'm debating putting my ear to the panel, when the doorknob turns, and I jump back just in time to appear extra guilty to the man in a business suit who'd opened it.

"Sorry," I mumble, backing out toward the counter area.

"No problem," he says, opening the door wider to let out another suit wearing an identical robot expression. I finally catch a glimpse of Mom and Dad behind them. Mom has that crease in the middle of her forehead that she gets when she can't puzzle something out. Dad looks . . . well, I wouldn't say he looks pleased, but he looks like he's *here* for the first time in a while. Like he's finally woken up or something.

My parents usher the suits to the door, with me trailing behind like a misbehaving puppy. The first guy gives my mom and dad each a business card. "It was a pleasure speaking to you, Mr. and Mrs. Mok. Please feel free to contact me if you have any questions whatsoever. We pride ourselves on finding win-win situations for everyone in these types of dealings."

Neither I nor my parents move as the guys disappear down the sidewalk. They look out of place, since we're not exactly Wall Street in this part of town. The weird tension they leave behind is strong enough that the tourist family looks up and stares. Then my mom shakes out of it and heads behind the counter.

"Who was that?" I ask.

Mom waves the business card as if clearing the air. "Oh, nothing to worry about."

Which is exactly what she would say if there *were* something to worry about. I catch a glimpse of a Kale Corp logo on the business card.

"That guy was from Kale Corp?"

Mom shoots me one of her looks and walks into the kitchen. I realize she's worried that the customers will hear, which is kind of unsettling in itself. I don't get why those Kale Corp guys would be here. Unless they're launching their own brand of teas, which I wouldn't put past them.

"It's nothing. They just wanted to talk."

Right. That's why Mom looks like the Mafia just came in offering protection. I'm trying to decide how far to push this, when Dad cuts in.

"It's better if we tell him," he says in gruff Cantonese. "It will probably be on the news soon."

Mom makes a gesture that's half annoyed shrug and half nod, which my dad apparently takes as assent.

"Kale Corp wants to open a store here," he says.

I frown. "In Chinatown?"

"Here," Dad says. He circles his finger to indicate our surroundings. Oh. He means *here*. In our strip mall.

"You mean where the grocery is?" The Chinese grocery at

the end of the parking lot has been around for as long as we've been here. Bryan and I used to spend hours watching the octopuses swim around the fish tanks. Mrs. Lau, the matriarch of that supermarket, is getting on in years, but that shop is still an extension of her personality. She's always there chatting up the customers, pushing their newest barrel of salted duck eggs, showing people how to pick a good papaya.

"Would they really kick Mrs. Lau out?"

"I don't know. I haven't talked to Mrs. Lau. Kale seems to want people to leave voluntarily. Maybe they'll offer her money."

There's something about the way Dad answers. As if the question of Mrs. Lau closing her store isn't the most relevant issue right now. "Wait," I say. "If they want to buy the grocery, why were they talking to you?"

In the moment it takes for Mom and Dad to exchange a look, a suspicion forms.

Mom sighs. Her gaze goes from the empty hot-water pot to the sink, scanning for things that need fixing, as always. But this time, I'm not sure she's registering what she sees. "These days they open more than just their grocery store. They have their specialty stores and cafés that they put next door."

Maybe my brain has completely called it quits, because it takes me forever to figure out what she's actually saying: Kale Corp wants to turn our teahouse into an organic specialty store. Maybe the horror of it shows on my face because Dad speaks up. "It's all very early, Danny. They haven't bought the building yet. We don't know what will happen."

"Could—could they just kick us out?" Granted, I've done my fair share of complaining about our shop, but still, it's ours. I think of all the years my parents poured into building this place, the early mornings and late nights, all those cups of tea poured, all the homework assignments I did at the back table. I think about our regulars coming in every morning after their daily exercise in the park. These thoughts and more cram into my brain, but all I manage to choke out is "Where would everyone play mahjong?"

Dad smiles. I think it's supposed to be comforting, but it just looks like he's pulling his cheeks to the side. "Don't worry about things that haven't happened yet."

I look to Mom, who's attempting her own, less toothy version of the comforting smile. She's better at it than Dad, but she still looks like she's taken a sip of moldy tea. She pats me on the shoulder.

"These processes take a long time," she says. "Many things can change."

That's not exactly comforting.

It's like we were in the freeze frame of a movie, and now someone presses play. Mom walks toward the dining room, and Dad goes back into the office. I stand, stunned, for another moment before retrieving my backpack from where I'd left it by the office door.

As I heft the bag over my shoulder, I catch another glimpse of Dad at his desk. He's motionless again, but this time, instead of staring at his spreadsheet, he's staring at the Kale Corp business card.

WET AROMA OR DRY?

Welcome to another installment of Thoughtful Tea Talk, when we brew our mugs, sit down, and discuss the ins and outs of tea tasting.

Today's question is for our olfactory-obsessed friends. How do you best like to smell your tea? Do you like to sniff it dry, right out of the bag? Or wet after a good soak in hot water?

I'm partial to dry aromas. There's something about that dry-roasted smell that reminds me of strolling through a forest.

What about you?

Posted by Hibiscus, 4:25pm

Bobaboy888 (5:42pm): Wet aroma, all the way. That gives you the best sense of what it'll taste like as a tea.

Hibiscus (6:02pm): But you lose all the crispy notes when you smell it wet. And the smells all blend together.

Bobaboy888 (6:49pm): Crispy notes? What are we talking about, fried chicken? Anyways, I can detect different aromatic notes just fine from wet leaves. Maybe the issue is not the state of the tea, but the smeller.

Hibiscus (7:05pm): Yes, I'm sure you're a regular dachshund.

CHAPTER FIVE

CLEMENTINE

I'M NOT SURE WHY I'M SO BOTHERED BY THE KALE Corp news, but I'm still thinking about it when I get home. Maybe it's because I really love that strip mall. There's a teahouse with excellent oolong, a grocery store with tasty and cheap box lunches, and a gift shop that single-handedly enabled my brief but intense Hello Kitty phase. Every store in the mall is a mom-and-pop with its own personality. It's one of those places that's uniquely Chinatown, and it's hard to think about it being replaced by a chain store that's the carbon copy of two hundred others around the country.

I'm mulling this over in my room when I hear pots and pans clanging in the kitchen, a sure signal that Mom got off work early and is decompressing via food therapy. I've often thought she could start a YouTube channel called "Cooking in Yoga Pants." It certainly seems to help her de-stress, and watching her wash and chop vegetables has this soothing ASMR effect for me as well.

I shuffle down the hall and find her in her yoga-wear ensemble, looking like a unicorn with her hair in a sharp bun atop her head. She's rinsing a colander full of basil under the tap. A jar of pine nuts sits open next to her. My mouth waters.

"Hey, Clem," she says.

"Hey." I sidle up next to her. The whole kitchen smells like torn basil, which as far as I'm concerned beats any air freshener hands down. "Have you heard anything about Kale Corp moving into the mall on First and Hudson?"

Mom tosses a few brown leaves to the side. "I don't think so. Why do you ask?"

"Josh from the newspaper mentioned it."

"Hmm." Mom gets this distant look that means she's scanning her memory. I sense a drop in her guard and snatch a basil leaf to chew.

"Hey!" Mom mock slaps my wrist, but she's still mulling over my question. "I can check with my contact at the local business council. He should know about new companies moving in."

Mom's pretty quick at gathering information when she wants to be. After we put the pesto chicken in the oven, she texts her contact and then runs to her office for a quick phone call. She has an answer for me by the time Dad gets home for dinner.

"The rumors are right," she says between bites of linguine. The pasta is al dente in a way that only happens when Mom doesn't try to brainstorm a story while cooking. "Kale Corp is in the process of purchasing the strip mall from its original owners."

Dad's making quick work of his chicken, forking pieces in

quick succession and popping them into his mouth. At six foot three, he eats a lot, though he says it's a lot less than he used to. He pauses between bites long enough to ask, "The whole mall? Is it final?"

"Pretty close," says Mom. "The sale's not final yet, but I think they plan on opening their stores one way or another."

I scrape pesto from the edges of my plate. "That's really sad."

"Oh?" Dad gets this look on his face that says, "You will bare your secrets for me, and I will print them on the cover of the *New Yorker*." "What about it makes you sad?"

Maybe he's good at his job, because I start talking. "It's just that Chinatown keeps disappearing, bit by bit. Remember all those small shops we used to go to? That bakery with the pork floss buns? And that karaoke store that looped videos of dreamy Asian women in giant sunglasses and sun hats. They're all gone now. It seems that every few months, more stores close and big corporations move in."

"Why do you think that's a bad thing?"

Okay, he's definitely interviewing me now. "I guess I like these places and don't know where else I'd find them. There's plenty of Kale stores around the city, but only one Chinatown. It's mostly nostalgia and convenience for me, but I expect it'd be far worse for the people who are directly affected. I mean, where would those store owners go?"

Dad's expression sharpens as he reaches for his rhetorical rapiers. "What if Chinatown's residents want a Kale Corp store?"

I don't back down. He'd be disappointed if I did. "Maybe, but people don't exactly do a survey of the residents when these takeovers happen, right? The corporations just move in. And I can't imagine any of the displaced store owners would be happy about it."

Finally, Dad drops his journalist face. "Yeah, I agree with you. It's a pity to see the old stores and residents go away. And I don't think it's in the best interests of the community."

"The real question," says Mom, tag-teaming into the conversation, "is what you're gonna do about it."

That's classic for my parents. They're really into the "empowering your kids, teaching them to be self-starters" thing. After eighteen years as their daughter, you'd think I'd be prepared for that question, but I don't have an answer ready. "I don't know. Writing about it doesn't seem like it would help. I don't think Kale Corp's stockholders are avid readers of our school paper or my blog."

Mom wraps the elastic tighter on her unicorn bun. "Despite my general belief in the written word, I'd tend to agree with you on that."

Dad jabs his fork in the air, not bothering to swallow his food before speaking again. "How serious are you about all this?"

I'm a little wary, both of getting stabbed in the eyeball and of his question. "What do you mean?"

"I mean, are you upset enough about Kale Corp moving in to do something about it?"

Yup, my parental shenanigans detector is definitely going off now. "Maybe. Why do you ask?"

"Have you heard of Chinatown Cares?" he asks.

The name sounds vaguely familiar. "Maybe I've seen some flyers for them or something."

Dad leans forward, all businesslike. I probably look just like him when I'm trying to pitch a new investigation to Ms. Curtis, our newspaper adviser. "I covered an art exhibition for them a while ago. Their focus is activism and charity work, and they put a lot of energy into making Chinatown the kind of community its citizens want. If you fancy putting your money where your mouth is, I could put you in touch with them." His eyes sparkle. "You could try interacting with the world for a bit instead of just writing about it."

I cross my arms. "What kind of activism is this? Are we talking about knocking on doors or lying down in front of bulldozers?"

Dad laughs and leans back in his chair. "I don't know. Which do you prefer?"

My parents are no strangers to messy activism. Mom was tear-gassed a few times when covering police protests a while back.

"After knocking on a few doors," says Mom, "you might prefer the bulldozer option."

I roll my eyes. Things are busy with the paper, and I have college applications coming up. But on the other hand, I kinda do want to "put my money where my mouth is." It seems hypocritical to be putting together this big spread on Chinatown for our paper if I don't take any concrete actions to help the neighborhood.

"Sure," I say. "Put me in touch."

Dad emails his contacts at Chinatown Cares and gets a reply three minutes later saying they would "absolutely love" to show me around. Before I know it, we've made plans for me to drop by the next day after school.

Their office is not super far. I take the bus and walk one block to a squat L-shaped building next to a small parking lot. The building's wooden siding panels look like they couldn't decide to be green or brown, so they settled on an in-between shade that could be called either moss or puke depending on the generosity of the observer. The front door opens to a big room with several desks spread out in clusters. A few people are working at their computers.

"Hi," I say uncertainly. "I'm Clementine Chan?"

A Chinese woman stands up. She looks maybe a little bit older than my sister, with olive skin and straight black hair pulled into a ponytail. When her eyes settle on me, she clasps her hands in excitement. "Yes, Clementine! We've been expecting you."

Her handshake is surprisingly firm. I notice she has really long fingers. "My name is Rui." She pronounces her name "Ray," though I see the spelling on her desk nameplate. She gestures toward an older East Asian guy with salt-and-pepper hair and horn-rimmed glasses. "And this is Silas."

Silas shakes my hand. "Good to see you. Can we get you anything to drink?" He speaks with a slow, laid-back lilt that reminds me of surfers discussing the tide. I show them my stainless-steel water bottle, and Rui gives me a thumbs-up.

"Why don't we talk in the conference room," Rui says. She leads me toward a door on the back wall, though she deviates from our trajectory to grab a notepad and pen from her desk. I get the impression that she's figured the shortest path between every two locations in this office.

The conference room itself is moderately large and haphazardly decorated. Most of the walls are bare, although one patch on the far end has pictures of rallies as well as group photos of mostly Asian people in front of various storefronts and apartment buildings. I suspect that someone once had grand plans of decorating the entire room but got distracted.

"We met your dad a while ago at the art exhibition. He was so friendly," says Rui as she settles down across from me. She opens her eyes wide and leans forward as she talks, giving her an almost-nervous look, but I don't think she's nervous, just very deliberate. Next to her, Silas reclines in his chair and hooks one arm over the back. His mug has tea leaves floating in it, which makes me like him more.

Rui folds her fingers and fixes a friendly gaze at me. "So what can we do for you?"

"Oh, well . . ." I guess I thought they'd take the lead—give me a list of options or something. "Honestly, I'm not sure I know enough to answer your question. I'd just heard that Kale

Corp was moving into that strip mall, and it made me sad to see parts of Chinatown gradually getting displaced."

I can tell from Rui's easy nod that she likes my answer. "One of the store owners from the Hudson Street Mall reached out to us after Kale's representatives paid them a visit. It's a growing trend these days for big corporations to move in. We're seeing the typical gentrification pattern—young professionals earning higher wages are moving into Chinatown, which attracts luxury developments and drives up rent prices, making it harder for the original residents to stay in their homes. On the commercial side, new businesses often cater to those more affluent professionals, so the original residents are priced out of those services as well."

I shift uncomfortably at her words, wondering if our family's apartment would count as a luxury development. It's new, and we do have a doorman and a gym. I usually think of myself as belonging in Chinatown because we're Chinese, but my parents would definitely qualify as young professionals with higher salaries.

"Anyways," Silas chimes in with his deep drawl. "These corporate takeovers are hard to fight. There aren't as many protections against being displaced for businesses compared to, say, apartment renters. Which seems shortsighted, because where are those apartment renters going to buy food and necessities? That grocery store in Hudson Street Mall is one of the last affordable groceries around. It'll be an uphill battle to save them, but we'll do what we can, and we would love to get more of the community involved."

"Especially students," says Rui, smoothing some flyaway hairs from her forehead. "There are so many things we do that high school students can help with. Petitions, rallies, door-to-door canvassing. The earlier in life we get people aware of these issues, the more likely we are to make big changes in the long run."

Rui is clearly passionate about this topic, and her enthusiasm infects me. "We have some great people at my school, and I think they'd be interested in helping if they knew more about what was going on. Maybe I could put up some flyers and see who might be interested?"

Rui gives me a big smile. "That's a great idea."

CHAPTER SIX

DANNY

NOTHING STAYS SECRET IN CHINATOWN FOR LONG.
Our neighborhood gossip channels were already first-class back in the day, but nowadays, all the aunties and uncles have smartphones and group chats. They're always sending things to each other between sips of tea, be it pictures of their grandkids or news segments about baby ducks being rescued from sewer drains. With those well-greased communication systems in place, it's pretty much impossible to keep anything secret from anyone. The FBI has nothing on the auntie network.

I don't know if my mom told someone about the guys in suits or if one of the aunties mentally snatched the news from the 5G, but suddenly, one morning, everybody's talking about Kale Corp. I hear snippets of conversation when the old folks come in from their a.m. calisthenics at the park. As the mahjong tiles get pulled out one morning, I pass Uncle Tony and his best friend, Uncle Lian.

"Bamboo Village teahouse closed last year, and now this,"

says one in Mandarin. "Soon there won't be any places for old geezers like us." That comment is followed by some muttering about nianqinren, young people, who they mention with the same tone other people use to talk about aliens or bitcoin investors.

Uncle Tony catches sight of me. "Danny! What Pu'er do you have today?"

I circle around to their table. "Hi, Uncle Tony. We still have the 2003 Aged Green Stamp, and the 1990 Old Tree Raw Pu'er, which I think you had last week, right? And yesterday we got some cakes of 2010 Gold Blossom. I don't think anyone's tried that one yet."

Uncle Tony's eyes light up like a pirate with a treasure map. "Make us a pot of the Gold Blossom."

"Sure thing!"

A good chunk of my gloom lifts off as I head back to the kitchen. Uncle Tony's a Pu'er connoisseur, and he's always enthusiastic about sampling new acquisitions. I always try to brew my A game around him.

First step is to reboil the water in the hot-water pots. We do keep one of the pots at 95 degrees Celsius, but freshly boiled is better for Pu'er. It's early in the morning, so we still have a plentiful selection of teapots, and I pick out a good unglazed vessel of Zisha clay. After a couple minutes, the water's ready. For most customers, I'd put tea leaves into the pot, pour water over it, and serve it out, but for Uncle Tony, I just load everything onto a tray. He and Uncle Lian perk up when I appear.

"Would you like me to brew the first cup for you?"

"Yes! You're getting very good at it these days."

I'm kind of honored that Uncle Tony would say that, and I do every step extra carefully. First, I rinse the cups with boiling water to warm them. Then I carefully break the right amount of tea leaves off the cake. Since the leaves are pretty compressed, I peg it for a longer brewing time. The first rinse is six seconds long, and that goes straight into the discard bucket. For the second brew, I count to twelve before serving it into their teacups.

The uncles take thoughtful sips, and I wait for their reaction.

"Not bad," says Uncle Tony. "Kind of woody. Very smooth."

"It's a little more humid than I like," says Uncle Lian, furrowing his brow.

"That might improve after it sits out for a few months," I say.

Uncle Lian nods his agreement and pats me on the arm. "Thank you! Well done."

I leave everything there so they can brew the rest themselves.

My family personally samples each tea we select for the shop, and Dad's even gone to visit many of the producers in Taiwan and China. Back in the day, he occasionally brought me along too. We toured farms and factories, soaking in everything the producers had to say. A lot of these plantations were passed down from generation to generation, and each had its own way of making its best tea. I learned about growing conditions, weather, soil, and nutrients. Harvesting and roasting. I listened to lectures about judging a tea's progress by its smell, how partially roasted tea has a tea smell and a fire smell, and how you know that the tea is done when the two smells meld together.

Dad also took me to tea shops back then, where we attended classes with the brewing masters. Here too there were so many details, so many techniques perfected over generations. I learned about picking the right pot shape and material for the specific tea I was making, about caring for a teapot so it absorbs tea oils and eventually contributes its own flavor to each brew. There's the importance of temperature regulation—details like leaving the pot lid open so it wouldn't get too hot and cook the leaves, or pouring hot water over the top of the brewing pot to ensure an even temperature distribution. The tea that those masters brewed was good, so very good. When you drank with them, you felt like you were part of something bigger than yourself, an art form, tradition, and beverage break all in one.

Of course, Dad hardly goes on these trips anymore, and I don't go at all. But I do practice my brewing from time to time, and I squirrel away the tags on new teas we buy, just in case we start making trips again.

Serving Uncle Tony took up most of my morning time, so I scramble to grab my bags for school. As I head for the door, I glimpse Auntie Lin and Mom huddled in the corner. They stop talking in the most obvious way when I walk by, and Auntie Lin pauses from fiddling with her jade earring to give me this overly bright smile.

"Danny! How's school?"

It's cute how they hush when someone nears—a meaningless

effort since even Auntie Lin's whispers carry clear across the room.

"School's good, Auntie Lin. See you this afternoon."

As I leave, Auntie Lin hisses to my mom, "I tried their frozen baozi once. Not good at all. No flavor!"

Well, Kale Corp's frozen bao might be bland, but they sure sell a heck of a lot more of them than we do.

The specter of all this hangs over me as I walk to school. Having your parents keep things from you is bad enough. Having the entire tea shop gossiping behind your back, apparently trying to shield you from the obvious truth that your family's restaurant is on the line . . . well, that messes with your head.

I mean, I'm not obtuse. I see what's happening in my neighborhood, the old shops disappearing one by one. There was this one gift shop that Bryan and I used to stop by all the time, owned by a friendly old man who'd let us read from the manga shelf for free, but only if we'd finished our homework for the day. Maybe Uncle Paul, as we called him, should have charged us, because he eventually couldn't afford his rent. To be fair, I don't think giving freebies to neighborhood kids was the primary reason he went out of business. From what I pieced together in the years following, what happened was this: Uncle Paul's street used to be a busy shopping street, with clothing shops, plant stores, and restaurants. But one by one, neighboring stores went out of business, and a whole bunch of art galleries opened up in their place—the type of galleries that are open to the public only a few hours a day, if at all. Foot traffic dwindled, and so did the gift shop's sales.

Eventually, Uncle Paul closed the store and moved across town to live with relatives. Another art gallery opened in its place.

A few years after he closed shop, I ran into Uncle Paul again. He saw me from across the street and called me over, making a big fuss over how much I'd grown. We walked together a bit. He told me he was retired and in the neighborhood to have lunch with friends. He missed running his shop but counted himself lucky to have children who could support him.

As we walked, we found ourselves on the street where his gift shop had been. The art gallery in its place was sleek with large windows. A handful of people milled inside, strolling between rainbow-colored acrylic sculptures that looked like upside-down mushrooms.

The two of us stopped to look in the window.

"What do you think those are?" asked Uncle Paul.

"I don't know. Plants maybe?"

Uncle Paul grunted. "I don't know how they charge a thousand dollars for something like that."

"Are they really a thousand dollars?"

He shrugged. "Let's see," he said, and he opened the door to go in. I followed a little nervously. The sleek artsy vibe of the place didn't feel like my usual stomping grounds.

The two of us stood around the closest sculpture for a bit, looking above and below for a price tag. Apparently the piece was called *The Fork of Infinity*, though I couldn't figure out what part was the fork and what part was infinity. And then we looked up, because a lady with orange stilettos, horn-rimmed glasses, and a fake smile was coming toward us.

"Hello, gentlemen. Thank you so much for your interest. Unfortunately we are currently open by appointment only. Would you like to set a time to come by later?"

I'll never forget the look on Uncle Paul's face as her words sank in.

"No, no thanks," he said. "We'll leave."

I felt so bad for him that day. And even then, part of me had wondered what it would have been like if it'd been us, not him. How it would have felt to lose our restaurant and have it turn into a place we couldn't even enter without an appointment. Now, with those Kale guys showing up, all those questions come back. I dunno, maybe I'm just being paranoid. Maybe my parents were right when they told me there was nothing to worry about.

Heck, maybe Auntie Lin will decide that she loves Kale Corp baozi and start serving them at her dinner parties, but I'm not putting any money on it.

Bryan and the rest of the crew are at the usual locker bay. Jess is hanging off Nate's arm, and Meiling is rearranging her collection of hot sauce bottles. I'm not in the mood to shoot the breeze, so I do that thing where you conjure invisible thoughts and slip casually by. I almost think I get away with it too, until Bryan shows up at my locker a few moments later.

"Okay, now you're taking antisocial to a whole new level. Skipping out on dinner is one thing. Now you're doing the invisible man bit too?"

There are disadvantages to staying friends with the guy who was Spider-Man to your Flash in kindergarten.

"Kale Corp is moving into our strip mall."

Bryan blinks. "What?"

"Kale Corp's apparently buying our strip mall. Now they want us all to move out."

Bryan has that look he gets when he's trying to decipher Little Lin's Chinese-language interviews. Minus the lovestruck moon eyes. "Move out? For real?"

I slam my locker shut. "All I know is that two guys in Mafia suits showed up at the teahouse a few days ago waving papers and saying words like 'win-win situation.'"

"No kidding. So what's going to happen to the shop?"

"I don't know. My parents keep saying it's no big deal, and things are still in the early stages, but these guys didn't look like they were planning on going away."

Bryan doesn't answer, but I can tell that he gets what a big deal this is. He's spent so much time at our tea shop that Mom's been known to let him man the cash register if she needs a bathroom break. He's run through the aisles of that grocery store with me, and we both got our green belts from that kung fu studio on the corner.

The hallways are crowded as we make our way to class. It must be flyer day, because the bulletin boards are swarming with kids from rival organizations trying to edge each other out for prime flyer space. Survival of the fittest. They really should hand out jousting rods and helmets.

A flash of red catches my eye. Did that flyer say "Kale Corp"?

I double back. By the time Bryan cranes his neck around to look for me, I'm already crouching down to look at a bright-red poster. There's a picture of the big Chinatown arch. Underneath, it says, "Fight the Kale Corp takeover! Save Chinatown. Email Clementine Chan for more information."

Bryan's voice floats over my shoulder. "Is this a newspaper thing?"

That's what I'm wondering too. Everyone knows Clementine Chan, or at least the whiplash feeling when she speed-walks past you with notebook in hand, simultaneously engaged in three conversations at once with her newspaper staff editors. She's a small person, but the breeze is considerable. Or maybe it's just the psychic force of that much sheer competence.

"It doesn't look like a newspaper thing," I say.

Bryan shrugs his backpack higher up his shoulder. "How do people have so much time?"

"Maybe by not marathoning a new Netflix show every week?"

"Hey, I need my afternoon downtime. School's stressful."

I give a noncommittal grunt, trying to imagine what my mom would say if I told her I couldn't bus the tables because I "needed my downtime." Actually, I'm trying to figure out how many pieces she'd chop my corpse into before throwing it to the birds. I do wonder what it'd be like to go home and chill after school like Bryan does. Or even spend all these hours on the newspaper like Clementine. I guess Fragrant Leaves is my extracurricular.

Bryan heads off to history, and I settle down for math. Mr. Aspenwood spends a lot of time going over identities with complex numbers. I understand it just well enough for my mind to start wandering, but probably not well enough to do the homework later.

Or maybe I'm distracted because I can't stop thinking about that flyer. Why would Clementine Chan be doing something related to the Kale Corp takeover? I don't think she's connected to any of the businesses there, and first semester senior year seems a strange time to start a new extracurricular. I wonder what she plans to do. Being on the paper probably gets her first dibs on the latest news. Could she know something I don't?

Usually the thought of signing up for anything makes me queasy, even something small like joining a bake sale. As far as conflict goes, I'm more of a "write sarcastic comments from my couch" type of guy instead of a "face down the Man" type of guy. But then, until today, my family's tea shop has never been in the Man's crosshairs either. It doesn't help that the sad commentary from the old folks this morning is still knocking around in my head. God knows I don't have much free time, but this is big. The tea shop is basically our lives.

When math class ends, my bag's already packed and I'm the first one out the door. The hallways are streaming with people, which gives me some cover. I don't know why it feels like I need to sneak around. It's not like anyone would care about me going back to check out Clementine's poster. Still, I have this weird urge to pull a hoodie over my face, if SoCal autumns were cold enough for hoodies.

I feel this huge wave of relief when I see the flyer, as if part of me had worried someone might have stolen it last period. But nope, it's still there. The relevant words are all on it. Chinatown. Kale Corp. Clementine's email address. I take a furtive look around before snapping a quick picture. Then I stuff my phone in my pocket and hightail it back to my locker.

CHAPTER SEVEN
CLEMENTINE

I MAKE THE FLYERS MYSELF. I THOUGHT ABOUT pulling in some favors with my art director, Felicia, but it felt too much like an abuse of power. Also, I'm strangely self-conscious about telling people what I'm planning. Somehow, it seemed more discreet to plaster posters with my name all over the school than it did to pull one of my newspaper colleagues aside and tell them about Chinatown Cares.

At least I'm an old hand at hanging posters. Every Tuesday morning, all the flyers on the bulletin boards around campus are stripped clean, and then it's basically a free-for-all as every student organization covers them back up with new, exciting proclamations. I get there early and claim some pretty good real estate, and then I start refreshing my email.

"You haven't posted anything on your blog recently, have you?" asks Adenike after I pull out my phone for the fourth time this passing period.

"I'm just seeing if anyone's emailed me about the Chinatown

Cares Youth Council."

I've already told her about meeting Rui and Silas and agreeing to help them start up a student arm. Nike thinks it's a great idea, though she's too busy with her own things to join. Besides newspaper editing, she's taking a bunch of APs and fundraising for a big church trip over spring break.

Honestly, most kids at our school have full schedules, so maybe that's why my in-box sits empty the entire day.

"Maybe everyone's busy at school right now, so they won't have time to email me until later," I tell Adenike during lunch.

She glances around the cafeteria. A cluster of guys are rehearsing a TikTok dance next to the trash cans. Another table's playing Jenga with cafeteria brownies.

"Give them time to think it over," she says. "A lot of people probably haven't even seen the flyer yet."

Maybe I should have chosen a brighter red for the paper.

Over the next hours, I come up with numerous excuses to casually stroll by my posters. The first and fourth times, it's to confirm that my email was printed correctly. The second and fifth, it's to make sure they haven't been postered over. I also do a few walk-bys to check the contrast of the black words against the red background.

Still no emails.

In a burst of self-control, I banish my phone to the dining room at 4:47 p.m. so I can do my homework without repeated refreshing. I finish my chem lab write-up at 6:58 p.m., and at 7:01 I start checking again.

An email pops up at 7:07 with the subject line "Chinatown flyer." I tap through to the message before the subject line fully settles on my in-box screen.

Hey Clementine,

I saw your flyer about Kale Corp. I'd be interested in hearing more about how to help.

Danny

I check the email address for the last name. Danny Mok. He's in some of my classes. If I remember right, he usually hangs out with Bryan Yip and a few other Asian kids. We don't talk much. Actually, I'm not sure if we've ever spoken at all.

I tap reply but end up staring at a blank draft. I'm not quite sure what to say. What if he's the only person who writes me? Better to wait for other replies.

But there are no emails the next day, or the day after that. I can tell Adenike feels bad for me because she offers me extra Starbursts from her locker stash.

"Do you think it's weird if I ask him to meet up and it's just the two of us?" I unwrap a strawberry Starburst—the fourth I'd shamelessly accepted that day. "Maybe you could come to the first meeting so it won't be that awkward. You could always drop out afterward."

"Like a blind date setup except for extracurriculars?" She throws up her hands. "Oh, silly me. I completely forgot that I have no time for another activity. Have fun changing the world, you two!" She gives me an exaggerated wink.

I twist the Starburst wrapper into strawberry-scented rope. "Seems reasonable to me."

"You just need to be up-front with him," she says. "It'll be a little awkward, but if he's really invested in the cause, it shouldn't make a difference. Even if it's just you two, you're still working with that organization, right? So it's not like you're going to be charting a path completely by yourselves."

She's right. I know she's right. I bury my face in my hands.

"Clem, you faced down Principal Griego when he didn't want us to print that article about teacher salaries. You can face—what's his name again?"

"Danny. Danny Mok."

"Right. Maybe you can ask him to meet you in the newspaper office."

"Fiiine."

I open up his email and hit reply.

Hi Danny,

Thank you so much for getting in touch!

"Good start," says Adenike over my shoulder. "Your choice of one exclamation mark is spot-on. Friendlier than none, less hyperactive than two."

I elbow her away from my screen.

I would love to meet up and chat more if you like. Do
you want to drop by the newspaper office after school?
I'm there most afternoons, so just let me know a time
that works for you.

I hand the phone to Adenike, who scans it over and gives it
a thumbs-up. "I knew you could do it."

I roll my eyes and press send.

TEAPOT ENVY

Hey guys, I just saw the cutest teapot at the store. Isn't it gorgeous? I love the floral detailing. What do you think, should I pick it up?

Posted by Hibiscus, 6:30pm

Bobaboy888 (6:45pm): That porcelain makes me cringe.

Hibiscus (6:53pm): Yes, I'm well aware that beauty offends you.

Bobaboy888 (7:23pm): Don't you mostly brew oolong? You shouldn't be using porcelain. You want a clay pot that can absorb tea oils and add its own flavor over time.

Hibiscus (7:35pm): In case you haven't noticed, good clay teapots cost a lot. I'm not exactly rolling in dough.

Bobaboy888 (7:55pm): I'll give you that point. But if you must do porcelain, why not go for something smaller like a gaiwan and save up for clay, instead of spending your hard-earned dollars on a pot that will murder your tea?

Hibiscus (8:12pm): So basically, you're saying that

buying this teapot would be like inviting a serial killer into my home.

Bobaboy888 (8:32pm): Yes. And who wants Charles Manson sitting in their cabinet?

CHAPTER EIGHT
DANNY

THE NEWSPAPER OFFICE IS HARD TO FIND. CLEM-
entine said it was by the staircase in the southeast corner of the
school. Since I can't navigate my way out of a paper bag, I end
up using my phone compass to figure out what corner that is.
Then it turns out that the door in question is tucked *behind* the
stairs, so you can't easily see it from the hallway. But I finally
find it after a few minutes of circling.

The place smells like leftover pizza. There's a girl with enor-
mous hoop earrings and a *Vegetables Are Poison* T-shirt typing
furiously in the corner. Clementine's easy to spot at the center
table. Her long black hair is in a loose braid over one shoulder,
and the collar of a button-down peeks out over the neckline of
her sweater. You could totally take a picture and caption it *Por-
trait of an Ivy League Shoo-in*.

She fiddles with her braid as she works, and she glances up
at the sound of the door. "Danny," she says with a smile. "Glad
you could make it."

Well, that was a friendly enough greeting. Less activity fair hustle than I expected. But something's off. I thought I was late. I'd even made sure to open the door extra quietly so I could slip in unnoticed. But there doesn't seem to be anyone else here.

I glance at my watch. "Is this the place for the Chinatown meeting?" Did I get the day wrong?

"Yeah, you've got the right place." Clementine starts tapping the back of her pen against her notebook. She looks almost apologetic.

In the awkward silence that follows, I notice that the girl who hates vegetables can type really fast. It's like a constant stream of key clicks from her corner.

Clementine blinks a few times, and then she seems to regain her bearings because she perks up a little. "You know what? It's a little stuffy in here, and I don't really want to bother Nadia. Do you want to take a walk?"

All this is giving me a strange vibe, but she's right about it being stuffy. I think there's pizza grease settling into my hair.

"Okay," I say.

She smiles. It's a nice smile. Her entire face lights up, and she loses a bit of that intimidating-editor vibe. "Great. Let me just pack my stuff."

She stuffs her notebook into her bag and leads the way out the door, but her brows knit together as we pass under the doorframe. By the time we're outside, she's preoccupied again. I wonder if I've missed a memo or something.

"Do you like boba?" she asks.

"What?" I realize I'm displaying the verbal skills of a caveman, but I can't help it if *she* keeps saying random things.

"Oh." I swear she blushes a little. "There's a boba shop on the corner. I figured it would be a nicer place to chat."

If Clementine were Bryan, I'd start wondering if this was some scheme to get me on a date or something. But this isn't Bryan. This is Clementine, A-plus student and overachiever extraordinaire. Yeah, she's cute, and yeah, I've noticed. But Clementine's pretty in the way that you'd expect her to be. Like she's so good at everything else—turning the newspaper into her personal empire, bulldozing through AP classes—that of course she'd be good-looking too. It just wouldn't cross her mind to be otherwise. Clementine's attractive like a Greek god is attractive. But you'd never try a pickup line on Athena, because she'd bust your head open with an ax, and then where would you be?

"Sure, I like boba," I say. "I mean, is there anybody who doesn't?"

"Fantastic!" Clementine's shoulders visibly relax. She speeds down the sidewalk and starts talking a mile a minute. "I'm sorry to drag you out here. It's just that I'm in that newspaper office twenty-four seven, and I really needed some fresh air. We always get pizza when it's deadline time, and the windows don't open, so the grease smell just gets trapped. I've been trying to get air filters, but it's amazing the hoops you have to jump through to get the budget for replacement filters. Plus, my assistant editor thinks the fans would be too loud."

Whoa there. I'm having a hard time keeping up, both with her walking and her mile-a-minute monologue. If this is how she is before drinking a cup of sugary, caffeinated boba tea, maybe we should be getting some chamomile instead.

"The boba's on me," Clementine says as we walk into the shop. "Because I was the one who called the meeting."

Okay, now this is really giving me first-date vibes. Bryan could totally pick up some moves from her. "It's okay. I can get my own."

She tosses her braid back over her shoulder. "No, I insist. They have a two-for-one special. We've gotta take advantage of it."

A lifetime of watching my elders get into literal wrestling matches at the cash register, yet I just weakly nod my agreement. My mom would die of shame if she were here. But really, I'm just too confused to argue.

Before I know it, the barista's handed me a squishy see-through cup of ice-cold milk tea, and we're headed to a table.

"So," says Clementine as she settles into a chair opposite me. "How did you get interested in the Kale Corp acquisition? Or are you just interested in helping Chinatown in general?"

Despite her endless chatter earlier, she looks like she actually wants to hear my answer. My mind flashes back to the businessmen in the back office. I guess there's nothing secret about Kale Corp taking over our tea shop, but it still feels weird talking about it. "My family's shop is in that mall."

Clementine's eyes widen. "Oh, which one?"

"Fragrant Leaves. The teahouse."

"Fragrant Leaves!" She claps her hands together. "I've been there! It's such a nice shop."

"Uh, thanks." I hope she doesn't ask me if I remember seeing her there, because I don't.

Clementine takes a long sip of her bubble tea, repositioning her straw occasionally to pick up more pearls. "Then I can definitely see why you'd want to fight Kale Corp coming in."

"Yeah," I say. "I'm kind of over all those yuppie businesses and luxury apartment dwellers coming in and taking over."

Clementine's smile freezes slightly. "Yeah, you know those luxury apartment dwellers, ruining it for everyone." There's the slightest edge to her voice, and I realize I have no idea where Clementine lives. Did I just inadvertently insult her? If she really is a Chinatown newcomer, why is she even in this fight? Is it just for the glamour of it all?

Both of us have stopped talking. *Way to make things awkward, Danny.*

Clementine clears her throat. "Anyways," she says, plowing on, "I've been talking to Chinatown Cares—that's the organization I'm working with—and they have some ideas for legal challenges and putting public pressure on Kale not to open that store. And there's plenty of opportunity for us to help out. Teens can do a lot, you know—planning rallies, gathering signatures. I mean, the only thing we can't do is the actual legal work 'cause obviously you need several years of law school for that, and I guess we'll let Rui and Silas take the lead on communicating with store owners. . . ." She's speaking faster and faster, until abruptly she puts on the brakes. "So . . ." Clementine shoots me a nervous glance, the way Meiling used to look when Bryan handed her his diarrhea-prone pet hamster. "Before we go on, I should tell you that I didn't really get as many responses as I'd hoped for."

Clementine had been talking so quickly that I almost don't catch that last part. "As many responses as you'd hoped for?" I echo as my brain scrambles to catch up.

"Yeah . . ." She fiddles with the portion of her straw that's outside the cup, bending it into itself segment by segment. It's the visual equivalent of fingernails on a chalkboard.

"So, uh . . . how many people signed up?"

She cringes the slightest bit. "Just you."

"Oh."

I guess that explains it.

She grimaces apologetically. "Sorry to spring that on you."

Clementine seems to be expecting me to say something. My brain stumbles back into the picture, trying to piece together the last few bits of conversation but not doing a very admirable job of it. "So, uh, is this still happening?"

At this, Clementine comes to life again, and the upbeat tone comes back into her voice. Talk about emotional whiplash. "Well, it's completely up to you. I know you were probably expecting a bit more when you signed up."

To be honest, I'm not quite sure what I expected. I guess I thought that I'd come into a meeting with a bunch of people who were just as energetic and with-it as Clementine. I figured they would decide things, and I'd tag along if they made sense. I definitely didn't expect to be sitting here in a boba shop as the only volunteer.

I know a hopeless cause when I see one, and this seems like one of those things where it's safer to get out earlier than later. Much better to let Clementine down now before she gets any more invested. She probably won't even be all that disappointed. I'm sure she has ten million other projects she could be working on.

Clementine interrupts my thoughts. "But even though it's just the two of us who signed up, you should know that we'd have plenty of support from Chinatown Cares. Their staff members are super supportive and incredibly nice."

In the back of my brain, a voice starts on constant loop. *We're the only two who signed up.*

I'm starting to feel queasy. Part of it is the awkwardness of this whole boba nondate. But beyond that, it's slowly dawning on me that everybody in our strip mall is going to lose their stores, and nobody at school cared enough to even respond to the flyer.

Am I surprised? On second thought, not really. People have their own lives. But it's not a good feeling, to know that the thing your parents poured their lives into for decades is just another poster to ignore in the school hallways.

Clementine leans toward me over the table. "I know this is a lot to process." She's surprisingly earnest, her dark eyes wide and purposeful. "I just figured . . . it'd be a pity not to at least try and fight the takeover. I've spent a lot of time in that mall. I've been to your teahouse, I've shopped at that gift shop, and I've watched the octopuses crawl around the grocery store's fish tanks. There are a lot of good things in that corner of our neighborhood, and I feel like those good things should stay, you know? And even though people don't seem to care now, I feel like they would if we just asked them to pay a little more attention."

It's the octopus that gets me. I guess Bryan and I aren't the only ones who like to watch them slither around. And now I'm seeing how Clementine's eyes shine as she makes her pitch. I'm feeling the energy and hope coming off her, and suddenly I'm thinking that maybe this isn't just another project for her. Maybe she truly does care, and maybe she's right that we could get other people to care too.

At least, I want her to be right.

Clementine stops talking. The words she'd been uttering nonstop crash into each other in the unexpected silence. She gives a little embarrassed shrug, which collapses one side of her button-down's upturned collar. "Anyways, I'm talking too much. I mean, I'm sure you have stuff to do, and I totally understand if this is too much of a curveball. I just wanted to let you know that I'm still in if you are." She tucks a strand of hair behind her ear and gives me a shy but surprisingly charming grin. "Not to put you on the spot or anything."

I guess it's my turn to say something again.

"You don't have to give me an answer right away," she adds quickly. "You can think about it."

"No, that's cool. I don't need time to think it over. I'm in."

Did I just say that?

Clementine blinks. Her mouth opens into a little O. "Are you sure? I don't want to pressure you or anything."

It's like my mouth is moving without my permission. "Yeah. I mean, the teahouse is a big part of my life, and I feel like I should be taking some action."

I've officially split into two separate people. Half of my brain is watching and freaking out, as the rest of me smiles back at her, spouting platitudes about never knowing unless you try. Smiley-platitude me sounds pretty convincing, to be honest.

Clementine looks at me for a moment or two, and then she smiles that brilliant smile again. "That's great, Danny. I'm really glad to have you on board."

I get back to the tea shop later than usual. Mom's at the register.

"Why so late?" she asks. "You go somewhere with Bryan?"

"No, I was meeting with a classmate."

"School project?"

"Yeah." I guess we could call it that?

She waves me over and smooths down my hair, frowning at it as if she could intimidate it into behaving. "You need to bring a comb to school. Your teachers see you like this?"

"It just gets messy again after I comb."

"Maybe you should cut it."

I shrug. "Maybe we just have to accept that I got your good hair genes. But better I get my hair from you than from Dad, right?"

Mom's mouth quirks. She ruffles the top of my head, which undoes her earlier efforts, before pushing me toward the kitchen. "I got you some seaweed snacks. They're on your table. And can you do the dishes?"

There's nothing like a giant pile of dirty plates and cups to make you second-guess your decision to join an ill-fated pseudoclub with only two members. I'm still not sure how I ended up staying on board. A moment of insensibility? I guess Clementine was so excited about it that I got swept up as well.

I soap up the sponge, wondering what I've gotten myself into. Do I even know what we'll be doing? She'd said something about public pressure on Kale Corp, but what does that even mean? I get this mental image of a crowd of people pushing on the Kale Corp headquarters until it topples over. If only.

I think back to that list of things Clementine was rattling off—petitions, rallies . . . Whatever she has planned, I hope she remembers that it's just the two of us. I already have a lot on my plate, no pun intended. Clementine might be able to spend long hours improving the world and her college application, but I don't have the bandwidth.

I should start my homework, since I got home late. Instead, I dig into the bag of seaweed snacks on my desk and log on to Chinatown Linktropolis. There's a raging debate going on about whether red bean or lotus paste mooncakes are better.

Someone's also linked to the latest *Babble Tea* post. The title is "Communi-tea."

Curse the blog gods, tempting me with an atrocity like this when I really have work to do. There are a lot of annoying people online, but Hibiscus pushes all my buttons.

I don't remember when exactly Chinatown started becoming *trendy*, but a few years ago, articles about "hidden Chinatown gems" and "unique cultural finds" started popping up everywhere. Before that, Chinatown was just Chinatown. The place that I lived, plus the other folks who lived and worked here.

You might think it's a good thing that the neighborhood suddenly became popular. And maybe it would have been, except that the "Chinatown gems" everybody pushed always seemed to be trendy places run by white guys who sneak French words into their Asian-inspired restaurant names. For some reason, a "Chinese restaurant" by itself was lowbrow and bargain basement. But call it an "Asian gastropub," add in a craft beer selection, French desserts, and bespoke fortune cookies, and suddenly we have something exciting! Avant-garde! Our family baozi recipe is just a meh immigrant dish, but add in European influences and call your dipping sauce a soy-ginger aioli, now that's worth paying top dollar for.

When the tourists started pouring in, a few of them did drop by Fragrant Leaves, but they turned up their noses at the decorations and rolled their eyes when Mom couldn't understand their rapid-fire English. They'd take pictures of typos on our menu for Instagram and then peace out for the wine bar down the street.

I remember this one woman. She had these giant sunglasses, a weirdly lime-green dress, and a purse that looked like it was patched together from the skins of multiple endangered species. If that didn't peg her as an influencer, the fact that she and her friend started posing for photos before they looked at the menu certainly did. They spent ten minutes blocking the aisles and complaining about the lighting in voices they thought no one could hear. Mom finally intervened when one of them asked Uncle Tony to switch tables so they could stage their food photos closer to the window, at which point they apologized profusely and attempted to butter Mom up with compliments about the teahouse and promises to "tell everyone!" what a "cute little place" this was.

A few days later, I looked up the lady's account. There it was, a video montage of her delightful trip to Chinatown. One photo out of the ten she posted was of our tea and pastries. She called our food exotic and misspelled our last name. The vast majority of the caption consisted of her gushing about the Asian-inspired gastropub down the street. She had at least five pictures from there—sipping a cup of wine, spilling the filling out of her lettuce wrap (made with cilantro garlic aioli, naturally), and eating a freshly baked "Great Wall" soufflé.

I dunno, maybe the lighting was better there.

It's like the tourists who visit Chinatown want a Chinese experience, but not *too* Chinese. They like the idea of checking out another culture, but only if the culture conforms to their comforts. I never saw that particular influencer again—Chinatown's a destination for people like her, not her usual digs. The only internet personality who sticks around is Hibiscus, who seems to be a local. It kills me, 'cause she clearly knows and visits all these mom-and-pops that nobody else pays attention to, and she could do so much to bring attention to them. But instead, she just talks about how much she loves Chinatown while sweetly suggesting we change everything about it.

I click through to "Communi-tea." (Gag.)

> The idea of community has been on my mind lately, thanks to some recent changes around my neighborhood. I've been thinking about the way people come together and support each other. There are geographic communities, activity-based communities, interest-based communities . . . This blog, for example, has been an amazing community over the years. It sprang up around the topic of tea, yet you have all become more than fellow hobbyists, but friends as well. Thank you all for being you.

You know what boggles my mind? The fact that Hibiscus can string out a bunch of platitudes, and her comment feed just blows up with people high-fiving her about how brilliant she is. For a post that's basically just a riff off a bad pun. This would be annoying on a regular day, but having just come back from a meeting where it was pretty clear that people in our "local community" don't give a horse's ass about Fragrant Leaves, it's especially grating. I scroll down to the comment box.

It's a sad commentary on society to see what we consider to be a community these days. Communities used to be things that spanned decades. They were places where people ran up against each other over the course of their lives, sometimes in good ways, sometimes not. But they had to figure out how to coexist, to support each other and work out their issues.

Nowadays, anything's a community. A housing development is community. A blog where people log on for 10 minutes a day and don't even know each other's real names is a community. People come and go, log in or out as they want. And somehow that's community?

I feel a bit better after hitting the submit button, as if I'd let out some of the pressure in my head. I finish my homework quickly, and that night I sleep well. By the next morning, I'm much more optimistic. The idea of joining this Chinatown Cares Youth Council doesn't seem so bad when I'm well rested. After all, it's just an extracurricular. How horrible could it be?

My new calm lasts approximately two minutes, aka the time it takes for me to open my eyes, blink the sleep out of them, roll over, and grab my phone.

In my in-box is an email from Clementine.

Hi Danny,

Thank you again for signing on to the youth council! I was just tossing together a list of ideas for getting things off the ground. Would love to chat more and get your thoughts on the following.

1. We should meet with Rui and Silas at Chinatown Cares. They're wonderful, and they'll be so happy to meet you.

2. Do you know other business owners in your strip mall? It might help with the outreach if you did.

3. I'm going to ask Principal Griego about whether we can table at the cafeteria. That'd be a great way to get word out to our classmates.

4. What's the best way to contact you? Email? Text?

Thanks, and talk soon!

Clementine

Oh my God.

I throw my pillow over my face. Does she ever turn off? I think through last year's biology lectures, trying to figure out the likelihood that Clementine might be another subspecies of human being. *Homo energeticus.* I have no idea how I'd even start to reply to her email, so I don't.

By the time I get to school, I've managed to push the whole Chinatown Cares thing to the back of my mind. I'm feeling less antisocial than usual, so I say hi to Meiling and Jess at the locker bay. They wander off to first-period orchestra, leaving Bryan to hover over my shoulder as I stuff all my things except my math book into my locker.

"Jess said I use too much cologne," he says, sniffing the back of his forearm.

"If you're putting cologne on your arm, she's probably right."

"Hi Danny!"

We both turn to see Clementine standing at the entry to the locker bay with a book bag slung over her shoulder. She's wearing a polka-dot blouse with a denim skirt. I pull my eyeballs up so I don't get caught checking out her legs—which are nice, not that I was looking. She's way too awake for this hour. I wonder if she's dropped by the boba shop.

"Just wanted to say hi!" she says, somewhat uncertainly. "I hope you don't mind that I sent you an email this morning. Is email better for you, or text?"

"Uh . . ." Next to me, Bryan is staring openly. Think round-eyed, open-mouthed emoji. "Either email or text is fine." *I'm equally likely to blow off messages in either.*

Clementine smiles, and once again I'm surprised by how the space around her brightens when she does. "Fantastic. I'll catch up with you later!"

Bryan doesn't remember to close his mouth until after Clementine's disappeared around the corner. Then he turns to me, and this sly grin appears on his face.

"It's not what you think," I say before he says anything that'll make me regret having ears. I close my locker extra loudly as a backup measure.

"What? I didn't say anything," Bryan says.

"I ended up contacting Clementine about that flyer we saw in the hallway."

"Oh yeah, for the Kale Corp thing? So is there a new club starting up?"

"Kind of."

"What do you mean kind of?"

There's basically no way for me to explain it that will not end up with Bryan giving me crap about this. "I was the only one who signed up."

"Oh." Bryan looks confused. "So is it still happening?"

"Well, Clementine gave me an out, since I was the only volunteer, but I told her I'd help her."

"Wow." Bryan nods thoughtfully. "So you just joined a two-person club. You must be really dedicated to the cause, huh?"

"Yeah." He's taking this more in stride than I thought. "I wasn't sure about it at first, but then Clementine started talking about how important the old Chinatown shops were, and basically how they're cultural pieces that wouldn't come back if they disappeared. And I don't know, it made sense somehow. She made a good pitch. Newspaper editor, you know. She's got a way with words."

Bryan stares at me for a moment, and then he slaps his thigh and busts out laughing. "Dude, you should listen to yourself."

"What?" I glare at him, but he just keeps laughing and makes a big show of wiping his eyes. People around the hall turn to look at us.

"You totally just said yes because she's hot." Bryan clasps his hands together, all exaggerated choirboy earnestness. "They're important cultural pieces that won't come back."

I throw my hands in the air. There's no way to shut Bryan up when he gets like this, so I just concentrate on moving out of the area as quickly as possible. "Good grief, man. Yes, my family's restaurant is at stake, but I just signed on to get some action."

Bryan trots at my elbow like a golden retriever slathered in hair gel. "So you really gonna fight the Man?" He furrows his brow. "Should I help or something?"

"Oh, hell no." One awkward encounter between Clementine and Bryan is plenty. Besides, I'd take a bullet for Bryan, but I'd also be the first to tell you that he's completely useless as far as getting anything practical done.

Bryan shrugs off my words. "So . . . is Kale Corp going to leave a horse carcass on your doorstep now?"

"One of the aunties would probably find a way to stir-fry it."

Bryan snorts at that. "With extra ginger."

He peels off into history class. I shake my head and duck into math. Leave it up to Bryan to turn everything, even our family's livelihoods, into some kind of attempt to get laid. As I go to my desk, I think about everything that comes next and wonder about what this fight will mean.

I'm definitely not thinking about the way Clementine's eyes light up when she talks about the Chinatown cause or about how I caught a whiff of strawberry shampoo when she tossed her braid over her shoulder just now. I mean, what kind of Neanderthal do you think I am?

CHAPTER NINE

CLEMENTINE

I'M TRYING TO BE EXTRA CAREFUL NOT TO COME
on too strong with the Chinatown Cares thing. I know I can
get intense sometimes, and I don't want to freak Danny out.
So I made sure to gather all my ideas into one bulleted email
instead of sending them haphazardly one by one. I mean, if I
were discussing newspaper ideas with Adenike, we'd be texting
back and forth all day, but Adenike is used to me. I don't know
Danny well at all.

"Let me get this straight," says Adenike, fighting to keep
the corners of her mouth down. "You were careful to show self-
restraint by limiting yourself to four bullet points in your initial
email to him."

I pop an orange Starburst into my mouth. "Why? Do you
think that's too many?"

"Oh, my dear Clementine. I suppose you'd have to ask him
to be sure. Maybe next time you see him, you can check to see
how much of the whites of his eyes are showing. How did the

rest of the meeting go, by the way? Was it as horrible as you thought it'd be?"

"It *was* kinda stressful," I admit. "I mean, the moment he walks into the newspaper office, I can tell he's wondering why no one's there. And Nadia's in the office, so I don't want to have this whole awkward conversation in front of her. So I suggested grabbing boba, but I was super self-conscious about how to do it, because I didn't want it to seem like I was just trying to get a cute guy on a date."

"So he's cute?"

I stop chewing midbite. Did I say that part out loud? "No."

Nike raises her eyebrows.

"I mean yes, he is, but that's irrelevant. The point is—"

Adenike whips out her phone. "I don't know why I haven't looked him up yet. . . ."

I bat half-heartedly at her as she moves her phone out of my grasp. "The point is that I was trying *not* to make it look like I was hitting on him. Because I *wasn't*—"

A picture loads on Nike's screen. She pauses to study it, and then she nods appreciatively. "You're right. He has a pleasant face. Love the hair too. He looks kinda like the guy in that C-drama you watched last year."

I can't help peeking over her shoulder. She's looking at what must be Danny's online yearbook picture from last year, so it's not the most flattering photo, but his crooked smile and unruly hair have a certain charm.

I hit the power button on her phone. "As I was saying, I was doing my best to keep it casual and not awkward, and I was up-front with him about the whole situation, like you told me to be."

Adenike relents and puts her phone in her bag. "And how did he take it?"

I deflate a bit. "I don't know. I'm not quite sure what to make of him, to be honest. I mean, he was a little standoffish at first."

She nods sagely. "Unfortunately looks and personality don't always correlate. Don't worry, there are plenty of other fish."

I roll my eyes. Adenike gives me a hard time, but neither of us is desperate to get our love lives going—not with everything else going on senior year. The last time I dated anyone was in sophomore year, when I had a thing with someone on the newspaper photo staff. It fizzled out, and he's since switched to yearbook.

"Well, if you'll let me finish, Danny was kind of distant at first, and he was definitely surprised to be the only volunteer. I totally thought he was gonna drop out. But"—I emphasize that last word with a finger and raised eyebrows—"he stayed on. He was kind of mellow about it all, actually."

"Mellow is good," said Adenike. "You need more mellow in your life."

I fish out my phone. "I especially need more mellow this morning, since Bobaboy left another comment on my blog last night." And now I have time to reply.

"Really?" asks Adenike. "You're gonna go straight from stressing about Chinatown Cares to stressing about your blog?"

"I swear." I'm already typing furiously. "Bobaboy is like ninety-five years old. His screen name should really be GetOff-MyBobaLawn. It's like, nothing's good enough for him unless it's five hundred years old and has the full blessing of our ancestors."

Adenike pats me on the back. "Maybe it's a good thing you're getting into the Chinatown Cares thing. Less stress for all involved if you step away from your blog a bit."

CHAPTER TEN

DANNY

EVENTUALLY I TELL CLEMENTINE THAT MONDAY
works best for visiting Chinatown Cares 'cause they're usually
slow days at the tea shop. In the time between scheduling our
meeting with the mother ship and the actual day of, Clementine tells me they'll "absolutely love" me at least twenty times.
If I'd made a drinking game out of it, I'd be well on my way to
a liver transplant.

We meet up after school to take the bus over. As far as silver
linings go, Bryan's not around to make snarky comments this
time, and the awkwardness is less palpable when we greet each
other. I think I'm also building up some immunity against her
energy levels, because I'm feeling less of that shock of exhaust-
ing expectations every time she looks at me.

"Do you take the bus often?" Clementine asks as we get
on. She looks nice in one of those blouses that tie at the neck,
which makes me wonder if I should have picked a less wrinkled T-shirt. The seats are full, so we grab on to the straps that

hang down. The top of Clementine's head is about level with my nose. She definitely uses strawberry shampoo.

"Pretty often," I say. "I have my permit, but my parents are usually using the car to run errands."

"Yeah, I have my permit too, but my parents don't trust me to drive myself yet."

My phone buzzes. I fish it out of my pocket to see that it's Mom asking when I'll be back. I type back, *In an hour*. As I put my phone away, I see that Clementine's brought hers out too, and she's frowning intensely at it. She types something, stops, and then types something else.

"Everything all right?" I ask.

She startles and puts her phone away. "Yeah, everything's fine," she says somewhat sheepishly. "I swear, comment threads are the devil's invention."

"Yeah, I'm pretty sure they have their own circle of hell."

She smiles in a way that makes me feel as if we're both in on some secret. I'm startled at how special it makes me feel. A few moments later, Clementine leans toward the window and pulls the bell.

It's a short walk from the bus stop to the Chinatown Cares building. As I walk in, I'm a bit surprised at how low-key the atmosphere is. I'm not quite sure what I expected. A bunch of hipsters with nose rings? Jugs of milk and pepper-spray-blocking goggles? But it looks like a real estate agent's office.

Rui and Silas don't quite live up to Clementine's promise that they'd loooove me on sight, but they're friendly enough, and they don't seem put out by the fact that there's only two of us. I suppose, given the size of their building, that they don't have all that many people on staff either. After introductions, they hustle us into the conference room, and soon everyone has notebooks and pens out and they're doing that thing where they're looking at each other enthusiastically and waiting for the magic to happen.

I should probably have brought a notebook. Or some magic.

"Danny's parents own Fragrant Leaves teahouse," says Clementine.

"That's right, you mentioned that!" says Rui. Suddenly, all her attention is focused on me. "How are your parents handling the Kale Corp news?"

Mostly they're pretending that it's not actually happening. At least when I'm around. "They don't really talk about it."

"No worries," says Silas. His drawl sounds even slower next to Rui's quick chatter. Out of the people in this room, he's the only one who doesn't carry himself like he has a direct hookup to intravenous caffeine. "These things take time to process. Rui and I will be reaching out directly to all the business owners pretty soon. Is that all right with you, or would you rather talk to your parents yourself?"

I mentally catalog all the things I'd rather do instead of talking to my parents about Kale Corp. Pull out my fingernails, run around the schoolyard naked singing Little Lin hits, die . . .

"It's fine with me if you reach out to them."

"Fantastic," says Silas.

Rui leans in, raising her eyebrows for extra emphasis. "We're going to try to hit this from all angles," she says. "As I mentioned, you two will be super helpful in getting the community informed."

I don't quite follow the entire conversation after that. There's some talk of public action and petitions. Clementine is nodding like a bobblehead doll, and I start wondering why someone would name their company Kale Corp. Was the founder a fan of green smoothies? Did focus groups decide that a high-fiber leafy vegetable was the best way to part health-conscious rich people from their money?

"What do you think, Danny?" asks Clementine.

The green smoothies disappear in a puff of cruciferous-scented smoke. Everyone's looking at me.

"Sorry," I mumble. "What was the question?"

"Rui and Silas were thinking we could start by gathering signatures for a petition."

"Oh." I do my best to look with-it. "Where?"

"All over," says Rui brightly. "You can do it at your school, and you should definitely talk to customers and store owners at the shopping center. It might also be a good idea to do some door-to-door canvassing."

Clementine's nodding enthusiastically again. Is there anything she's *not* totally gung ho about? I can't tell if she throws herself into all her extracurriculars or if she really is this dedicated to Chinatown. "That sounds like a great idea. Maybe we can start off with familiar territory. School, perhaps?" She turns to me. "Or your shop?"

Honestly, I'm beginning to question the life choices that brought me here. The image of Clementine and me awkwardly holding clipboards in the mall parking lot as aunties and uncles give us the side-eye makes me queasy. Pushing petitions at school in front of everyone from the chess team to the cheerleading squad doesn't sound much better. I never thought I'd say this, but going door-to-door talking to strangers is sounding like the least scary option.

"I'm up for canvassing," I say. "But maybe we can start with the broader community?"

Rui nods. "That works great for us. Just let us know when you'd like to do it."

CHAPTER ELEVEN

CLEMENTINE

OUR FIRST OFFICIAL CHINATOWN CARES YOUTH Council initiative is door-to-door canvassing on Saturday morning. I did some canvassing for the last election with my mom, so I have some idea what to expect. I know to bring a wide-brim hat, sunscreen, and plenty of water. I suggest those things to Danny the night before as well, and he texts back.

> sunscreen, hat, water, got it.

I do an inventory of our other supplies. Flyers informing tenants about their housing rights, check. Petition forms, check. Clipboards, check. Extra pens, check.

I'm supposed to meet up with Danny at the neighborhood where we're canvassing. It's kind of exciting stepping out for our first official outreach event. Up until now, we've been talking about doing stuff instead of actually doing it. But now we're heading out into the real world. Maybe we'll even make a difference.

Danny's already waiting for me when I hop off the bus, looking a little sleepy under his baseball cap. He's more dressed up than he usually is, in a short-sleeve button-down over gray slacks and sneakers. Maybe it's the button-down, but for the first time, I notice how broad his shoulders are, as well as the lean muscles of his arms. I guess he does spend a lot of time carrying teapots full of boiling water.

"Hey." His lips quirk in a crooked smile that makes my stomach do an unexpected flip.

"Hey yourself," I say, channeling my best on-task editor persona. Last thing I need is to start blushing around my only volunteer. I'm starting to get the hang of working with Danny these days, though he's hard to read. I still perceive this reluctant vibe from him sometimes, but he's shown up to enough meetings now that I do think he wants to do this.

"Can I take the bag?" he asks, reaching for it with a (nicely sculpted) forearm.

"We can split the weight," I say, handing him a thick stack of flyers. "Here's the rundown. First, we have flyers letting the residents know about their tenant rights and the resources they can access through Chinatown Cares. We'll leave those at every doorstep and go over the information with anyone who has questions. If the residents are open to speaking to us beyond that, we tell them about our petition."

It takes him a few moments to digest this. "Okay, where should we start?"

"How about this one?" I point to an apartment complex with units that open to outdoor walkways.

"Sounds good to me," he says.

"Great. But first . . ." I pull out my phone and motion him closer for a selfie. "Let's take a photo for the newspaper Instagram."

Danny gets this expression like he just swallowed a spoonful of lemon juice. "Sorry, I'd rather not." He fidgets with a button on his shirt and looks away. "Feels a bit too self-congratulatory."

I reel back. Where the heck did that come from? "It's just for awareness. People can't support us if they don't know what we're doing."

Danny's still giving me that skeptical look, and I put my phone back in my purse. "Never mind. Let's just go."

Honestly, I'm kind of offended. That's the thing about Danny. It's like, one moment he's perfectly nice, and then all of a sudden he's super prickly. I guess Adenike was right: good looks don't always match up with a pleasant personality.

Neither of us talks as we walk to the apartment complex, and I'm thinking up all kinds of reasons as to why there's nothing wrong with taking selfies. I mean, I'm a journalist. I document things.

It's almost a relief to get to the door of the first apartment. I raise my hand to ring the doorbell and grudgingly make eye contact with Danny to make sure he's ready. He has the grace to look a little guilty at least as he nods his go-ahead, or perhaps I'm just imagining it. The doorbell chimes. There's no answer.

We leave a flyer and move on to the next unit, where no one

answers either. Danny knocks on the third door, with the same result.

"So," says Danny, scuffing his sneakers on the ground after door number four. "Do you think they're all actually not home on a Saturday morning, or are they just hiding?"

We get our answer at the next unit. Danny rings the doorbell. There's silence again, and then we hear a bit of shuffling from inside.

"Is that whispering?" Danny mouths at me.

A high-pitched kid's voice comes through the door. "Why aren't we at home?" The last words are muffled by shushing.

Danny and I look at each other. His shoulders start to shake, and I bite my lip to keep from giggling.

"Guess we should move on," I say.

Things are less tense between us after that. We move from door to door, until someone finally answers. It's a middle-aged woman who listens politely as we hand her pamphlets and thanks us. When we move on to the petition, though, she cuts us off. "I'm sorry. I'm very busy right now."

We thank her and move on.

Danny puts his backpack down and swivels the knots out of his back. "Seems like we just have this one unit left. How about we take a break after this?"

"Sounds like a plan."

He lets me do the honors. An older Asian man opens the door. He smiles and nods enthusiastically when we give him the pamphlets. It's encouraging enough for me to start in about the petition, but I can tell he's having some trouble understanding my English.

"Do you speak Chinese?" I ask.

"Cantonese," he says.

I turn to Danny. "You can speak Cantonese, right?"

"Oh." He startles a bit, as if surprised that he does. But then he jumps in and starts pointing at the clipboards and explaining things. He's impressively fluent, at least it looks that way to me. I catch a few words like "Kale Corp" and "Hudson Street." The old man is nodding along and making what sound like understanding noises. When Danny offers his pen, the man signs the petition and smiles at us before he closes the door. We wait until the latch turns, and then we high-five.

"Not a bad way to finish this building," I say.

"This calls for a celebration," Danny says. He reaches into his backpack and brings out a wrinkled paper bag. "I snatched some pastries from the shop before I left, and I remember seeing a park across the street. Wanna sit down over there and have a snack?"

"My stomach's growling at the thought."

We round the corner and head toward the street. The park on the other side looks like one of those old Jasper City institutions that've been nurturing families for decades. Giant trees tower over picnic benches and an admittedly patchy lawn. A woman jogs by with a Great Dane, while a handful of kids scream from atop a rust-colored play structure. One of those shady trees looks really great right now. I'm eager to get there, but I realize as we're crossing the street that my foot hurts.

"You okay?" Danny asks. "You're limping."

Guess I wasn't hiding it as well as I thought. I stop at the other side of the road and give my ankle an exploratory swivel. Yep, definitely a sore spot on my right heel. I grimace. "I wore some new shoes yesterday and got a blister. I thought I'd be okay today if I wore sneakers."

He furrows his brow. I'm kind of touched at how concerned he looks. "You think you need to call it a day?"

"No, I don't think so. It's an old blister and the sneaker's not pressing too hard on it. I just should've put a Band-Aid on before I came out today."

Danny weighs my words. "Well, it might help to sit for a bit."

The trees let through the perfect amount of sunshine, a smattering of speckles that dance with the wind. We plop down on a greener patch of grass. Danny brings out a paper bag.

"I have flaky sun cakes right here," he says. "And two egg tarts."

"Oh my gosh." I can feel my saliva glands aching as he hands them over. The sun cake is perfectly light, with white flakes that fall onto the grass with each bite despite my attempts to be neat. And the lusciously creamy egg tart, with its perfect amount of caramelized sweetness and rich buttery smell, is a darn near religious experience.

"This is amazing," I say.

"My mom makes the best egg tarts," Danny says with a matter-of-fact pride. "That's what the aunties say."

We're silent for a while, which is just fine with me because this egg tart and I need some quality time.

Danny washes down his last bite with a swig from his water bottle. He puts a hand on the grass and jumps to his feet in a surprisingly fluid motion. "Tell you what," he says. "Since your foot is hurting, why don't you stay here while I run down to the high-rise on the corner to see if we can get in? That way, if it's a bust, you won't have gone all that way for nothing."

"Oh, are you sure?" I feel bad taking it easy so early in the day.

He gives his lopsided grin. "Yeah, no worries. I'll be right back."

It's a beautiful day. A little warmer than I'd like, but there's a breeze. I admit it's nice not to be on my feet. I sit back and feel the prickly grass on my palms and the wind in my hair. A short distance away, a group of five-year-olds pick the leaves off an unfortunate bush and pile them onto the sidewalk.

Danny jogs back a short while later. He gives me a thumbs-up and plops cross-legged next to me, clutching a plastic bag like a sack of pirate's booty. "I buzzed the resident that Rui told us to contact, and he said he'd let us in no problem. I also dropped by the corner store and picked up some Band-Aids."

He proceeds to show off the contents of his bag one by one: Band-Aids, a tube of Neosporin, two bags of Flamin' Hot Cheetos, and two bottles of red Gatorade.

When I raise my eyebrows at the last two, he shrugs mischievously. "Canvassing is tiring. We need our electrolytes."

He made a good call with the Gatorade—it's blissful to have

an ice-cold beverage on a day like this. Danny takes a Flamin'
Hot Cheeto and dips it in his Gatorade before popping it into
his mouth.

"Did you just dip your Cheeto in the Gatorade?"

His grin is unapologetic. "It's actually really good. Only with
red Gatorade, though, because Flamin' Hot Cheetos are red.
Regular Cheetos would need orange Gatorade. There's a science behind it."

There's something different about him. Sitting here in the
grass, chatting about Cheetos, Danny's more relaxed and hap-
pier than I've ever seen him. He projects a playfulness that
draws out the same in myself.

"Science, huh?" I say.

"Definitely. But don't take my word for it. Try it yourself."

I'm curious, though part of me worries that this is just an
elaborate prank to get me to do something gross. I shoot him
a suspicious glance, which makes him grin even wider. Then I
dip a Cheeto and pop it into my mouth.

I gag. "It's disgusting."

Danny shrugs. "Not everyone can have a refined palate for
snacks."

I throw a Cheeto at him, which he handily catches and dips
into his Gatorade. He soaks it in there a few more seconds
than necessary, making deliberate eye contact as he does. The
gaze he turns on me is part teasing, part smoldering challenge,
almost flirtatious. The kind of look that seeps into your bones.

I shield my eyes, thankful that the whole Cheetos thing

gives me an excuse to look away. "Ew . . . gross."

"Sooo good," he says around a mouthful of Gatorade-soaked Cheetos, which I admit kind of undermines the whole smoldering attractive mystique. When I look at him again, there's laughter in his eyes.

Finally, the Cheetos are fully consumed. The cheese-flavoring-contaminated Gatorades are closed up and packed away for toxic waste disposal, and my blister is all bandaged up. I'm well hydrated and ready to go.

"You sure you're okay to do another building?" Danny asks. "If you need a few more minutes I could take a few floors by myself."

Under different circumstances, my inner feminist would be insulted that he keeps offering to do stuff for me. It's not like I'm a delicate flower. But I don't get the feeling that Danny's asking in a condescending way. I'm also surprised that he's offering to canvass solo, because I can tell this isn't exactly his thing. I doubt he'd choose to spend his morning this way if his family's restaurant were not at stake.

"I'm all right to walk," I say with a playful smile and an arch of my brow. "Now that my wounds have received the best medical care."

Danny blinks, a stunned expression flashing across his face. It passes so quickly, though, that I'm not sure I didn't imagine it. And then he grins again. "It's the egg tarts. They have healing qualities."

I can't argue with that.

The apartment building on the corner is a high-rise with a gray concrete facade. The security guard pays us no attention as we buzz the apartment Rui told us about. A few minutes later, an older Asian man comes down and opens the door.

"You kids working with Chinatown Cares?"

"Yes, just doing some outreach," I say.

He gives us a thumbs-up and wishes us luck. Danny and I get back to work. The response we get in this building is the same mix as before. Most people don't answer the door, and a few others accept the flyers but clearly want us to leave.

We're at the ninth floor when a woman in red sweatpants opens the door. When we start our spiel, her face lights up. "I love Chinatown Cares! They helped my friend when her landlord was trying to push her out of her apartment. He was refusing to fix things and raising the rent, and the Chinatown Cares people helped her know her rights."

The lady looks carefully over our flyers and asks all kinds of questions about the seminars and services being offered. Her eyes open wide when I tell her about the Kale Corp petition. "I go to that shopping center all the time. I'll definitely sign."

As she takes the pen, a gray streak rushes across her living room and makes a break for the apartment door. Something furry brushes past my legs, then streaks down the hall.

"Chloe! My cat!"

Danny and I exchange horrified looks. Then we drop our things, and all three of us give chase.

Chloe the cat appears to be some kind of long-haired gray,

and she must have really yearned for freedom, because she's totally booking it. She runs to the end of the hallway and stops there, but when the lady goes to catch her, the cat ducks between her legs and zigzags past Danny and me. Then the feisty feline darts through an open door into the stairwell.

"Who propped open the stairwell?" fumes Red Sweatpants Lady.

We run to the stairs. The cat's already out of sight.

"Ma'am, if you want, we can split up," says Danny. "You could go down, and Clementine and I will go up."

"Okay," says the lady. "One sec." She disappears into her apartment and comes out with a Ziploc bag full of cat treats. She also gives us a towel "for wrapping the cat."

As the lady's footsteps echo down the stairwell, Danny and I trade weirded-out glances. He gives me a crooked smile and stuffs his hands in his pockets. "Shall we?"

We start the trudge up. I'm looking at the towel under my arm and wondering how exactly we're going to get the cat to agree to being "wrapped."

"How tall is this building again?" Danny asks. He's starting to breathe harder from the exertion.

"Twenty floors?" I say. "Or was it twenty-five?"

It's a workout. On the bright side, none of the doors on other floors are propped open, which hopefully means the cat is still in the stairwell somewhere. I feel terrible that we managed to lose the pet of our one enthusiastic supporter.

The building is twenty stories high. I know that because on

floor nineteen, we can see that there's one more level to go. Danny rounds the corner, stops abruptly, and puts a hand on my shoulder. The gesture is surprisingly confident, and the pressure of his hand on my shoulder grounds me. He points up the stairwell. There's our fuzzball, at the very top of the stairway. Her fur's sticking up, and her back is arched.

"I'm not sure it's a good idea to grab her right now," I mutter. "Maybe we should get her owner."

"Her owner's probably nearing the first floor by now," says Danny. "I don't know if we can keep the cat here that long."

"Well, what's our alternative? Get ripped to pieces?"

He lowers his arm, leaving my shoulder warm where his hand had been. "I used to help Bryan corral his cat for vet visits. Let's see what we can do." Before I can make a skeptical reply, he starts talking softly. "Hey Chloe, how are you doing? That was a bit of a climb wasn't it?"

The cat waves its tail back and forth.

Danny keeps talking. I don't completely catch everything he's saying . . . something about how the pigeon watching isn't what it used to be and the various habits of local mice. Miraculously, the cat seems to be calming down. Danny places a cat treat on the floor and backs away. As Danny talks, Chloe very carefully creeps toward the treat and sniffs it.

"Yeah, have a few, Chloe. They're tasty."

The cat takes a bite. Danny puts some more on the floor in front of the cat, leading her closer to us.

Danny looks back at me. "Towel," he mouths.

I feel like a cat commando, sneaking up that staircase. Danny reaches back for the towel, his fingers brushing my arm before landing on the fabric. The skin of his fingertips is calloused but warm. His voice is shiver inducing—friendly, low, and hypnotic as he keeps up his cat-whisperer monologue. He holds the towel casually in his arms, fiddling with it, adjusting it into some configuration I don't quite follow.

The next part happens so quickly, I have trouble catching it all. Danny attacks, moving almost like a cat himself. There's a fluid coiling of limbs, a rush forward, a scuffle. Yowls fill the air, and then Danny's holding what looks like a cat burrito. A very wriggly cat burrito.

Danny holds the sides down tight. I really hope he's got a firm grip on those claws. "It's okay, Chloe girl," he murmurs. "We're just going to get you home."

We're careful walking down. Danny keeps talking to the cat, emanating calm through his pores while I trudge nervously alongside him. I try not to imagine Chloe bolting out of Danny's arms, pulling us off-balance, and sending us tumbling down the stairs.

We run into Chloe's owner on the twelfth floor. She's ecstatic to see Danny's bundle, and we make our way back to the apartment, where Danny very carefully hands the cat over.

"We're so sorry to let your cat out," I say.

The lady waves our apology away. "No, no, it was my fault for not paying more attention. Thank you for everything you do for Chinatown, truly."

We wish her a good day. I gather up the flyers we'd spilled on the hallway floor and glance at my watch. "It's almost noon.

I told my parents that I'd be back for lunch."

Danny shrugs his bag onto his shoulders. "Should we call it a day? We covered a lot of ground this morning."

We're too exhausted to talk much on our way back to the bus stop. My foot has started hurting again, and my thighs burn from that stair workout. Still, there's something about having chased a cat up a high-rise and successfully captured it that makes you feel at least somewhat accomplished, no matter what your original goals were for the day.

"What do you think?" I ask Danny when we're almost at the stop. "Should we try something different next time? Maybe the customers at your strip mall would be more open to signing petitions."

"Yeah, maybe." His forehead creases, though, and he gets that distant vibe again. I can almost see the walls come up around him, his body language closing off. It's jarring after getting along so well all morning. I'm about to ask for his thoughts in more detail, but then my bus comes around the corner.

"I'll see you at school?" I ask.

He blinks and then seems to remember himself. "Oh, yeah. I'll see you Monday."

As I get onto the bus, Danny exclaims loudly and smacks his forehead.

I turn around. "What?"

He laughs. "We forgot to get the cat lady to sign our petition."

CHAPTER TWELVE

Danny

CANVASSING WAS A LOT LESS PAINFUL THAN I thought it would be. Yeah, we got a lot of doors shut in our faces (or never opened at all). Yeah, it was tiring, but it was also fun to hang out with Clementine. I mean, she can be a bit much at times, but there's something about her optimism and energy that makes an early Saturday morning feel more worthwhile.

But when Clementine suggests getting signatures at our shop next week, my good mood evaporates. Suddenly I'm nervous again, and defensive, and I'm not sure why. I mean, we're trying to save the shop, so of course it makes sense that we'd collect signatures there. But somehow, I feel protective of Fragrant Leaves.

And I don't like the idea of bringing Clementine there.

As the bus lets me off near the store, I'm thinking about how worn down our building is. How we never got around to fixing the paint peeling in two corners and how the air conditioner rattles when it starts. The laminate paneling on the walls is old—like, older than I am—and the furniture, too.

Fragrant Leaves isn't like that boba shop Clementine took me to for our first meeting. We don't have baristas writing cute messages on cups. It's just me, my mom, who doesn't follow your English if it's spoken too quickly, and Dad, who slogs through the day like the dining room's filled with thick grass jelly.

But in the end, it doesn't matter. Because there's no way, practically speaking, that Clementine and I can save our shop without actually spending time there. So when I see her on Monday, I tell her it's fine to do the store next weekend.

The night before she comes, it occurs to me that I should give my parents a heads-up. I poke my head into the kitchen, where my mom is doing the last of the cleanup before we close up shop.

"Mom, one of my classmates is coming to the shop tomorrow."

Mom looks up from the half-loaded dishwasher. At the end of the day, she's muted, her movements slower. Even the red flowers on her blouse look dimmer.

"For school?" she asks.

"Yeah, it's that project I mentioned before." I guess that's close enough. It's a school organization after all, even if it's not for class.

"Okay," says Mom. Almost as an afterthought, she adds, "You need to work harder at school." Never miss a chance to nudge your kid toward straight A's, even if the last two times your kid turned in an assignment late, it was because he got caught up helping customers.

She scratches her arm with a gloved hand, leaving a cluster of bubbles on her sleeve. "Aiya, Danny, wipe that off for me, will you?"

I glance at her blouse. "The bubbles are popping already. It'll be gone before I get there."

Mom raises her eyebrows. "Your mom wiped your butt for six years. You can wipe some soap water off your mom's sleeve."

I chuckle. "Touché."

"What?"

"I'm just saying you raise a good point, Mom." In my defense, by the time I grab a bit of paper towel and come back, the soap really is almost gone.

Mom pecks me on the cheek while I soak up the remaining dampness. "Thank you, Danny."

She continues with the dishes, and I'm left with this feeling that I'm somehow sneaking around behind their backs.

BLACK BELT TEA
ON A WHITE BELT BUDGET

I went to a workshop the other day about gongfu cha. For those of you who don't speak Mandarin, the word "gongfu" is often transliterated into English as "kung fu." Yup, think Bruce Lee and badass pandas. Literally translated, gongfu means hard work, or effort. So you can see why it's used to talk about the martial arts.

Like martial arts, which has a long tradition of discipline and training, gongfu cha is the discipline of brewing and serving a perfect tea experience. All aspects of tea making, from water temperature to brewing time to your posture and the height from which you pour, have to be practiced and perfected. I found the workshop to be fascinating, and the oolong we sampled at the end was otherworldly.

I want to re-create the experience at home, but it's much harder without the fancy tea bowls and equipment. Also, I don't always have time to prewarm the teacup or rinse the tea leaves like I'm supposed to. Which leads me to the question: Is it possible to do black belt tea on a white belt budget and schedule?

So I open the floor to you, my dear readers. How do people feel about infusers instead of brewing cups? Do we really need to prerinse the tea leaves or warm the cups? Is it legit gongfu cha if you're not letting tea and water overflow onto the tray? Could I use slightly hotter water to balance out a cold cup?

I also want your opinions on the ceremonial aspects. How important do you think it is to sit up straight instead of tilting when pouring the tea? Some tea masters circle the water they're pouring on the leaves, while others keep the water in a strong uninterrupted stream. Are these superstitions, or do they add to the experience?

Posted by Hibiscus, 7:30pm

Bobaboy888 (7:50pm): Gongfu cha for Dummies. By all means, take a method that's been perfected over thousands of years and put in your optimizing shortcuts. What could possibly go wrong?

Hibiscus (8:15pm): Good to see you too, Grandpa. Did it hurt your soul when those young upstarts added a motor to your horse and buggy?

Bobaboy888 (8:47pm): Transportation technology is completely different from food or art. You can always get somewhere faster. But there are some things that just shouldn't be messed with Chicken noodle soup, pepperoni pizza . . .

Hibiscus (9:34pm): Really, you're taking a stand for pepperoni pizza?

Bobaboy888 (11:38pm): Don't tell me you're one of those people who go for ham and pineapple. Wait, who am I kidding? I'm talking to someone who uses Papyrus font on her blog graphics.

Hibiscus (9:55am): Sorry I didn't get back to you last night. I was too busy dancing around my pizza oven with a giant slab of Canadian bacon.

CHAPTER THIRTEEN
DANNY

SATURDAY MORNING IS A DISASTER. ACCORDING TO
Mom, Dad looked absolutely exhausted when he woke up, so
she made him go back to bed. It's just me and her opening up
the store, and a big group of tourists comes in just as we realize
the milk for our egg tarts has gone bad. I take over the counter
while Mom makes an emergency milk run. I get several grumpy
comments as I'm frantically running from hot-water pot to cash
register and back. Auntie Lin yells at one of the complainers
to be patient, which almost makes the whole fiasco worth it.
Almost.

Mom finally returns with the milk and helps me catch up
with the orders. When everyone's finally served and the tourist
group meanders out to its next stop, the two of us collapse onto
chairs in the kitchen and catch our breath.

"Thank you, Danny," Mom says, smoothing down her flyaway visor hair. "I don't know how we'd run this store without
you."

Honestly, I don't know either. It seems like it's always something like this, some last-minute emergency, a crisis that needs to be fixed right away. Even when I'm relaxing, I'm constantly on edge, waiting for the next thing to come up.

Mom looks dreamily toward the dining area. "Remember when you used to follow the waiters and 'help' with the cleaning?"

I do have vague memories of following behind the staff with my broom and dustpan. "I was probably just spreading the dust around, wasn't I?"

"You were still learning the proper methods," Mom says diplomatically. "And it didn't help that you always wanted them to give you piggyback rides."

"I'm surprised they put up with me as much as they did."

Mom laughs. "You were the boss's son! What do you expect them to do?"

"Oh." Now that she put it that way, I feel like kind of a brat.

Mom gives me an affectionate pat on the shoulder. "It's okay. Dad and I kept you under control most of the time, and the staff all loved you. And look how you've grown up!"

As Mom goes back behind the counter, I take five minutes to decompress, by which I mean check a thread on *Babble Tea* for new comments. Then I realize that it's almost time for Clementine to arrive, so I meander into the dining area and try to play it cool. Apparently it doesn't work, because five minutes later, Auntie Lin calls out to me.

"What are you doing, looking at the door so much, Danny?

Waiting for your girlfriend?" She cackles at her own joke.

I turn away from the door, trying to pull together some shred of dignity. "I'm just trying not to lose track of time." Then I wipe off a few tables to make myself look busy, and Auntie Lin laughs again. Apparently, the idea of me having a girlfriend is a source of endless hilarity.

I'm half-heartedly scrubbing at a grease stain when I see Clementine coming across the parking lot. I stand up nonchalantly and put my rag away, like I totally haven't been checking the clock every ten seconds. Auntie Lin stacks her mahjong tiles as if she hasn't been exchanging amused glances with her fellow players and smirking nonstop.

Clementine's hair is down today. Instead of her usual braid, she just has the sides pinned back, which makes her look softer. As she approaches the door, she's typing on her phone with a rather satisfied expression. Then she puts it back in the bag and smiles at me.

"Hey!" she says. That smile's gonna be the death of me.

"Welcome to the shop!" I say.

Auntie Lin deliberately turns back to her game. Thank God.

Still, I find plenty to be nervous about. There's a smudge of dirt on the ground right next to my shoes. When was the last time we mopped? And now that the mahjong game has started again, the clash of tiles rings in my ears. Somehow I'm simultaneously self-conscious about how few customers we have and how loud those few customers are.

Clementine's peering around like she's genuinely excited to

be here. I'm not sensing any reservations or judgment, and that relaxes me a bit.

"So!" She clasps her hands together. "Show me around!"

There's something endearing about the expectant look she turns on me, and something within me rises to the occasion. I gesture expansively toward our surroundings. "Welcome to Fragrant Leaves tea shop, your one-of-a-kind Chinatown tea experience." Clementine's eyes crinkle, and the rest of my nerves fall away. "This is the dining room, with the mahjong crew at their usual table. They're here pretty much every morning."

The mahjong crew is still engrossed in their game. Maybe they don't plan to embarrass me after all. I move closer to Clementine and lower my voice.

"Over there is what I call the politics corner, where the uncles like to sit and talk about world affairs. We try to keep them in that corner so they don't offend the rest of the guests. There's an unofficial schedule these days. The Taiwan independence group comes on Tuesdays and Thursdays. The pro-China group comes on Wednesdays and Fridays. And they must never meet, because that would ignite World War Three."

Clementine raises her eyebrows.

I nod toward an uncle strolling by the door. "Over there is Uncle Tony, who likes to walk up and down the edge of the store doing pressure point exercises. See how he's tapping his eyebrows? One hundred taps at each acupoint, no more, no less. He's here at eight a.m. sharp every morning, and he always wants a piping-hot pot of fancy imported tea."

"It seems like you have a lot of regulars."

"Yeah." I'm getting animated now. "And they're great. Like, Uncle Tony? He sold air conditioners before he retired. When our old one broke down, he came in one day and installed a new one for us just like that. He wouldn't take any money, and believe me, it takes some real resolve not to take money from my mom when she wants to give it to you. We've had other regulars fix the plumbing in our bathroom and power-wash the walls. There was also this one stretch of time when we had some middle school kids coming in after school. At first they were totally trashing the dining room, but then Mom put her foot down. By the end of the year, they were not only cleaning up their own stuff, they were busing the other tables too."

"I love that." Clementine's eyes move across the room like she wants to soak it all in. "It sounds like a special place."

Telling Clementine about all this reminds me how proud I really am of this restaurant. The delight on her face warms me, and I get this urge to gather all the things I love about Fragrant Leaves and bring them to her. "Yeah, it is. It feels like more than a shop, you know. It's a community."

Clementine looks behind the counter to where my mom is coming out from the kitchen. "Is that your mom?"

"Yeah." I lead her behind the counter. "Mom, this is Clementine, my classmate that I told you about."

Clementine is all smiles and earnestness. "You have such a lovely shop, Mrs. Mok. Thank you so much for letting me visit."

I can tell by the way Mom spreads her fingers like a hug

emoji that she's charmed. "Thank you! So you two are working on a project?"

Alarm bells go off in my head. "Hey Clementine, how about I show you the kitch—"

But Clementine is already off to the races. "Yes, we really want to keep Kale Corp out of this mall." Mom's eyes widen at the words "Kale Corp." I imagine a trapdoor opening under my feet. Clementine doesn't seem to notice anything awry. "There are so many irreplaceable shops here, including your own lovely teahouse, and we have so many things planned—rallies, petitions, press conferences . . . We really want to get the community behind all of you."

"Oh." Mom looks at me, and I can tell she's still trying to puzzle out Clementine's words. "Danny told us it was a school thing."

"It's a school committee," says Clementine, "but it's so much more than that. It's a community initiative. It's a fight for justice. We want to do all we can to keep Chinatown the unique and vibrant neighborhood that it is."

"Ah, I see." Mom meets my eyes in a way that makes me think we're going to talk later, and I stare back like a raccoon caught in floodlights. Then Mom breaks her gaze and waves at the counter displays. "Anything you want to eat or drink, just take it, okay? Make yourselves at home."

CHAPTER FOURTEEN

CLEMENTINE

I FEEL SLIGHTLY UNEASY AFTER DANNY'S MOM goes into the kitchen.

"Did I say something I wasn't supposed to?"

Danny stares after his mom. For a moment, I think he didn't hear me, but then he shakes his head. "No, Mom's just busy."

"I see." Maybe I just imagined the weirdness. And his mom really was very nice.

Weirdness aside, I'm really enjoying my visit. It's one thing to come here as a customer, but it's a whole new experience to have Danny introduce the place to me, to hear his stories and see the place through his eyes. I'm kind of embarrassed about the review I wrote about this shop a while back. To be fair, the write-up was mostly positive, though I did have opinions about the decorations and the music. It makes me glad that I blog anonymously.

"So! Where should we start?" I ask Danny. "The mahjong players look like they're taking a break. Should we try them?"

Danny's expression is reminiscent of a prairie dog right before a hawk swoops down. "Well, um, they still look like they don't want to be interrupted. Maybe we should—"

An old lady in a flowery blouse waves at us from the mahjong table. "Danny! Who's your friend? Come! Come! Introduce us!"

Prairie-dog Danny cringes. He tilts his head toward the mahjong players with a resigned smile, catching my eye. "Shall we?"

Tiles are scattered all over the mahjong table. One seat is empty and three older aunties sit on the other sides, sipping their tea.

"Auntie Lin," he says to the lady who called us over, "this is Clementine."

She beams, her jade earrings bouncing as she looks at each of us in turn. "This your new girlfr—"

"No," we both say before she can finish.

The auntie snorts and says something in Cantonese that I don't catch. I look to Danny for translation, but he just drops his eyes, and I swear he blushes a bit.

Auntie Lin turns a keen eye on me. "You have boyfriend already?"

Her question takes me off guard. "Uh, no. I—"

She gestures toward Danny like an Asian Vanna White. "Danny's a good boy!" she says. "A little shy, but good-looking, yes?"

Her laugh is infectious, and I find myself smiling back. "Very much so." Oh my God, did I just say that? A prickle of heat spreads from my temples to my scalp.

Danny steps in. I can't look at him. "Actually, Auntie Lin," he says, "we're here to talk about Kale Corp moving in."

"Kale!" Auntie Lin straightens in her seat and crosses her arms. "Your mom tell you about that?"

Danny shakes his head. "It's been in the news, Auntie Lin. Everybody knows about it now."

Auntie Lin clucks her tongue. "Terrible frozen baozi. Terrible. They make things and put them in freezer bags and say it's Chinese food." She shakes her head. "It's not Chinese food."

I seize the opening, as well as the welcome change of topic. "Exactly, Auntie Lin. I am so glad you agree. Because what we're doing today is about preserving the real Chinatown. We want to support old institutions like Fragrant Leaves that have been a cornerstone of the community for decades. Those large corporations moving in just don't have the deep roots or cultural awareness of mom-and-pop shops like this one."

Auntie Lin looks at me with a puzzled expression, and I realize I've lost her. "You don't like Kale Corp either?"

Danny clears his throat and starts speaking gently in Cantonese. He gestures at the petition. I catch a few English words here and there—"Chinatown Cares," "petition"—but everything else goes over my head. My Mandarin's bad enough—my Cantonese is basically nonexistent. As Danny talks, Auntie Lin becomes more animated, and her eyes light up in comprehension. She interjects a few times with what sounds like agreement. Then she smiles at me.

"Okay, I will sign!"

She puts down her name with a flourish, and then she passes it around to the rest of her mahjong partners, who I realize have also been listening. The last auntie to sign hands the clipboard back to me, but I pass it right along to Danny.

"This is your wheelhouse, I think."

He hesitates for a moment, but then he nods and adjusts his grip on the clipboard. There's a confidence in his posture that wasn't there five minutes ago. The two of us go from table to table, and I watch as Danny talks to each of the customers. I'm impressed by how at ease he is with all the regulars. I mean, he's nice enough at school, but here it's like he's a completely different person. It's not your usual barista/customer dynamic. I can tell that these people think of him as family. And though I can't understand most of what he says, I know he's got this.

As we make the rounds, I'm mostly just following along, letting Danny do his thing. I find myself transfixed by the openness in his face, the unaffected honesty in his posture. At one point he looks up and our gazes meet. I'm startled, and slightly embarrassed to be caught looking, but then his eyes crinkle and he grins. Warmth blooms in my chest as I smile back.

After a while, he turns to me. "I think that's about everyone," he says.

I look around the shop. Two hipster-looking twenty-somethings are at a corner table, sipping tea and surfing their phones.

"What about those two?" I ask.

Danny shakes his head dismissively. "Those guys are just here for the social media cred."

I give him an incredulous look. "Seriously? You're going to turn down someone's signature just because they're wearing trucker hats?"

"I mean," Danny stutters, "I just don't think—"

I snatch the clipboard from him and take it to the corner table. I'm a little fidgety, partly from annoyance and partly because I've been feeling a bit useless for the past half hour. I channel it all into a winning smile. The girl and the guy at the table look wary when I approach, but they listen politely when I give them my spiel and sign without hesitation.

I give Danny my best "I told you so" look as I hand the clipboard back.

"Two more signatures. And it really wasn't that hard."

His cheek twitches as he takes the clipboard. "So we're done?"

I can tell he wants to move on, but I'm still annoyed. "Why were you so sure they weren't gonna sign the petition?"

He shrugs. "You were right. I was wrong." The way he says it, though, it sounds more like *Go away.*

Before I can reply, there's a scrape of chairs, and two of the mahjong players stand up to leave.

"Danny! Clementine!" Auntie Lin waves at us. "We need more people!"

Danny freezes. He gives me a sidelong glance and answers

before I can make sense of what's going on. "We have school-work to do, Auntie."

Auntie Lin slaps away his words. "You can't work all the time."

A grudging smile appears on his lips. "Auntie Lin, the only time you ever say that is when you need mahjong partners." He gives me a glance that's part cautious and part amused. "Do you play mahjong?"

My mouth drops open. "I mean, I've played a few times with my grandparents, but I'm not even sure I know all the rules."

Auntie Lin's still waving like an air traffic controller angling for a pay raise. "Just for fun! I won enough money for today. We use just chips, no money." When we don't budge, she walks over and takes my arm in both hands. "Come. You're Chinese. You need to learn to play mahjong."

And that's how I end up at the mahjong table with a tile ruler in front of me and a whirlwind of panicky thoughts in my head. Danny, kitty-corner to me, catches my eye. "Sorry," he mouths. I'm not sure what he's apologizing for—being prickly earlier or getting me looped into mahjong—but there's no time to won-der. Everybody's stacking tiles into neat walls. I do my best to work fast, but the septuagenarians are building circles around me. When Danny finishes his side, he nudges a few stacked tiles toward my part of the wall, which I gratefully accept. His fingers brush mine, sending a flash of warmth up my arm.

Once the stacks are made, people start drawing tiles four at a time. I'm doing my best to keep up. Auntie Lin and the woman next to her have full-on poker faces. The clink of tiles, which might have been soothing in another context, are constant auditory reminders of my inadequacy. If this is "playing for fun," what would playing for money be like? I sneak a glance at Danny, who catches my eye and grins.

"You look like you've done this before," I say under my breath.

"Sometimes I sub in for people who need to leave the table." His voice is low. "Breathe. You're doing great."

The game starts. I know the basic rules. You're trying to make sets of three, either consecutive or three of a kind. You draw a tile every turn, and sometimes you can claim what other people discard.

The first time I claim someone's discard to make a set, everybody congratulates me so enthusiastically that you'd think I won the game. That makes it slightly less embarrassing when I then claim a discard out of turn and Auntie Lin stops to explain the rules to me. About ten minutes into the round, Danny flips his tiles over with his ruler.

"Hu le!" He won.

As Auntie Lin howls in outrage and the refined Auntie Esther laughs, I slip out of my seat.

"Oh, no, Clementine, not yet!" says Auntie Lin. "You have to do at least four rounds. Everyone has to have a chance to start. Otherwise it's bad luck."

I laugh, but I'm not nearly as reluctant as I was the first time. As we start again, I'm still the clumsiest at the table, but I don't make any more major gaffes. Danny keeps finding subtle ways to help me, nudging stacked tiles in my direction, signaling me with a glance when it's my turn. He's really understated about the way he does it. I'm not sure the aunties notice half the time.

Auntie Esther wins the next two games, which garners a lot of complaints from Auntie Lin. A few minutes into the fourth game, I'm surprised to see that I'm only one tile from winning. I wait and wait for my winning tile to show up, but it sure takes its time.

Finally, Auntie Lin flips her tiles down. "Hu le!"

As she collects her chips, she shows me a six of bamboo. "You looking for this, Clementine?" she says with an evil gleam in her eye.

I can't believe it. "Yes! I was waiting for so long!"

Auntie Lin winks unapologetically. "Yes, I know. So I hung on to it."

I shake my head, laughing. "You are too skilled at this, Auntie."

Auntie Lin points to me. "She's a good one," she tells Danny. "You should win her over! Buy her gifts! Take her out to dinner before someone else snaps her up." At this point, Auntie Lin's comments are just one absurdity on top of all the ones before, and I'm beyond embarrassment. Danny and I just look at each other and grin. Perhaps it's my imagination, but we hold each other's gazes a moment longer than we need to.

It's getting close to noon, so I thank everyone and tell them that my parents are expecting me at home. Auntie Lin pointedly asks Danny if he's going to walk me to the bus station. We both step out the door, chuckling from the ridiculousness of it all.

"Sorry about the aunties," he says after the door closes. "They can be a bit much."

"Don't be," I say. "They were delightful. This entire shop is lovely."

He gives a half smile, putting his hands in his pockets and bowing his head as we walk. "Yeah, I guess I go back and forth on it. Sometimes I love it here. Sometimes it's kind of stifling. I feel like I've spent most of my life just in those two rooms."

"Do you think you'll stay close by for college too?"

Danny makes a face. The wind's making a mess of his hair, and I have an urge to finger brush it into place. "I got that letter with my college counselor assignment a few weeks ago, but I haven't set an appointment or anything. I guess I'll probably apply to places around here. What about you?"

"I'm still trying to figure it out. My mom is from the East Coast, and she talks about Boston like it's a magical place. Also, my sister's at Brown and she really likes it there."

"You could probably go wherever you want," he says.

I'm more flattered than I expect at his words, maybe because I kinda assumed he didn't know much about me. "Maybe? It's hard sometimes to keep perspective, because Claudia was this huge overachiever, and so were my parents. It's kind of hard being in their shadow."

He gives a crooked smile. I notice that he has a single dimple underneath one corner of his mouth. "Well, I'd say you definitely fit into the overachiever bucket."

I laugh. "Well, when I'm not annoying the newspaper staff to death."

Danny runs his fingers through his hair as we near the bus stop. "I can see why your mom likes the East Coast. My family visited New York City when I was twelve for my cousin's wedding. My mom said the city was too crowded, but I thought it was the greatest thing ever. I thought it was so cool how all the skyscrapers just went up around you on all sides, and how you could hop into a subway station and come out somewhere else. I'd love to go back one day."

He has this dreamy look in his eyes as he describes it, one I've never seen on him before. "Maybe for college?"

He pauses uncomfortably, and I get the sense he's trying to decide how much to say. "I've thought about it, but New York City is really expensive, and my parents need me here."

"You mean at the shop?"

"Yeah. They depend on me a lot to help out." He sounds so resigned.

"Maybe you could still apply to some places just in case. If things work out, maybe your parents could hire help or something. I feel like there's always a solution if you look hard enough."

Danny gives me a sidelong glance. "You think so?" He's half smiling, but there's also a challenge in his voice. "So let's say you're talking to a single mom on minimum wage. Or an undocumented immigrant. Would you still say it's all about looking hard enough to find a solution?"

"Are you comparing your situation to those people?"

"No," says Danny. "I'm just curious how far your idealism goes."

Idealism. The word irks me, because I don't think Danny meant it in a good way, but I feel like I can't say anything without sounding super privileged.

We're silent for a while, watching the cars go by. That undertone of joy I'd felt from Danny just a moment before is gone. My mind goes back to that conversation earlier in the day with his mom.

"Um . . . sorry for harping on this, but was I not supposed to tell your parents about our Chinatown project? Your mom seemed surprised when I mentioned it."

Danny flinches. "Oh . . . Yeah, I hadn't told them the whole story yet. I told them it was a school project."

"Why wouldn't you tell them? I think they'd be really proud of you for getting involved."

He shrugs. "It's complicated. They've never really talked to me about restaurant issues. They consider it something for adults to worry about."

"Oh." What he says doesn't surprise me, exactly, since I'm sure a lot of parents are that way. But it still strikes me how different it is from the way my parents do things. "Well, maybe as you get older they'll start seeing things differently."

"Maybe," he said. "But I don't think it's just an age issue. My parents don't really get the idea of changing the system. In their heads, when things get tough, you're just supposed to put your head down and work harder. You take what life gives you and you trudge forward as best you can."

"So you wouldn't call them idealists?"

He meets my gaze, his mouth quirking to acknowledge the barb in my question. "No, I'd say we're all a very pragmatic family."

My bus rounds the corner just then.

"Oh, before I forget." Danny hands me a crumpled paper bag. "You like the egg tarts, right?"

I open the bag and peek inside. A buttery smell comes out that just about makes me melt. "Oh. Was it that obvious?"

He grins. "Kinda."

He really does have a nice smile, or maybe it's just my stomach talking. I stuff the tarts into my purse. "Thank you. These make the whole morning worth it."

A mischievous glint appears in his eye. "You're welcome. I was feeling charitable after you complimented my looks to Auntie Lin."

"Ha!" *Please don't blush again.* He must think I'm such a dork. "Well, it's not the *most* outrageous thing I've said for baked goods."

"Wow, you must have told some pretty good whoppers, then."

"What can I say? I like sweets." I shrug, trying to reclaim some of my dignity. "Thanks for being a good sport about that. Those aunties are so lovely, I figured it'd be better just to play along."

An expression I don't quite recognize flickers across his face. A moment later, it's gone, and he grins again. "Yeah, no worries. You just gotta roll with it when the aunties get going. But they love you. You should definitely come by the shop more often."

"Oh, don't you worry about that," I say. "Now that I've had these egg tarts, you won't be able to get rid of me."

CHAPTER FIFTEEN
DANNY

I CATCH MYSELF SMILING AS I WATCH THE BUS drive off with Clementine. Images from the morning linger in my mind: Clementine at the mahjong table, biting her lip as she frowns at her tiles. Clementine lighting up at the sight of egg tarts. The two of us trading a celebratory fist bump after collecting signatures from everyone.

The aunties can be a bit much, but Clementine was cool about it all. Which is a relief, because I find myself hoping that she meant it when she promised to come back to the shop. Also, it's good that she clarified that she was just humoring the aunties by playing along with their matchmaking. Always better to get everyone on the same page. We wouldn't want things to start getting weird, not that I was reading anything into her actions or anything.

In the afternoon, I cover for my mom at the register. After a while, Dad comes out of the office. Sleeping in this morning was good for him. His eyes are brighter than usual. He hands me the comics page of the Chinese-language paper.

"It's funny today," he says. "See if you can read it yourself, or I can read it to you later." He sees the cup of oolong I've brewed for myself on the counter. "Can I try?"

"Yeah."

He circles the cup under his nose and then takes a slow, thoughtful sip. I hold my breath until he nods his approval. "You've always had a good sense for brewing."

He's said it before, but it still lifts my mood.

After Dad spells me at the register, I look over the comics (which I can half decipher based on what few Chinese words Mom taught me to read), and then I sneak in a few hours of homework before dinner. It's only around closing time, when Mom comes by my desk as I'm finishing up my English reading, that I remember the awkward conversation Clementine and I had with her this morning.

"So," she asks, "what is this *school project* you are working on with Clementine?"

"Oh, uh." I push my chair back from my desk. Guess it's time to come clean. "It was Clementine's idea."

Coming clean doesn't mean I can't blame it on someone else.

I continue. "Clementine was putting up posters about the Kale Corp takeover at school. She wanted to put together a group of kids to work with Chinatown Cares."

Mom narrows her eyes. "Work with them how?"

"Just petitions and things like that."

"What do petitions do? Kale Corp going to listen to signatures?"

To be honest, I'm not so sure myself. It seemed to make more sense when Rui and Silas were talking about it. "I don't know. It's public pressure or something."

Mom's quiet for a bit. I wonder if she's mad at me for butting into adult business. "These things are a waste of time," she says.

So I'm not getting an *Attaboy, Danny. Thanks for doing your part.* Not that I expected fireworks in my honor, but her words still hurt more than I care to admit.

"I'm just trying to help the restaurant," I say.

Mom waves her hand, as if dispelling my words. "You want to help the restaurant? There's dishes that need cleaning over there."

"I do the dishes all the time."

"Good. And if you still want more things to do, just ask me." She looks toward the office door and lowers her voice. "See how tired your dad is every day? Petitions won't make him less tired."

A knot of frustration forms in my chest. I mean, I've had my own doubts about how much work Chinatown Cares was going to be, but I'm annoyed that Mom's shooting it down without knowing anything about it. It's not as if I'm signing up for new extracurriculars every other week. All I do is work at the restaurant. I even skip out on hanging out with my friends on busy nights. And the one time I decide to do something new, something that helps our entire family, my mom thinks it's a waste of time.

"I know Dad is tired," I say. "But it's not like doing more dishes will fix that. We've been trying to 'do more dishes' for years. I want to try something new."

Mom's cheek twitches, and I worry for a moment that I've pissed her off. But then she shakes her head. "Don't let it interfere with your schoolwork," she says. And after a moment she adds, "And don't bring it up too much around Dad."

FUSION TEA IN A MULTIETHNIC WORLD

Things have been kinda hectic in real life. There are big changes happening in my community, pushed along by strong societal forces. It's making me think about how people from different backgrounds influence each other, and how that can have far-reaching consequences.

I've been spending so much time thinking serious thoughts that I'm in the mood for something more lighthearted. Something experimental and out there. I want to be a bit wacky in the kitchen. This morning, I was making a cup of jasmine white tea, and I thought, "What if this had a bit of cream and sugar?"

I know, I know, I'm turning in my Chinese person card right now. But hear me out. What's wrong with a little bit of experimentation? I mean, Chinese people have black tea with milk and boba all the time.

So I made jasmine white tea with cream. It wasn't bad. The cream does overpower the tea flavor a little bit, but that's not necessarily a bad thing. If you're in the mood for something creamy and want just the slightest hint of tea flavor, this might be great, especially before bed.

All this has given me an idea for a new blog series: "Fusion Tea in a Multiethnic World." It'll be like the tea equivalent of Korean taco trucks, mixing inspiration from lots of cultures to create exciting new combinations.

Now, dear readers, I need your ideas for what to do. Iced chrysanthemum tea with sugar and raspberry ice cubes? Pu'er cha with vanilla and cinnamon? Jasmine with peppermint extract?

The sky's the limit.

Posted by Hibiscus, 7:00pm

Bobaboy888 (8:30pm): I have a name for that mocha iced oolong cinnamon latte I invented for you. We can call it the Babbler, and we'll serve it up with a side of hot dogs and waffle fries.

CHAPTER SIXTEEN

DANNY

MOM COMES BY ONE EVENING WHILE I'M DOING homework. "That group you and Clementine are working with. Are they called Chinatown Cares?"

I shake the afterimage of capacitor diagrams from my brain. "Yeah," I say, a little wary.

"They come by this morning." She holds out a flyer with the words "Business Owner Meeting" at the top. "Everybody's talking about Kale Corp. They want us to go to a meeting tomorrow night at the grocery store."

That's not news to me, since Clementine texted me about the meeting yesterday. I guess Rui and Silas want to make formal contact with the store owners as a group. They also want me and Clementine to attend.

"Are you going?" I ask my mom.

She makes the expression she does when she smells something off in the fridge. "These groups . . . they always come in saying they'll make big changes. They start projects, make extra work for everyone, and then the next thing comes up and they disappear."

That's cynical, even for Mom. "Why would you say that?"

"We had young people come by maybe seven, eight years ago? Same thing. Wanted to save Chinatown. Had all these ideas. And they realized that it's not so easy. Not just put up a few posters, and all the customers come in through the door. They ran out of money. Some got new jobs. Some had families and got too busy. Everyone disappeared. But we stay."

Now that she mentions it, I do remember some enthusiastic Rui look-alikes coming through during my elementary school days. "I think the Chinatown Cares people have been around for a while," I say cautiously. Silas does talk a lot about fights of years past.

Mom gives a skeptical shrug. "I'll go to the meeting. Mrs. Lau wants me to go." She pauses. "I hope they don't make Kale Corp mad. Right now they offer a lot of buyout money to leave, but they don't have to."

"I'll probably be at the meeting too," I say. "With Clementine."

Mom purses her lips. "You're still spending a lot of time on this project."

"Yeah."

Mom shakes her head as she walks off, leaving me extra frustrated. With the way she's reacting, you'd think that I was selling drugs instead of volunteering for a nonprofit. Do my parents think I'm that incapable of judging things for myself?

The next day rolls around. When it's close to time for the meeting, I tell my parents I'm going to wait for Clementine at the bus station and head over with her.

I'm jittery as I wait for Clem's bus to arrive. I'm not sure when the thought of seeing Clementine went from *oh so awkward* to something I look forward to, but I'm eager to see her, especially since we didn't run into each other at school today. She comes off the bus looking really nice in a pleated skirt that brings out her trim waist. Her hair's held back with a blue headband in addition to her braid, and she smiles at me.

"Hey!" she says. "So how're you feeling about this meeting?"

"I don't really know what to expect."

She gives a little shiver. "I don't either." I get the sense that we're both nervous. The difference is that she's nervous-excited, while I'm nervous-worried. My mind flashes back to what my mom said about young people diving enthusiastically into a cause, only to move on with their lives a few months later. I don't think that's true for Rui or Silas, but what about Clementine? She'll be going off to college next year. Is Chinatown Cares just another stepping-stone for her on her way to greatness? It feels messed up to be wondering this as we're walking side by side to the grocery store.

"How was your day?" I ask.

She grimaces. "All right. I had to punt on layout tonight for the newspaper. My staff's annoyed at me."

"Oh, are you sure you wanna be here? I'm sure Rui and Silas would understand if you were busy."

"No, it's all right. It's just that we're doing this big China-town spread that I was really involved in planning, but the writing's all done. It's just the layout, which they can handle. And I'll make it up to them." She looks at me, clearly eager to change the subject. "How are you?"

My first thought is to shrug her off with an *I'm great*. But then I think, she just told me about her issues with the news-paper. Maybe I should be honest too. "I'm all right. I didn't sleep much last night. The restaurant was busy, so I didn't start my homework until after dinner."

Clem's forehead creases. "Are you running around like this all the time?"

"Not all the time." I feel defensive at the pity on her face. "We've just been short on help recently. That's why I want to stay close for college. To help with things."

"You want to stay, or you feel like you should stay?"

I'm regretting being honest now, especially if it means we'll be playing therapist for much longer. "I mean, it's not my life's ambition to wash dishes, but I want to see the shop do well."

"Have your parents actually told you they want you to stick around?"

I think about the restaurant's financial troubles, how we've slowly let our staff go, and how Dad's spreadsheets always put him in a funk. But it feels like it'd be a betrayal to tell Clem-entine about all this. "Asian parents don't really tell you things. They just convey their expectations through mind control."

She laughs at that. "Must be a useful genetic trait. I'm just wondering if your receptors are as accurate as you think."

There's a layer of smugness there that gets under my skin. "You don't really need to read minds to see piles of dirty plates or lines at the cash register."

Clementine's forehead creases. "Isn't it still worth talking about, though? Your parents seem like nice people. I feel like they'd want you to succeed."

I stiffen. "Are you saying that they can't possibly be nice people if they want to keep me here for college?"

She blinks. "That's not what I meant. I just think parents can surprise us sometimes. What's life about if you don't pursue your dreams?"

"Look, I get the sense that your parents are all for you pursuing your dreams, and that's great. But sometimes one person's dreams affect someone else's. Our family's dream is to run this teahouse. I can't just give that the middle finger."

Maybe she catches the bite in my voice, because she backs off. "You're right. I'm sorry to pry. It's just that, I don't know, Danny. I think you're really great, and you have so much going for you. And you seem so happy whenever you talk about New York. If things with your parents really are as you describe, then maybe there's nothing to be done. But if it's actually a misunderstanding, wouldn't it be a pity if you never figured it out?"

I'm caught off guard by the softness in her voice and the way she looks at me, as if she sees past my arguments and bristle and finds something precious. It's surprising enough to take the edge off my anger, and any retort I have disappears. We walk in silence for a while. I'm aware of her movements next to me, the breeze off her skirt as it just misses brushing my hand. What is it about Clementine that always keeps me off-balance?

The automatic glass door of the grocery store opens for us. There aren't many customers now that we're past the after-work rush. Yang, the cashier, waves at us from the checkout line and motions us toward the back. Clementine squeals when she sees raspberries on sale and makes me promise to remind her to buy them on the way out. We go through swinging doors to some kind of storeroom/office. Boxes of instant noodles are stacked along the back wall next to a small altar with oranges and incense. Chairs have been set up in the middle, most of them filled already. Mrs. Lau sits at the front, next to Rui and Silas. My parents are a few rows back, and I recognize some of the other store owners as well.

We take a seat to the side. There's a lot of pent-up energy in the room. Mrs. Lau is the only one who looks relatively at ease, sitting next to Rui and occasionally leaning over to speak to her. Everyone else is looking around, fidgeting, picking up their phones and putting them back down.

Silas glances at his watch and moves up toward the front of the room. He clears his throat and the room quiets down.

"Thank you very much for coming," he says. I kinda expected him to be less surfer-like when he was speaking to a crowd, but he's still speaking super slowly, with one hand in his pocket. It doesn't make him seem unprofessional, though. Maybe I'm biased, but his whole laid-back vibe makes him more approachable. "I'm Silas from Chinatown Cares. I'm sure you know that we're here today to discuss Kale Corp acquiring this shopping mall. We first heard about this from Mrs. Lau and have been in contact with some of you since then. We wanted to call this meeting so we would have an opportunity to speak with you and give you a chance to speak with each other about your thoughts. On that note, does anyone have initial impressions or comments on the situation?"

There's a silence. Everyone's looking around, getting a feel for what's going on. Then Mrs. Lau speaks. "It happened so quickly. One day, they were here and asking us to get out."

"They want to turn this mall into a fancy juice bar and vitamin store," says Mr. Yook, an older man with a gravelly voice who owns the Chinese medicine store.

Master Zhuang from the kung fu studio speaks up from the back of the room. "They keep sending their people here to talk to us. They pretend to be really nice, say they'll give us money."

"This is just a building to them," says Lily Zhu, the soft-spoken owner of the Szechuan restaurant. "There are lots of strip malls. Why not go somewhere else? We've been here thirty years. Many of my customers don't have cars. They might not follow us somewhere else."

There's a pause. Neither of my parents is saying anything, and I wonder what that means.

"It's a good amount of money they're offering, though," says a woman with pearl earrings. I recognize Leah Wong, who owns the travel agency.

"Good for a while," says a loud voice from the back. I turn around to see Mike Mao, the gift shop owner. "But what do we do after that? This money's not gonna last us forever. And then where will we put our stores? Go somewhere with rent that's twice as high? Hike up our prices?"

Silas puts a hand up, raising his voice over the murmurs. "As you can see, it's a complex situation. And I want to be up-front with you about what we're facing. With business evictions there are far fewer legal protections. Our lawyers are working tirelessly, but it's possible that they won't be able to do anything on that front.

"What we *can* do is place pressure on Kale Corp not to move in. The sale is not yet final. We can raise community awareness about what's at stake. We can get the news media involved, do interviews and press conferences. We can try to rally the community behind you."

Mr. Yook smooths back his bluish-black-dyed hair. "That sounds like a lot of work."

Silas nods. "It will take energy and time on your part, so we leave it completely up to you individually to decide what you want to do. The more people we have, the more leverage we have, but this isn't the kind of thing you sign on to just because everybody else is. Joining this fight because of peer pressure won't be sustainable in the long run, and so I would like everyone to be understanding about other people's choices. It's your lives, your shops."

Again, everybody is quiet. I sneak a look at my parents.

My mom has her arms crossed over her chest, and her lips are pursed. Dad's staring at a spot a few feet in front of him. Is it weird for them that I've been working with Chinatown Cares already? I wonder if they feel like this forces their hand. I haven't even had a real conversation about it with Dad yet, though he didn't seem too surprised when I mentioned I'd be at the meeting.

Mr. Yook shrugs and adjusts his heavy black glasses. "Well, what do we have to lose?"

"Sleep, our youthful beauty," says Mike Mao from the back, and everybody laughs.

Lily, the restaurant owner, rubs her hands as if trying to stay warm. "I don't know if I want to push them. If we cause too much trouble, maybe they'll kick us out with no money at all."

"That's exactly what they want you to think," says Mike Mao, scratching the edge of his receding hairline. "They want to intimidate us into not giving them trouble."

Another sober silence.

Master Zhuang crosses his arms. "Well, the risk is worth it for me. I've been here for twenty years. I have my customers. I want to stay." He turns to Leah Wong from the travel agency, his next-door neighbor. "What about you, Leah?"

Leah doesn't answer for a while. "It's tricky for me. My industry is changing, and I was thinking of moving to a home office anyways. The buyout money would help."

Silas jumps in. "Don't feel like you have to give answers now. We don't want to put anyone on the spot. While you think things over, we can tell you what we're already working on."

He gestures toward me and Clementine. As everyone turns to look at us, the hairs on my arms stand up—well, the ten hairs that my Asian genes have graced me with. "Danny and Clementine are volunteers from the local high school. I'm sure many of you know Danny from Fragrant Leaves tea shop."

Clementine gives a shy smile and a little wave. I do my best to shrink myself smaller.

Silas looks us over with a pleased expression, as if he's showing off some particularly good specimens of Jasper City High School student. "Clementine and Danny have been collecting signatures for a community petition. We already have a good number of names, and we can give you each petition forms to keep at your stores. We can also talk about rallies and special shopping days to raise your profile in the community." He looks around, and from the way all eyes fix on him, it's clear he has everyone's attention. "I know your stores are important to you. I know this move from Kale Corp has a huge effect on your lives. I just want to let you know that Chinatown Cares is here to help you however we can."

Clementine and I go to the Chinatown Cares office to debrief the next day. The conference room feels spacious and sterile compared to the ramen-packed meeting room from last night. I kinda miss the smell of incense.

Rui's in good spirits, chipper despite yesterday's late night. "What did you think of the meeting?"

I shrug. There were so many people last night, saying so many different things, that my brain completely failed to put it together into any coherent picture. "It was good, I guess."

"It was fascinating," says Clementine. "I loved hearing everyone's thoughts."

Silas claps me on the back, heartily enough to sting. "Your parents had a lot of questions afterward."

I cringe. "Yeah, sorry, they're kind of jaded. I guess they've been burned by nonprofits before."

"Don't apologize," says Silas. "It's perfectly natural for them to have questions. The sad truth is that many well-meaning people stride into these situations thinking they have a solution, and they end up making things worse. It's good that your parents are discerning. Though they might not be as opposed to working with us as you think."

"Really?" I can't keep the surprise from my voice, and Silas smiles in low-key amusement.

"Really truly. They spent a long time talking with me, and they seemed pretty open to different options."

I take a chug from my water bottle, for lack of anything better to do. Truth is, I'm surprised. Surprised and kind of angry. I don't think I've heard a single thing from my parents about Chinatown Cares except "Don't do it" this whole time. I didn't even talk to them after the meeting. They'd gone back to the shop directly after, I'd walked Clementine to the bus stop, and then we'd closed up the shop like the meeting hadn't happened. But apparently they were willing to have a "pretty open" conversation with Silas?

Rui does that thing where she opens her eyes wide, as if what she's about to say is the most amazing thing ever. "A majority of the stores are leaning toward fighting the move, which is great. We can do a lot with that kind of enthusiasm." She looks us over. "How do you feel about being a liaison between us and the stores? You can keep an eye on the pulse of things. Communicate with the business owners and keep us up-to-date on what they need."

And that's how Clementine and I become the Hudson Street Mall gofers. Over the next weeks, we go from store to store, giving them petitions to sign and posters to hang. My mom starts making pointed comments about how I need to be wise about the way I spend my time.

The aunties get used to seeing Clementine on Saturday mornings and sometimes after school. I get used to stashing a few egg tarts to slip to her when she comes. And both Clementine and I get used to the constant teasing about our love lives. The aunties are shameless in their matchmaking, and Clementine humors them. It's totally for show, though—she's said as much before.

During one of our Monday afternoon update meetings, I'm sitting with Silas in the Chinatown Cares conference room. Rui and Clementine are in the corner going over poster designs. I should probably get back to the restaurant, but I'm dragging my feet. Clementine tucks a strand of hair behind her ear, nodding thoughtfully at something Rui says. I catch myself staring and fumble with my backpack.

"You've planned a lot of these rallies before, haven't you?" I ask Silas.

Silas breaks into a faint smile. "We've done our fair share," he says, "for better or for worse. As long as people see potential for bigger profits in Chinatown, evictions are going to keep happening. Older stores are going to close. Long-term residents will have to move out. It's like playing Whac-A-Mole. That's why we've started thinking in recent years about longer-term solutions."

"What do you mean?"

"Chinatown Cares is in the early stages of forming a community land trust," Silas says.

"What's that?"

Silas leans forward. It's the most enthusiastic I've ever seen him be about something, though to be fair, his version of enthusiasm still involves talking at about three-quarters of anyone else's normal speed. "It comes down to the core question, you see. What forces should shape a community? Usually, neighborhoods are driven by the market. Whoever pays the most for a building gets to move in. There's no thought to what might actually be good for the people there."

"Isn't that how real estate works?" I ask.

"Well, it's certainly what we're used to," says Silas. "But just because it's what we're used to doesn't mean it's the only way. Imagine, for example, if a piece of land were owned by a nonprofit with a board made up of community members. When the nonprofit sells or rents out the buildings on that land, it takes into account not just profits, but what's good for the community too. We call that model a community land trust."

"And Chinatown Cares is starting one?" I ask.

"We're trying to," says Silas. "There's actually a great piece of land we have our eye on, an old boarding school we'd like to buy and convert into affordable housing with some commercial spaces. It takes money, though, so we're fundraising and lobbying with the powers that be."

"It does seem like a very different way of doing things." It's hard to wrap my mind around, but it makes a great deal of sense.

"Yeah," says Silas. "And it'll take time. But that's the goal."

VICTIM BLAMING

Bobaboy888 (6:02pm): Victim blaming. That's what you're doing.

Hibiscus (6:24pm): Oh my gosh, are you still stuck on the habanero jelly incident? The label was printed in clear, 20-point font. How was I supposed to know the taste tester would think it was marmalade?

Bobaboy888 (7:34pm): That episode was atrocious, but I'm actually talking about your tea shop reviews. You have this underlying assumption that mom-and-pop stores are getting kicked out because they're not working hard enough. "Serve more iced tea! Play better music! If you do better, you'll survive!"

Hibiscus (8:12pm): Constructive criticism isn't victim blaming. I think these old shops provide so much to the community. But the reality is, competition is growing. Like it or not, we all have to adapt.

Bobaboy888 (9:46pm): Whoa, AP Bio. Look at you with your evolutionary terms. You talk about competition and adapting like it's this march toward progress. But is that really what's happening on the ground?

Hibiscus (10:01pm): Lemme guess, you're going to be my exclusive on-site correspondent. What's the description they put after your name? "Bobaboy888: Curmudgeon at Large"?

Bobaboy888 (10:25pm): Har har. Look, Chinatown's trendy. We get hip people with lots of money moving in, so landlords raise rents and kick people out because they can make more money from an art gallery/wine bar than they can with grandma's shop on the corner. Do the original Chinatown residents want art shows with the latest selection of Cabernet? No. But the rich newcomers do, and they've got more money to throw around.

Then you come along and tell all those mom-and-pop shops (who, by the way, have served generations of satisfied customers) that they need fog machines in their entryways because that's what that new dance club down the street has, and look how well that club is doing! Never mind that they serve tea, not cocktails, and that their regulars think a cosmo is a warehouse store with cheap rotisserie chicken.

The question is this. Who are you trying to impress? Whose money are you trying to earn? Who gets to decide what Chinatown is supposed to be? The people with the power and connections or the people who've called this place home for decades?

CHAPTER SEVENTEEN
DANNY

AS THE PETITIONS CIRCULATE, THE HUDSON STREET
Mall stores start planning a rally and shopping day to attract press and community attention. Lily from the Szechuan restaurant volunteers to do a two-for-one lunch special. The gift store and Chinese medicine store will offer 20 percent off. Even Mom and Dad come through with a "free pastry with large cup of tea" deal. Master Zhuang wants to have his kids do kung fu demonstrations onstage, which makes Rui positively giddy.

"Can you imagine the little white belts? Soooo cute!"

I think back to my Chinese school days, when Master Zhuang taught us kung fu forms after class. We did a show at the end of the year where one kid constantly punched in the wrong direction and another kept shouting "Hai!" too late with his kicks.

"Should be interesting," I say diplomatically. I'm exhausted because the sink clogged at the restaurant last night, and we had to stay late waiting for a plumber. Clementine's sitting next to me. This entire meeting, I've been alternating between trying to stay awake and trying to ignore the fact that Clementine's arm is one inch away from mine on the table.

"I'm encouraged by the enthusiasm from the store owners," says Silas. "A lot of them were worried at first about losing the buyout money if they spoke out. Which is fair. They have bills and expenses, loans to pay off." Silas's eyes flicker to me, so briefly that I almost don't catch it. Then he straightens and his tone changes. "Anyways, let's talk about speakers. I'm happy to share that Mrs. Lau has agreed to speak at the rally."

I must look surprised, because Silas smiles.

"She was hesitant at first, but we told her that these things work best when people tell their own stories," he says. "You're the experts on your own lives and experiences. We can't duplicate that as activists, no matter how good we get at giving speeches."

"Speaking of which . . ." Rui's eyes sparkle. "Have either of you given any thought to speaking?"

Clementine and I exchange a glance. I catch a whiff of strawberry shampoo as she brings her braid over her shoulder.

"Us?" says Clementine.

"We want to have people from all generations speaking. This Kale Corp takeover will impact people of all ages, and we want people to know that."

Clementine gets that "I'm ridiculously competent and thoughtful" look on her face. "I hadn't thought about it since I'm not affiliated with the mall. But if you think it would be helpful . . ."

"I think you should," says Rui. "You work so hard, and you

have a perspective as a young member of the community. Plus, if your fellow high school students attend the rally, they'll be more likely to listen to their peers."

I'm putting all my energy into my invisible man trick. If Clementine's willing to speak, they don't need me, right?

Rui turns my way. "What about you, Danny?"

Why does that trick never work anymore? "Um, I probably wouldn't be the best speaker."

Rui is unfazed. "Are you sure we can't convince you otherwise? You certainly speak English better than many of the other store owners, and you have a personal connection to the tea shop."

Clementine puts a hand on my arm, which is . . . distracting. "I think you're selling yourself short, Danny. You have a lot to contribute." She's all earnestness, and I admit, I'm kind of touched to see that much confidence from her. Then Clementine gives me a mischievous smile that makes my skin buzz where her fingers are. "Besides, it can't possibly be worse than chasing a cat up a stairwell, can it?"

"Actually, it's a lot harder," I say. "Cats can't tell if I say something wholly ridiculous. Cats in general are better audiences than people."

"Really?" Rui frowns like she's giving this serious consideration.

"Yeah, they mind their own business, and half the time, they fall asleep, which is pretty ideal."

Rui laughs, though she seems disappointed that cats didn't turn out to be the amazing audience I'd led her to hope for. "I know it seems intimidating, but we've worked with tons of people, and it's not as hard as you think. Everybody's nervous at first, but it almost always turns out much better than they expect."

She pulls out her phone and starts scrolling through videos of Asian grandmothers in front of microphones. Clementine pulls her hand back as we lean in for a closer look, a move I'm more aware of than I should be.

Rui gestures toward her phone. "We had a rally a while back about poor living conditions in senior housing. The landlord wasn't making repairs, and the situation was so terrible that the tenants decided they needed to speak out. See, here's Mrs. Tang speaking out about leaky pipes in her bathroom. And here's Uncle Charles and Uncle Qian talking about how the elevator wasn't fixed for months. Can you imagine? An elevator in a senior housing high-rise, broken for months on end. Thankfully, the residents were brave and took action." She scrolls through five or six more videos, offering commentary on each.

Wow, the "shaming with Asian grandmothers" tactic. Rui plays dirty. I can't really say it's hard to give a speech at the rally when all these old people who don't even speak English are stepping up.

Maybe Rui sees me wavering, because she smiles. It's the smile a tiger gives before it eats you for lunch, or before it entices you to commit to a public speaking endeavor that you'll forever regret. "How about you try writing down what you think you might say, *if* you were to give a speech? Maybe that will help you decide one way or the other."

CHAPTER EIGHTEEN

CLEMENTINE

NEW PRINTINGS OF THE NEWSPAPER USUALLY arrive on Tuesdays, and it's tradition for free members of the editorial staff to gather after school to ooh and aah over the final product. I love the look and smell of the fresh papers, bundled up in stacks with twine. They're crisp and smooth, and because we print on white paper instead of newsprint, I can run my hands over them without getting ink smudged on my fingers.

We've broken out the paper plates and divvied up the celebratory pizza, which is always tastier than layout-night pizza but somehow less fortifying. Josh is doing his best to keep grease off his beard, an effort that's hampered by the fact that he's eating two slices at once. Adenike taps a rhythm on the arm of the sofa as she pores over the opinion pages.

My pizza lies half-eaten next to me as I flip through page by page. Adenike has a great piece on the new initiative to hire diverse teachers, and Wei has a forceful editorial in favor of longer passing periods. The Chinatown feature looks amazing as well. A giant graphic of the Chinatown Gate spreads across the page, with articles tucked around it. The restaurant guide makes my mouth water, and an up-and-coming freshman writer did some fantastic research for the demographics fact box.

Nadia pulls up a chair behind me and shakes my braid as I read. "Can I do your hair?"

"Please do." Nadia's creations are works of art.

The gentle pull on my scalp is soothing as I read through the entertainment and sports sections. One review of a new buddy-comedy predicts the movie to be a "runaway success among less discerning audiences," which makes me giggle. Nadia ties off a new braid and snaps in a barrette just as I turn the last page.

"There," she says. "Keep it this way, at least for the rest of the day."

I flip my phone camera to selfie mode to check it out. Nadia's given me a half-up/half-down look, with a braided crown around my head and the rest falling around my shoulders.

Adenike wolf whistles from across the room. "Look at you, Fairy Princess Clementine."

I run my fingers carefully over the braids. "If I didn't have to wash my hair, I'd keep it in forever." I raise my voice to address the rest of the crew. "Great job on this issue, everyone, really. I'm ecstatic that this paper turned out so well, especially since I'm pretty sure I bombed my calculus test after copy night."

Wei pushes his wire-rimmed glasses farther up his nose. "We don't believe you."

"Well, I certainly hope you're right," I tell him. Truth is, I hadn't been so unprepared for a test in a long time. Between Chinatown Cares and the newspaper, my academics have taken an unfortunate hit.

As if summoned by thoughts of Chinatown Cares, the door opens and Danny walks in. I remember that I'd asked him to meet me here after school.

"Hey Danny." He looks good today, in a gray T-shirt that hangs flatteringly off his broad shoulders. His mess of hair is slightly less messy than usual.

"Hey—" He stops and stares at me, a stunned look on his face.

"What's the matter?" I resist the urge to pat myself down for unseen injuries.

He blinks, and then he seems to snap out of it. "Nothing." After a moment he adds, "Your hair looks nice."

"Thank you," I say. "Nadia is a wizard."

Nadia and Adenike exchange a meaningful glance, which I studiously ignore. Those two will read romantic fantasies into anything. Just because Danny likes Nadia's braiding doesn't mean he likes me in any nonplatonic way. And if there's any part of me that feels slightly hopeful at that romantic possibility, it's solely because I'm sleep-deprived.

I pack my bags and stand to go.

"You're leaving?" says Adenike.

"Oh, did I forget to tell you? We are doing some last-minute preparations for the rally."

"We're meeting with Ms. Curtis in fifteen minutes to go over next semester's budget," says Adenike.

I slap my forehead. "Oh no. I completely forgot. I'm so sorry." I feel the entire office's eyes on me as I run my to-do lists through my head. There are flyer designs to approve and coupons to xerox, some bullet points to run by Silas for my talk . . . Even with the weight of everyone's stares, I can't find a way to fit everything into my schedule this afternoon. Where's that cloning machine when you need it?

I turn an apologetic eye to Adenike. "I don't think I can miss this Chinatown meeting. Do you think you could go over it with her and email me what you decide on? We're usually on the same wavelength about this anyways."

Adenike presses her lips together, and then she sighs. "I can cover for you, but it's not ideal."

I give her a quick hug. "I'm so sorry. I'll make it up to you, I promise."

Adenike looks skeptical. I feel horrible, but the rally is just around the corner and we still have to finalize plans with half the store owners. "Ready to go?" I ask Danny, who's looking nervously between me and Adenike.

"Yeah," he says.

"All right, then."

PU'ER TIME

Do you have a secret Pu'er collection? My budget isn't really amenable to amassing vast stores of teas, but I do have a few cakes stashed away in my cabinet to age. Everyone once in a while, I take them out and wonder if I should brew something. I finally gathered up the courage to snap a photo of my stash and share it with you guys. What do I think? Should I dig in? Apparently Pu'er tastes best under dry storage after sixty years, but that's so long!

Posted by Hibiscus, 3:58pm

Bobaboy888 (4:15pm): Okay, I'll bite. You should brew a bit of your 2014 Hekai Mountain. I have a hunch it'll be at a good place right now.

Hibiscus (5:26pm): A non-sarcastic comment? Who are you and what have you done with Bobaboy?

BobaBoy888 (6:30pm): *shrug* I'm curious. And Hekai Mountain makes good teas.

Hibiscus (7:02pm): All right, I'll brew this one next week and post pictures.

Bobaboy888 (7:36pm): Careful with the photography. Your photos are so overexposed I worry it'll dry out the leaves.

Hibiscus (8:14pm): Ah, there he is. Welcome back, Bobaboy.

CHAPTER NINETEEN
DANNY

IT DOESN'T TAKE ME LONG TO REGRET AGREEING to write a speech. To be more specific, I started having second thoughts approximately ten minutes after mumbling my half-audible yes. Unfortunately, Clementine and I had already left Chinatown Cares by that point, and calling or emailing Rui and Silas to back out felt like too much of a hurdle.

I mean, I'm not a total slacker. I do make some effort at it. After a few days of procrastinating, I open up a blank document and type a few words.

My parents have owned Fragrant Leaves tea shop for the last 25 years. We serve a large variety of teas from Taiwan, China, and Southeast Asia. Our customers have been coming for a very long time, and I feel strongly that we offer an important service to the immigrant community.

I delete it all.

Meanwhile, Clementine the Energizer Bunny finally gets permission for us to table at the cafeteria, and I promise to man it with her. When I arrive five minutes before lunch, she's already set up with a huge sign that says, "Support Chinatown Small Businesses!" There are petitions to sign, flyers for rally day, and even "20 percent off!" coupons. Every surface of the table that's not holding petitions and flyers is decorated with candles and vases of silk flowers. I hope people don't get the impression we're advertising a well-decorated séance.

She greets me with an easy grin. "Hey! Take a seat!"

I plop down next to her. Tabling's not really my thing, but I can definitely think of worse people to hang out with for a lunch period.

"Ever done this before?" she asks.

"Nope."

"It's super casual. It'll be a breeze."

I'm convinced we'll spend the entire lunch period sitting awkwardly by ourselves, but a surprising number of people stop by. Clementine's enthusiastically chatting people up, hopping out from behind the table every other minute to hug someone new. I swear, she must be pulling energy from the air because I'm exhausted just watching from my chair. She hands out flyers left and right, and some folks from the newspaper promise to be at the rally. At one point the college counselor walks by and I avoid eye contact so he doesn't call me on the fact that I haven't set an appointment with him. It's not like I have that much to discuss. How hard can it be to apply to local schools?

About ten minutes in, Bryan comes and shoots video of us on his phone camera. Video editing is his newest fleeting hobby.

"Smile, guys, I'll put you on TikTok."

"Want to share that on the newspaper account?" says Clementine.

"Sure," says Bryan.

She gives him a thumbs-up as he walks off.

"Whew," Clementine says, collapsing into her chair. "How're you doing?"

"All right."

She furrows her brow. "You sure?"

Guess I'm not as good at disguising my feelings as I thought. Honestly, I feel kind of weird about this whole thing, and it's hard to hide it. I'd walked into this tabling session expecting to be ignored by our classmates, and I guess what actually happened is better. But there's something unsettling about watching Clementine work the crowd. It almost feels like she's holding court.

"Clementine!" A lanky teacher with long gray hair comes to the table and opens her arms to encompass everything on it. "How do you find the time to do all this?"

Clementine laughs. "Caffeine, mostly," she says.

The teacher chortles like Clementine's told the world's funniest joke. "Well, I think it's wonderful that you kids are doing this. Really great that you're taking the initiative to get involved in your communities and not just your school. It gives us hope as an older generation, you know?"

Clementine beams. "We try to do what we can."

There's a silence. I look at Clementine's stainless-steel water bottle on the table and wonder if it's more or less noticeable than I am.

Clementine glances at me, as if sensing my thoughts. "Ms. Curtis, do you know Danny? His family owns a tea shop in the Hudson Street Mall. Danny, Ms. Curtis is the newspaper adviser."

Ms. Curtis extends a long-fingered hand. "Nice to meet you, Danny. Best of luck to your family."

I mumble a reply.

She turns back to Clementine. "Fantastic job, both of you. I'll do my best to make it to the rally." She gives us this big cheesy wink and continues into the lunch hall. I imagine myself becoming bottle shaped. My hair morphs into a black cap made of environmentally conscious recycled plastic.

The flow of people slows after that, and we get some breathing room. Clementine breaks out a thermos of some kind of tomato-based noodle soup, and I munch on a PB&J. There's a Tupperware full of cookies in her bag next to the thermos.

"Those are for Adenike," she says when she sees me eyeing them. "I've been pushing too much newspaper stuff on her lately."

I make a sad puppy face. "No, no, it's okay. I'll just sit here and dream about cookies after a long, grueling hour of tabling."

She laughs. "Fine," she says, slipping one out from the Tupperware. "You can have one, but only because I like you."

I know she's just joking around, but my heart still speeds up a few beats at *I like you*. The cookie is lemon flavored, buttery, and soft, a calming counterpart to my earlier adrenaline rush. I nod toward the petition on the table, trying to play it cool. "Nice that we got some signatures."

Clementine reaches out a finger and pulls the clipboard toward us. "I guess so," she says.

"You're not exactly enthusiastic."

She shrugs. "I kind of hoped the Chinatown center spread would stir a lot of enthusiasm for this rally, but it doesn't seem to have made much of a splash."

"How do you know whether something makes a splash?"

"Oh, there are website analytics, and you just get a sense of buzz around the school when an article really resonates. I don't get that this time."

To be honest, I'm not surprised. I picked up a copy of the paper yesterday and looked over the Chinatown feature, since Clementine's been so enthusiastic about it. It was all right, I guess, but it felt . . . bland, for lack of a better term. Lots of facts and figures and restaurant recommendations, but the whole thing felt like a dehydrated version of Chinatown. Like they'd taken all the life out of it and left the dried-out skin on the page. But it's not like I'm going to say this to Clementine.

"That's a bummer," I say.

She shrugs. "How's the speech going?"

Ah yes, finish off the hour with the topic that Danny wants to talk about least. "I don't think it's going to fly," I say. "I wrote two paragraphs and deleted it all."

"Getting started is always the hardest part for me."

Clementine chews thoughtfully, looking so earnest that it's hard to think uncharitable thoughts about the Chinatown feature or her. "If you ever want someone to brainstorm with, I'd be happy to help. I find that talking it out gets me past blocks more often than not."

As sincere as that offer seems to be, the idea of sharing my disaster of a speech with Clementine the newspaper editor does not appeal. "Thanks. I'll keep that in mind."

She can totally tell that I'm blowing her off, but she doesn't say anything.

I open up my speech again that night, but I don't get much further. It's a disaster. I'm pretty sure that phishing emails impersonating overseas royalty are more convincing than what I've put on the screen in front of me. I give my computer dirty looks all evening and throughout the next day, wondering if I should just call Rui and Silas and tell them it's not gonna happen. I even get as far as picking up my phone, but as I'm walking to find a quiet corner, I catch a glimpse of my parents in the office, going over spreadsheets. My mom has a letter in her hand with the Kale Corp logo on top.

In my mind, a whole line of Asian grandmas walk onto the rally stage, deliver amazing testimonies, and shake their heads at me as they walk off.

So I do the unthinkable.

Hey, can I take you up on that offer of help?

Clementine responds almost right away.

> Sure. Do you have anything so far you can send over?

> Only a few paragraphs.

> Why don't you send that to me. Don't worry if it's terrible. First drafts are supposed to be terrible.

> Ha. You'll regret saying that.

> Hey, you saw me play mahjong. It's only fair that I get to see your terrible writing.

I laugh at that, and then I bite the bullet and send it. As I wait for her reply, I'm not as nervous as I expected to be. It's not as if I had any dreams of impressing her with my writing prowess. Plus, she has a point. After chasing a cat up a high-rise and playing mahjong with cutthroat grandmas, showing her my bad speech doesn't seem like as big of a deal.

My phone buzzes ten minutes later.

> It's a good start. We can work with this.

> Good pep talk.

Lol it is!!!

Uh-huh.

Meet me at the newspaper office after school tomorrow? We can go over it.

Deal.

Bring pastries. I edit better with pastries.

You're shameless.

She responds with a halo emoji. I smile goofily at my phone.

I show up at the newspaper office the next day with a big bag of sun cakes and egg tarts. The newspaper staff descends on me.

"I hear crinkling. I smell food," says the girl with hoop earrings.

"Out of the way, vultures!" says Clementine, wading through the crowd. "These are mine!"

I peek inside my bag. "Well, I did bring ten. I think there's enough for everyone."

A girl with a beaded glasses chain gives me a bear hug. "We will reward you richly for this. Do you want to be a newspaper mascot?"

Clementine grabs a sun cake and returns to her seat, patting the space at the table next to her. I catch a whiff of strawberry shampoo as I sit down. "Danny, you get the seat of honor due to your important contribution. Anyways, I printed out your speech."

She pulls a document out of her binder and places it in front of us. The margins and spaces between lines are filled with notes in purple ink and Clementine's neat handwriting. After another bite of sun cake, Clementine puts it down and picks up her pen, which seems to transform her. It's uncanny. All of a sudden, she becomes Editor Clementine. I kind of expect a pair of spectacles to materialize on her face.

"So," she says. "As I mentioned, you have a great start here. I think you're spot-on with the themes you want to hit. I'm just wondering if you can make them a little more personal."

"Personal?" That's not really my favorite word.

"Well, you have some great numbers here," she says, as patient as any third grade teacher. "It's nice to know how long your parents have run the restaurant and all that. But I feel like people could get those facts from Google. And what they really want to know is your story. What it's like to grow up at Fragrant Leaves, and how this Kale Corp takeover affects you personally."

"Personally?"

"Yeah." Clementine doesn't seem fazed by the fact that I've reverted to one-word utterances. The same word, to boot. "Maybe you can take us on a tour of your life a little bit. Let us see things through your eyes. People really respond to that personal touch."

I get this image of me driving a golf cart full of gawking tourists through Fragrant Leaves. *To your left, you can see our stack of ancient menus, filled with all kinds of exotic Chinese delicacies. . . .* The tourists' faces cloud over with pity as they hear about our recent troubles.

"I don't really want to put myself on display for some PR stunt."

"It's not a PR stunt." Clementine doesn't match my combative tone. She's still super calm, which annoys me. "It's your story. And I totally understand if you don't feel comfortable sharing every aspect of your life. But even a few glimpses of your day-to-day experience would really bring the speech to life. Remember that first morning I visited your teahouse, when you introduced me to everyone and we played mahjong with the aunties? That showed me, more than all the research I'd done to that point, what we'd lose if Kale Corp moved in. What if you could show the same to everyone else too?"

"Do I have to bare my life to the world for our tea shop to survive?"

A crease appears between Clementine's eyebrows. "Think about it as inviting someone into your house. You can keep them in the living room and show off your best family photos. You don't have to let them into your bedroom to snoop around in your drawers. If you really have nothing to share, that's one thing. But I think there are aspects of Fragrant Leaves that you love and want people to know about."

I fiddle with my collar, realizing for the first time how warm this room is. Is it not enough just to be a friendly space with good tea? Do we all have to hold heartwarming news conferences and have witty social media accounts like the celebrity chefs down the street?

"Sharing's always the answer these days, isn't it?" My voice is acerbic. "It's an Instagram world out there. We're all influencers now."

Now Clementine rolls her eyes. "What is it with you and influencers?"

I think of that lady who visited our shop with her dead-animal purse, gushing about Fragrant Leaves to Mom and getting our name wrong in the caption. Spending more time posing in the aisles than she actually spent drinking our tea. "It's all so shallow. Substance doesn't matter as long as you have the right filter."

"Just because something's shared with the public doesn't mean it's shallow or performative."

I don't like the way she's looking at me, as if I'm the one being ridiculous instead of her. "I'm just callin' it like I see it. And it's not like you follow your own advice either. You want me to get all personal, but your paper's Chinatown spread was just as superficial as my speech."

Clementine blinks at that. "What?" she says.

"You said you wanted to make a Chinatown spread that showcased how special our neighborhood was, but really, it read more like a travel guide." It feels like I'm playing dirty by attacking her newspaper, but I'm too annoyed to let it stop me.

"'There's three-dollar boba here, and four-dollar spring rolls there.' 'Here's a nice street corner for taking pictures or people watching.' 'Thirty percent of the population is Chinese, down from thirty-five percent ten years ago.' It's all encyclopedia and Google stuff. No one's gonna read that and understand what Chinatown really is."

She furrows her brows. "It's not the same thing. That's a newspaper spread. You're writing—" Clementine stops abruptly, and her eyes open wide. "Oh my gosh, you're right." She shakes her head, looking like she's just had her photo taken with extra-bright flash. "It's so obvious now that you mention it. Sorry, I need to—"

She crosses the newspaper office and picks up a copy of the paper. I can see her eyes moving as she scans back and forth, her expression settling into something in the space between frustration, annoyance, and grudging acceptance. She starts getting puzzled glances from around the office. I start to feel guilty.

Finally, she puts down the paper and comes back. "I'm kicking myself," she says wryly. She's calmer now, as she smooths a stray hair behind her ear, and she ignores the curious stares from around the room. "We should have gone about it completely differently, and now it's too late to redo it. But—" She gives me a significant glance. "If you were able to see what was missing in the Chinatown spread, maybe you can see why I suggested some more personal notes in your speech."

Wait, how did she turn my barbs right back at me?

Clementine slides my speech back to me. "It's your speech.

You should do whatever you want with it. But maybe think over what I said?"

I kinda feel bad about being so grumpy with Clementine, especially since she was doing me a favor. And as much as I hate to admit it, our talk does give me some ideas. I start noticing things about the teahouse and maybe, just maybe, start thinking about how it might fit into my speech. When a loud political discussion flares up in the dining room, I jot notes on a napkin. Same when the aunties pass extra-cute photos of their grandchildren. Soon I have a pile of napkins, but I'm not actually sure if I can string them together into anything coherent.

The other work with Chinatown Cares ramps up as well. Clementine and I post flyers all around the neighborhood. We shuttle petition forms back and forth and hand out schedules. She doesn't offer to help me with my speech again.

I get to the restaurant after school one afternoon to see Dad putting away clean dishes. He stacks them methodically and carefully, without all the clanging we get when Mom does it, albeit at a much slower rate.

"Did you just get back?" he asks, lifting a pile of plates into a cabinet.

"Yeah," I say. "But I'm heading out later to put up posters with Clementine."

"For Chinatown Cares?"

"Yeah. For the rally."

Dad wrinkles his face the way he does when a customer speaks

English too quickly. "You're spending a lot of time on this."

His words make me bristle. I already get grief about Chinatown Cares from Mom. Things are really going to get miserable if Dad starts getting on my case too.

"It's for a good cause," I say, not bothering to hide the edge in my voice.

Dad frowns at a plate, rubbing at a mark on it before putting it back in the dirty pile. "It might be a good cause, but don't waste too much energy worrying about stuff like this."

Maybe it's because I've heard this line one too many times, or maybe it's just that I'm exhausted. Whatever it is, something snaps.

"What exactly shouldn't I be worrying about?" I speak slowly and deliberately, aware of the grenade in my hand yet grimly determined to let it fly. "Should I worry about the loan that you took out to pay rent on this place?"

The dish Dad's holding freezes in midair, and the world crystalizes around me. I was guessing about the loan, actually. That slip from Silas brought back memories of bank forms on my dad's desk, snippets of conversation that ended the moment I came into a room. And though I hadn't been sure when I said it, the look on Dad's face tells me everything I need to know.

"How did you hear about the loan?" Dad demands, his voice clipped, shock clear on his face. "From Chinatown Cares?"

A pit opens up under my rib cage. It's one thing to suspect that your parents don't trust you with something important. It's quite another to have it confirmed. All the frustration from years past, all that anger I'd suppressed, kindles and expands in my core. "Is that really your first reaction?" I ask him. "Wondering who let me in on your secret? Because that's not the first question that pops up into *my* mind. What I want to know is why you'd share this information with someone you barely know, when you tell me nothing at all."

Footsteps sound, and Mom comes in from the cashier area. I guess I'd been speaking pretty loudly. She looks between me and my dad, puzzled.

Dad takes a deep breath. Slowly, I can see him gain control of himself. The shock from before is smoothed away, replaced by a responsible-parent veneer. When he speaks again, it's with the measured patience he used to use on me when I was seven. He might as well have stooped down and put his hands on his knees. "We don't tell you about these things because it's not for you to deal with. You're a high school student. Your job is to worry about your schoolwork."

That was the worst thing he could possibly have said. My smoldering frustration explodes. "It's always the schoolwork, isn't it? I don't know if you've noticed, but I have to worry about a lot more than my schoolwork. I have to worry about the dishes when they're not done. I have to worry about keeping the dining room clean when you guys are too busy to keep up. I might not have to 'worry' about money, but I certainly did give up my violin lessons when we didn't have enough of it. If you haven't noticed, Fragrant Leaves is my life too. My entire existence revolves around this restaurant, and you still share your secrets with Silas and not me?"

Dad reels. He actually takes a physical step back. The calm parent expression is gone now, obliterated, and the hurt in his eyes scrapes my heart raw. 'Cause it's more than just hurt. It's disappointment and loathing, aimed not at me but at himself, and it guts me.

I should take back what I said. I can't.

"Danny," Mom's voice is sharp, panicked. "Don't talk to your dad that way." She steps toward me, but I back away. My legs feel shaky, and I hope they don't collapse under me.

"Silas and Rui treat me like an adult." My throat's thick. It's hard for me to get the words out. "Why can't you?"

I grab my bag and push through the back door. The door swings shut behind me, and I'm greeted by the stark asphalt of the half-empty parking lot. My eyes burn. I'm breathing hard, and I swallow against the fast-growing lump in my throat. I don't think I've ever yelled at my parents like that before. I wonder if they're going to come after me, but the door stays closed.

I'm not sure where to go, so I just charge down the walkway toward the road, then turn onto the sidewalk. So many thoughts are flying through my head. I'm honestly not sure how my parents will react. Are they gonna ground me? Forbid me from going to Chinatown Cares? Cars zip past, their engines getting louder as they approach and softer as they pull away.

My phone buzzes in my pocket. I ignore it, but a while later it buzzes again. At this point, my feet are starting to ache from stomping around, and my head is beginning to clear. I should probably respond to my parents so they know I'm not dead. But when I pull out my phone, I see the messages are from Clementine.

The first one is from ten minutes ago.

> Hey, you ready to head out?

And just now:

> I'm gonna head out first and get started. Call me when you're free.

Crap. I totally forgot we were supposed to sync up about postering. I dial her number, and she answers on the first ring.

"Hello?" she says.

"Hey, I'm so sorry," I say. "I had, um . . . Something happened. I got distracted."

There's a pause on her end of the line. "Is everything okay?"

"It's fine." It's not fine. "I just . . . Where are you now?"

"I'm by the Chinatown Gate. Just started postering."

"Can I meet you there?" *Please don't ask any more questions.*

Pause. "You sure? If something's come up, you don't have to—"

"No, it's all right. I'll see you soon."

I hang up.

CHAPTER TWENTY

CLEMENTINE

I CAN TELL SOMETHING'S WRONG THE MOMENT
Danny steps off the bus. He comes out haunted, his eyes wide, and he barely registers the sight of me.

"You sure you're all right?" I ask.

He blinks, as if even that question is hard to answer. "Yeah, I'm fine. Sorry again about being late." He avoids my eyes and steps deliberately toward the Chinatown Gate. "Let's get to work."

The square by the gate is a popular tourist destination. Shops line a flagstone-paved open courtyard, and families run around, taking pictures and generally relaxing in the chill fall air. I hand Danny a stack of rally posters. He surveys the area again in a half-seeing way, and then he gestures toward the closest store.

"Start there?"

All right, then, I guess we're doing this. We walk the perimeter, putting papers up on bulletin boards and handing them to store owners. Danny marches half a step ahead of me, avoiding eye contact. Everything in his demeanor radiates misery. It's really starting to worry me. He's not prickly the way he was when we first started working together. It's more like he's in a trance, and whatever thoughts are holding him captive aren't good ones.

We work in silence until we finish the square.

"Do you want to put up the rest of the flyers along the road?" I ask.

Danny's staring off again. "Huh?"

That's it. I don't know what's going on, but it's awful to see him like this. I put a hand on his shoulder. He flinches under my touch, the muscles bunching.

"Hey," I say gently. "There's obviously something bothering you. Do you want to talk about it? I don't want to pry, and if you'd rather keep it to yourself, I'll totally respect that, but sometimes it helps."

I can almost see him running through different excuses in his head. The heat of his skin seeps through to my fingertips.

Finally, he deflates, letting out a sigh that leaves me surprised he's still standing. "I'm sorry. It's just . . . I picked a fight with my parents just now. I yelled at them, and then I stormed out. I'd never done that before."

I must look alarmed, because Danny catches my expression and chuckles. "It's really cliché teen angst, isn't it?"

He's making light of it, but I can tell this was serious. "Are you . . . Was it about the rally?"

Danny furrows his brow. "Yes and no. Remember that

meeting when Silas mentioned some of the businesses had taken out loans?"

"Maybe?" I have a vague memory of something like that.

His mouth twists. "One of the businesses was us." Danny lets out a breath and runs his fingers through his hair in a way that makes my chest squeeze. "It was the first time I'd heard about it. I knew things were bad financially, I just didn't realize we couldn't even pay our rent."

I'm stunned, both by the revelation and by the fact that Danny's chosen to share this information with me. I feel like I've been entrusted with something really personal, and I hope I can be a good enough friend to warrant it. "I'm sorry."

Danny lets out a ragged breath. "Yeah, but it's not even that. It's like, they never trust me with this kind of thing. The restaurant issues affect every aspect of my life, but my parents seem to think I'm perfectly happy staying in the dark and letting them take care of everything, which they're clearly not doing. Not that I blame them for the restaurant's problems. I know it's hard. It's just . . . they think I'm still eight years old and that I don't notice things going south. But I do, and it doesn't make it any easier when they try to hide it."

Danny wipes a hand across his eyes, and I look away to give him some privacy. It's hard for me to relate, because my parents are so completely different in how they raised me. But my heart aches for him.

I touch him gently on his elbow. He jumps, though he turns toward me instead of away. "I'm so sorry, Danny. For the record, your parents are wrong if they don't realize what a gift they have in you." His eyes soften at my words, and my awareness of our surroundings fades. When I speak again, it feels like we're the only two people in the square. "I've seen you in the restaurant, and I've seen how much of yourself you pour into it. You're amazing, giving, and a miracle worker with your regulars. I know your parents will see all that eventually, even if it takes them some time. In the meantime, you should know that I do."

A faint smile tugs on his lips, and he captures my gaze with his. "Thank you," he says softly. "I'm . . . I'm glad we got to hang out more this year, Clementine. You're pretty special too."

Silence stretches between us. In the natural rhythm of conversation, it's time for us to look away from each other, but neither of us does. I'm preoccupied now with the brown of his eyes, like dark, mellow Pu'er, and I get the urge to reach out and brush his arm with my fingers, to stand just a little bit closer. The way he's looking at me has shifted too, as if he's seeing me clearly for the first time, and the wonder in his eyes makes my stomach tingle. I swallow, my gaze flickering to his lips. Is it him that's leaning in or me? All I know is that there's some force pulling us toward each other, ever so slowly, irresistibly.

Someone slams on their car horn. We jump apart. The evening breeze is cool against my flaming-hot cheeks.

Danny looks dazed. It takes me a few moments to realize there's some kind of commotion at the intersection down the street. A car wasn't moving forward in the left-turn lane, and now everybody behind it is angry.

"The driver must be texting or something," Danny says.

"Huh?" Images and sensations flash through my mind. His lips, his eyes . . . the warmth off his skin. What were we talking about? "Oh yeah, definitely texting."

What just happened?

Danny clears his throat and scuffs his sneakers on the sidewalk. "Should we get back to work?" His voice is husky.

"Definitely." I'm kind of mortified. I'm not sure how I went from trying to comfort him to . . . But clearly, he wants to get past this moment. "Yeah, back to business. Let's make sure we get all these posters up."

CHAPTER TWENTY-ONE
DANNY

WELL, IF CLEMENTINE WAS HOPING TO GET MY mind off my parents, she certainly succeeded. Though maybe not in the way she'd intended. As we finish off our posters, I'm having a hard time keeping my eyes from drifting in her direction, gliding down the curve of her neck, lingering on her lips. Which is kind of ridiculous, right? Because she was just trying to be a supportive friend. If my pervy mind is hell-bent on imagining more to it, that's on me.

We finish up our posters quickly, and then, since we're close to the Chinatown Cares office, we drop by to say hi and hammer out final logistics.

Rui smiles at me. "Danny, how's your speech going?"

I cringe. Why don't things disappear when you refuse to think about them? "I'm still working on it. Do I need to give it to you beforehand?"

Rui shakes her head. "This is your story. We're happy to help you, but we'd never put words in your mouth."

I'm kinda surprised by that.

Clementine acts perfectly normal when we wait for our respective buses home, further proof that whatever happened was all in my head. She does put a hand on my shoulder right as her bus is arriving, which, to be honest, almost makes me jump out of my skin.

"You gonna be okay?" she asks. The lingering concern in her eyes almost unravels me right then and there.

"Yeah," I say. "Thanks for everything."

Her smile sends a glow through my entire body. I feel the imprint of her hand on my arm long after her bus disappears.

When I get back to the Hudson Street Mall, it's already dark outside. I feel a rush of nerves as I approach Fragrant Leaves. My hand freezes on the door handle, and I force myself to pull the door open. The entire front of the store is glass, so it's not like I can stay hidden even if I stand paralyzed outside.

So I take a breath and walk in. Only a few tables still have customers. Mom is tidying up the counter area. Dad's nowhere in sight. I come in cautiously, moving quietly between the chairs. At first, I think Mom doesn't see me, and then I realize she's studiously avoiding looking in my direction. I'm clear across the dining room by the time she finally raises her head, and I freeze under her gaze.

She jerks her head toward the back kitchen. "There's a pork chop and vegetables for you in the fridge. You can heat it up."

She goes back to her organizing and doesn't acknowledge me again.

* * *

Friday night before the rally, I take the bus home early and stare at my napkin notes. I copy them onto index cards and arrange them into an order that makes sense. For a while, I stand in front of the mirror trying to practice, but it's just painful. Every time I open my mouth, I hear my mom telling me to find better uses for my time, Dad saying that all this activism is above my pay grade. Maybe I should just back out of the speech, but I can't bring myself to do that either, so I just wallow in this impending self-enabled disaster. After a few more tries, I take out my phone.

There are a lot of new posts on Linktropolis, and I scroll mindlessly through. Hibiscus's ridiculous fusion tea series has a whole bunch of new posts. Since I figure nothing can possibly get me any grumpier, I click.

I shouldn't have underestimated her. *Babble Tea*'s front page is just atrocity after atrocity. Hibiscus starts out fairly tame, adding cream and sugar to various teas. But soon she's off to the races with peppermint extract in white tea and cinnamon foam art on Pu'er (Pu'er??). By the time I get to a badly drawn foam unicorn on a cup of chrysanthemum, my head's exploded and launched bloodied pieces of brain all over my bedroom floor.

What is it with everything fusion these days? Why does everything have to be nontraditional and hip? What's wrong with simply taking pride in our heritage and culture as it stands?

I text several links over to Bryan.

> Worst I've seen from her yet. I swear Hibiscus is out of control.

Bryan's reply comes a few moments later.

> I'm trying to imagine what my grandma would say if she saw me drawing foam unicorns in my teacup.

> Hibiscus calls it fusion tea, but she should be honest and call it "getting props from white people" tea.

Bryan laughs at that. A few minutes later, he sends a meme with a picture of a traditional Chinese tea setup on top and one of Hibiscus's pictures on the bottom. It's captioned *Traditional Tea Culture* on top in big white letters and *Influencer Tea Culture* on the bottom.

I officially concede that the speech is a lost cause and grab a few more screenshots from *Babble Tea*. Fifteen minutes later, I send a slideshow to Bryan called "Traditional Tea Culture vs. Influencer Tea Culture." Then I stuff my index cards into my bag and go brush my teeth. Right before bed, Bryan sends the slideshow back. He's added animated GIFs of teacups and a cartoon circus performer spinning plates on sticks. I was meaning to go to sleep, but it suddenly becomes extremely important to spend the next twenty minutes finding the perfect background music for our slides. We finally settle on a catchy T-pop song with words that resemble something like "I'm so beautiful!"

That's when I finally look at my clock. It's one a.m.

> Crap, I better go to bed.

> Good luck man. I'll catch you tomorrow.

My alarm goes off before sunrise. I groan and slap my phone, wondering what Clementine would say if I just slept through the entire rally. *I'm so sorry. I don't know what happened with my alarm. What a pity that I only woke up after the entire thing was over.*

It's a decent plan up until the part where she strangles me with her bare hands.

I make myself a double cup of oolong. It pains me to put it in a metal thermos, but desperate times call for desperate measures. Just as I'm pulling on my jacket, my phone buzzes, and I look out the window to see a silver Prius outside. Clementine, right on time, with the car she convinced her parents to let her drive this morning.

The streets are quiet as I race out into her car. Even Clementine's muted this morning, though the sight of her still sends a flood of warmth through me. She's huddled at the steering wheel with her own thermos. Her hair's in her signature braid over her shoulder, and she's wrapped a scarf around herself that's a stressful shade of yellow. I think she might be wearing makeup, because her lips look shinier than usual. It takes a few beats for my tired brain to drag my eyes away. I find myself thinking again of that moment yesterday, standing so close to her, staring into her eyes as if we could hold each other simply by looking. My mouth goes dry. I hope I don't make a fool of myself in front of her today.

We're both too sleepy to talk much. On the one hand, it greatly cuts down on my chances of saying something embarrassing. On the other hand, I have nothing to distract my wandering mind. Nothing to keep me from wondering if strawberry lip gloss actually tastes like strawberry.

When we pull into the parking lot, Silas and a few other guys are putting together a stage at one end of the lot. Rui is hauling speakers and sound equipment into place, pausing occasionally to give directions to a group of people holding stacks of posters.

"Clementine! Danny!" she says. "Grab some doughnuts. You can help put up posters and set up the petition desk."

I don't know what it is about doughnuts that make early mornings infinitely more bearable. Thankfully, I feel no need to fully understand something before stuffing it into my mouth, especially if the thing in question is filled with raspberry jelly and coated in crystalline sugar. As the glucose trickles into my brain, I start to feel human again.

After we're suitably fueled up, Clementine and I head to the petition desk to lay out clipboards and pens. Clearly, she's not distracted by what happened yesterday, because she's her usual supernaturally productive self. A guy from the Chinatown

Cares office circles us with his iPhone as Clementine finishes arranging the pens in an aesthetically pleasing fan pattern. We wave at the camera and smile.

The air warms in the parking lot as the sun climbs higher. I catch my parents pulling into their parking space by the tea shop, and I wave at Mrs. Lau as she heads into the grocery store. Master Zhuang gives us a thumbs-up from the door of his kung fu studio.

"How'd it end up with your speech?" asks Clementine.

I got tired of watching myself say inane things to the mirror, so I made inane videos instead.

"I figure your speech can make up for whatever dumpster fire I ignite."

She cocks her head, clearly trying to figure out whether I'm joking. "You need someone to practice with?"

"No, I'm good."

For a moment, she seems to waver between offering more help or letting it go. Apparently, she chooses the latter because she gives me a confident smile. "I'm sure whatever you have will be great."

Now I really feel like a jerk. I was a total ass when she tried to help me with my speech, and now she's taking the high road. I take a deep breath, gathering myself to apologize, when Clementine touches my elbow, sending a zing up my arm. "Look, it's Nadia!"

The fast typer with the large earrings comes running up to us. She's carrying a giant sign that says, "Tea, Not Kale!"

"I'm so excited!" Her earrings swing erratically. "Are you speaking?"

"We are!" says Clementine, sounding like she's talking about an impending lottery win instead of my imminent humiliation.

"Oh my gosh. I can't wait!" says Nadia.

My doughnut buzz flickers and disappears.

Clementine gestures toward the gift shop. "Twenty percent off at the gift shop today. They have a great Hello Kitty section."

It's very rare that I see someone's eyes light up with pure unadulterated greed, but it happens with Nadia. Clementine and I exchange amused looks as she zips off. The sun shines on Clementine's face at an angle, giving her skin a luminous cast. I have trouble looking away.

Thankfully, Bryan and Adenike show up just about then.

Bryan's first act is to inspect the empty doughnut boxes. "You guys got any more of these?"

Adenike eyes him like he's an escaped zoo animal.

More and more cars pull into the parking lot. Doors open and close. The sidewalks and stores start filling with people.

"Do you think there are more shoppers here than usual?" Clementine asks me.

I look around. "I think so?" But I'm not sure if it's indeed more people or if it just seems like more because I'm imagining every single one of them in the audience for my speech. Every time I check the time, it's moved forward more than I expect. Then, I'm looking at the clock as it goes from 10:59 to 11:00.

Rally time. I stare into those two zeros like the ominous voids they are. Then I look up to see Rui striding down the stairs, the inexorable march of destiny incarnate in an organized and enthusiastic package.

She grins at us. "Showtime!"

There's a crowd in front of the stage, and most are holding signs in support of our mall. I see Nadia in back, sporting a new Hello Kitty baseball cap. Clementine points out an Asian American couple waving enthusiastically from the middle of the crowd.

"My parents," she says.

It's hard to see them from here, but I now know where Clementine got her energy levels.

Bryan punches me in the shoulder. "Break a leg!" he says before he and Adenike join the crowd.

Rui takes the microphone, and the noise of the crowd dies to a murmur. She thanks everyone for coming and gives a brief overview of everything that's happened with Kale Corp. Then she calls up Master Zhuang to speak. He talks about the generations of kids who grew up in his studio and how he keeps his prices low because he wants people to be able to afford lessons. But now that he's getting kicked out, he doesn't know if he can find another place with reasonable rent. Moving too far would mean that his current students would no longer be able to attend.

After Master Zhuang comes Mrs. Lau from the grocery store, who talks through a translator. She tells about how she started the store, how her kids grew up there, and about the generations of families that have shopped there over the years. It's really moving. Mrs. Lau doesn't have Master Zhuang's presence, and her words are soft and halting, but that makes it all the more real. It reminds me that my family was one of the many who've shopped there. I was one of the kids who ran through those aisles.

I look at my index cards, and suddenly it clicks for me. These cards aren't just notes for a presentation. They're memories, proof of how special Fragrant Leaves is to me and so many others. And it dawns on me just how much is at stake. If we can't get momentum with this rally, I don't know how we'll save this place. Suddenly, I'm feeling the words in my hand more strongly than ever before.

Mrs. Lau finishes to cheers, and Rui dismisses us for a short lunch break. The restaurant is selling box lunches for rallygoers. Clementine and I pick some up and stake out a corner on the shaded sidewalk with other kids from our school. Clementine's parents come by to say hi, and Clementine introduces us.

Mrs. Chan's an uncanny vision of how Clementine will look in thirty years, with the same alert eyes and purposeful mouth.

"I've heard so much about you, Danny," she says with a firm handshake. From the corner of my eye, I see Clementine's eyes widen as she turns quickly away. "I wish the best for your restaurant. Kids like you will change the world. I know it."

Mr. Chan gives Clementine a healthy smack on the back, making her flinch and turn back toward us. He's super tall and seems to have forgotten that there's a pen wedged behind his ear. "This is great, guys! Three months ago, Clementine didn't even know what Chinatown Cares was, and now look at this!"

They leave to have their own lunch, promising that they won't bug us too much. As they walk away, I think about my parents in the tea shop, and my chest tightens at the contrast. I didn't even tell them I was speaking at the rally today. It was easier not to.

Still, it's hard to be depressed for too long with all the excitement around us. Everyone's in good spirits as lunch wraps up. Nadia shows off her newly acquired Hello Kitty key chains to an appreciative Adenike. Bryan regales Josh with stories about the octopus in the grocery store, and they run off to look for it. I'm mostly finishing my meal in silence, and so is Clementine. As Felicia and Bhramara leave on their own gift shop pilgrimage, the silence between Clementine and me starts to feel strained.

I lean over toward her. "Hey," I say. "I'm sorry." When she looks confused, I continue. "I'm sorry I gave you such a hard time about your suggestions for my speech. You were right. I did need to get more personal."

With the breeze blowing through her hair, Clementine gives off an air of contentment. Her cheeks are flushed with good-natured color, and while she's curious at my words, my comment doesn't seem to bring down her mood. "Why do you say that?" she asks.

"After I cooled down a bit, I did end up following your advice.

But I don't think I really got what you meant until I heard Mrs. Lau talk just now. She sounded so genuine, you know?"

Clementine nods, a half smile on her lips. "Yeah. She was great, wasn't she?"

"I know I'm kind of an ass about social media and influencers and that stuff. I dunno, I guess I've seen too many of them causing trouble at Fragrant Leaves. But you're right. Not all sharing is performative. Sometimes it's just sharing."

She's solemn for a moment, and she looks at me in a way that feels like she's wrapped a blanket around my shoulders. "Thank you for saying that, Danny. I appreciate it."

I could sit here looking into her eyes forever, but Rui chooses that moment to come by. "It's going great so far. I think we're going to start up again." She puts a hand on my shoulder. "You still up for speaking?"

I can feel Clementine watching me as I hesitate, and I sense her pride in me when I nod.

Rui smiles. "Great. Come on backstage, then."

There's no more time for worrying. Clementine squeezes my arm, triggering shivers through my frame. The next few minutes move faster than any segment of time has a right to. Rui calls everyone to order. The crowd gathers again. She gives a brief introduction with my name and my restaurant's name peppered in at random intervals. And then Rui's beckoning me on.

I'm light-headed as I walk onstage, as if I've had tea that's too strong for the time of day. Somehow I make it up the stairs without tripping, and I check out the faces below me. Bryan's watching me with a big grin, and Adenike's next to him, looking slightly less unimpressed with me than usual. When I bring out my notes and start talking, it feels different from all those times I practiced. This time, I genuinely have something worthwhile to say.

"Hello, everyone. I'm Danny Mok."

I feel eyes on me. More important, I feel that the crowd wants me to succeed. When I speak, it's less like reading a book report and more like that Saturday morning showing Clementine around the teahouse. I'm simply introducing people to everything I love about Fragrant Leaves, and from the openness in their faces, I see that they're eager to come along for the ride. When I finish, I'm so relieved at the applause that I'm light-headed again. By the side of the stage, I see Clementine beaming, Silas smiling, and Rui giving me an enthusiastic thumbs-up.

As I make my way offstage, I catch a glimpse of someone leaving the crowd. I only see his back, but there's no mistaking my dad's salt-and-pepper hair and bald spot. The sight stops me. Did he hear my entire speech?

But there's no time to think about that, because Rui comes at me with a huge hug, and Clementine follows up with her own. Rui's hug is friendly and energetic. And Clementine's feels . . . right. I catch a whiff of her shampoo. Her frame is smaller than Rui's, and she fits somehow. I don't want to let go.

Silas slaps me on the back. "That was fantastic, Danny. Just what we needed."

"I knew you could do it," says Clementine, stepping back to grin at me. I'm fighting the urge to pull her right back into my arms. "They don't even need to hear from me now."

Rui laughs. "You're selling yourself short, girl." And then she pushes Clementine up the stairs. Clementine surges on with the momentum of Rui's push, and then her steps smooth out and she strides onstage. The crowd falls silent, and you can tell right away that everyone is drawn to her.

Clearly, confidently, Clementine starts to talk—about the history of Chinatown, the immigrants who came to live and work here, the communities and the connection that would be lost if it all goes away. She's funny, she's eloquent, and she's beautiful. She's a force of nature. When I break my gaze away from her for just a moment, I see that everybody else is just as rapt.

Finally she finishes, and the audience erupts. Clementine gives them another brilliant smile and encourages them to shop at the stores and sign the petition. Silas pumps his fist in the air. Rui walks up onstage and works the crowd even louder. When Clementine comes jogging down the steps, I open my arms for a hug, and she runs into them, grinning up at me as she squeezes me around the waist.

"You were amazing," I tell her. I'm transfixed by the light reflecting off her lips.

"*You* were amazing," she replies.

"I'm going to kiss you," I say.

Clementine blinks at me, bewildered. My heart crashes to a stop as I realize what I just blurted out. What in the world got into me, declaring that I'm going to kiss her like some dude bro in a bad movie?

I jump back. "Sorry, I—I, uh . . ." I'm not even sure how someone goes about apologizing for this. I wonder if she's going to kick me in the balls. That happens in movies all the time. Did she ever train in martial arts?

Clementine breaks into that big grin again as she reaches for the nape of my neck. The brush of her fingers against my hair sends a shiver down my spine. Deliberately, she pulls me down so our foreheads touch, and then it's the most natural thing ever to fall even closer together. When our lips meet, it's electric, a jolt that goes through my entire body.

I guess she's okay with it.

I tighten my arms around her, pulling her closer and pressing my hands against the curve of her back. Clementine snuggles in, as warm and soft as I'd imagined. She smiles against my lips, and her low chuckle vibrates through my being. Her lip gloss is just the slightest bit sweet.

"Get a room," says Bryan loudly.

Clementine and I pull ourselves apart, and I look around, discombobulated. I can still feel Clementine on my skin, which makes it hard to focus. Everything smells like strawberry.

Apparently Bryan's made it backstage, because he's smirking at us. "Aren't you two supposed to be doing activism or something?"

Clementine jabs him with her elbow and he makes a show of doubling over.

"Thanks for your support, Bryan," she says. Then she looks around at the stage, the audience, and Rui up there still addressing the crowd, and she beams.

"Good rally," she says.

CHAPTER TWENTY-TWO

CLEMENTINE

WELL, I DIDN'T EXPECT THE RALLY TO GO LIKE this. Still, I can't complain.

Rui is still onstage, ushering the kids from the martial arts studio up for their demonstration. Master Zhuang is hovering at the other side of the stage, a mother hen with a black belt. I'm still smiling. I can't help it. As the kids take up a horse stance, I lean over, slide my hand across Danny's shoulder blades, and pull him in for another kiss. He smells like wood and soap. His muscles are firm and lean under his T-shirt.

Bryan makes gagging sounds. Adenike, who's joined us by now, puts her palm to her forehead and laughs silently. I'm not usually one for public displays of affection. And it's not like I came to the rally planning to kiss Danny. But it felt so right at that moment. And it feels right now.

The rest of the day passes in a rosy haze. The kung fu kids front-kick their way into the audience's hearts. A few more store owners talk, and Rui opens up the mic to people from the crowd. I try to count the number of customers coming and going from the stores, but to be honest I'm distracted, and so is Danny.

Thankfully, nobody seems to mind. Rui gives us this huge wink when she comes off the stage. She must have an extra eye monitoring the wings or something. Several other members of the Chinatown Cares crew call us lovebirds and give us sly grins and nudges.

I can't blame them. I mean, it *was* a pretty epic first kiss.

Later in the afternoon, my parents drop by to say bye. It's kind of a shock to see them—I'd completely forgotten they were here. I can tell Danny had forgotten too by the way he freezes at the sight of them. But Mom and Dad are upbeat and totally casual as they wish us a good rest of the rally—up until the part when Mom leans over and says, "I'd kiss you goodbye, Clem, but you seem to have had plenty of that already today."

She laughs as she links arms and walks away with Dad. I've never seen Danny turn so deep a shade of red. I do my best to melt into the asphalt, and when that fails, I make a mental note to put chili powder in my parents' toothpaste.

The day gradually winds down. We've been up since dawn, and I feel it more and more as time passes. By evening, even all that rally adrenaline isn't enough to keep the drowsiness from setting in.

"You good to drive home?" asks Rui. "You look like you're fading a bit."

"I'm okay now, but yeah, we'd better head home soon."

Danny and I are both pretty mellow on the drive back, basking on the residual warmth of the day. As I drive, I keep wanting to reach over and touch him. It's only my thorough indoctrination in driver's ed that keeps my hands on the wheel. Finally, I stop at a red light and muffle a yawn. Maybe the same thoughts have been going through Danny's head, because he reaches over and covers my fingers with his.

"I'm going to sleep so well tonight," says Danny. I love the way his voice sounds right now, low and rumbling with drowsiness.

"I know what you mean," I say. "I was going to—" I stop before I say that I was going to write a blog post tonight. I haven't told Danny about *Babble Tea* yet, and I realize that I'm not quite ready to deal with the awkwardness that might result. I suppose I could go back and take down my old Fragrant Leaves review, but that rankles my journalist instincts. I'll figure it out soon. Just not tonight.

Danny doesn't seem to notice my lapse. The light turns green, and I wrestle my faculties back toward driving.

"You know," he says, "giving that speech wasn't nearly as bad as I thought it would be. Thanks for your help."

"I'm glad. Your speech was really touching."

I'm kind of sad to pull in front of his apartment complex, and I turn to say goodbye. Meeting his eyes still sends a jolt through me. "What's your schedule like tomorrow morning?" I ask. "Maybe we could follow up with the store owners and see what they thought of the rally?"

"Yeah," he says, rubbing the sleep from his face. "Maybe a little later in the morning, though."

I laugh. "Okay. I'm game for sleeping in. Will you be at the shop tomorrow? Should I just go find you?"

"Yeah, that sounds good." He unfastens his seat belt, and a mischievous glint enters his eye. "So now I know you're a fan of kissing in public. How do you feel about kissing in private?"

My bones go soft at his words, though Danny immediately ruins the effect by adding, "Like, when your parents *aren't* watching."

"Oh my God." I bury my face in my hands. Maybe I'll mix cayenne into mom's kombucha too. "I'm sooooo sorry. My parents . . ."

Danny chuckles. When I peek out from behind my hands, he's leaning back in his seat and laughing. "It's all good. Absolutely mortifying, but they were really nice. They—" He stops. "I totally ruined the mood, didn't I?"

I grin despite myself. "Pretty much completely."

"Hmm." His expression becomes pensive, as if he were trying to solve a puzzle. "How about a redo?"

I raise an eyebrow. "A redo?"

"Yeah." Danny takes my hand, giving me a look that zings straight through to my toes. When he speaks again, his voice is gentle, earnest. "Today was a really good day, Clementine. I'm truly grateful I got to spend it with you. You're amazing. Beautiful, smart, caring, talented beyond belief. I'd been wanting to kiss you for weeks now, and I still can't quite believe that you feel the same way." Then that impish spark returns to his eyes. "But knowing now that you do, I'd like to kiss you good night. Is that all right with you?"

His words wrap around me like warm cotton candy. Instead of answering, I lean over the armrest toward him. My seat belt stops me from going very far, but Danny makes up the rest of the distance. I suppress a shiver and close my eyes, soaking in that delicious tingling sensation of waiting for someone to move closer, every one of my nerve endings alive for that first hint of contact—a breeze, a scent, the slightest brush of his lips.

And then we're kissing again, his lips soft, fiery, and sure, his teeth and tongue teasing mine. I can feel the heat radiating from his body, a comforting warmth against the chill fall air. I run my hands along his shoulders and down his back, taking in the lines and ridges of bone and muscle. His fingers brush the nape of my neck, sending a quiver down my spine. Time slows down. I'd be perfectly happy if this moment never ended.

When Danny finally pulls away, he takes my breath with him. It's dark outside, but there's enough light from the streetlamp for me to see the spark in his eye and for that spot just under my rib cage to ache in response. "I'll see you tomorrow?"

I hold his gaze. "Tomorrow."

CHAPTER TWENTY-THREE

Danny

I'M THE KIND OF PERSON WHO GETS GRUMPY WHEN I'm tired. (Is there a word for that? Tangry?) Tonight's different, though. I'm exhausted as I walk in the door, but I'm not grumpy at all.

I'm still thinking about Clementine as I lock the front door behind me, reliving that kiss in her car. My body is still warm in the places we'd touched, and I can taste the residual sweetness of her lip gloss. Finally, I come out of my fog to realize that Dad is on the living room couch, reading a newspaper. That kills my buzz a bit.

"Hey Dad." He's usually not out here at this time of night.

The last few days have been tense around the restaurant. Neither he nor Mom has mentioned the fight at all, and I've followed their lead. We're pretending it didn't happen, but it's not like we can disappear it for real. The residue of it lingers, like the smell of mold on old tea leaves. With a pit in my stomach, I remember Dad leaving the rally after my speech and how

I spent the afternoon marinating in post-kiss bliss while Mom and Dad managed the teahouse alone.

Dad puts down his newspaper. His expression's mild, but still I'm nervous. "You didn't tell us that you would be making a speech," he says.

"Oh. Yeah." Does he think I shared too much? Does he still think I'm meddling in their business? All the events of the day are closing in on me now, and I'm exhausted.

Dad absentmindedly fingers the mole under his right ear. "It was a good speech. I was glad to hear what the teahouse has meant to you over the years."

I stare at him, stunned. I was bracing myself for a scolding. I guess, between the fight earlier this week and everything from today, part of me thought I deserved one. But Dad doesn't look angry, just thoughtful.

"You don't mind that I did it?" I ask.

He studies me, taking a long, pensive breath. "When you first started helping Chinatown Cares, your mom was very worried. We remembered the other groups that came by, and we didn't want to see you put all this time and effort into something just to end up being abandoned and disappointed. We know what it's like to get our hopes up. But we've spent more time with Silas and Rui now. They're more experienced and responsible than the groups we've met before."

Again, I'm surprised. "I think they're a good group too," I say.

Dad nods. "We forget that you're eighteen now. It seems like yesterday that you were going into kindergarten." Do his eyes look shinier than usual? "We don't always tell you about what's going on with the restaurant, but I see now that you're able to understand more. I will try to remember that."

He goes back to reading his newspaper. After watching him a few more moments, I head to my room. I sleep well that night.

I have a brief impression of my parents attempting to wake me up the next day—Mom opening the blinds in my room, Dad shaking my shoulder and saying, "Come on, Danny, time to go," before I roll over and go back to sleep. Mom calls for me a few more times, and then they stop.

It's late morning when I wake, and my parents are gone. Whoops. I feel horrible taking this morning off after being gone all day yesterday too, but I gotta admit I feel well rested.

There's a text waiting for me on my phone.

Good morning 😊 Let me know when you're up and ready.

I wipe the drool from my cheek.

Do you not sleep?

Hey, I slept a good eight hours. I don't know what you're talking about.

I check the clock. Looks like I was out for ten hours.

I pull myself out of bed. I have horrible morning mouth, and my hair looks like it staged a rally of its own last night. I do my best to clean up, and then I grab some stale pastries and run out to the bus stop.

I've just gotten off near the mall when I see Clementine's bus coming. It makes me jittery, and I'm suddenly nervous about seeing her. Yesterday was almost surreal now that I look back on it. Part of me wonders what Clementine thinks of us now that the rally's over and we're back to a regular Sunday. Maybe she'll take one look at the pillow marks on my face and the rats' nest that's currently my hair and think, *Well, that was a bad idea.*

But then the bus pulls up, and she jumps off, looking as fresh as ever. Her cheeks glow, and she's wearing lip gloss again, which seems like a cruel trick. Her eyes sparkle when they lock on mine.

"Hey," I say.

"Hey yourself."

She gets this mischievous look, then plants a kiss on my cheek. "It's good to see you."

The tingle of her lips hasn't quite faded when she pulls out a giant clipboard. By the time I've accepted the fact that there's not another kiss coming, she's all business.

"Okay." She taps her pen on her clipboard. "I'm thinking we should go through the list of stores and check in with each one. We'll see how they felt about the day and compile it all into a report. Sound good?"

I hesitate, wondering if I should at least poke my head into Fragrant Leaves to see if my parents need help. On the other hand, we do need to get store reactions while memories are fresh, and it's probably more efficient to get this out of the way. I give her a salute. "Yes, ma'am."

She gives me an appraising look. "You're very attractive when you say that."

"I am, huh?"

Clementine shrugs. "Just sayin'." She nudges me with her hip and we start making our rounds.

Mike Mao, the gift shop owner, is happy to see us. "Lots of sales yesterday!" He pumps his fist in the air. "Twice the normal amount!"

Mrs. Lau from the grocery store is more subdued. She thanks us when we tell her that we enjoyed her speech. "Maybe a few more people came by yesterday," she says. "I haven't checked the numbers yet." She doesn't strike me as super convinced that the day made a difference.

Master Zhuang gives us high fives when we come by. "Great party yesterday! Great energy!" When we ask him if he got any new customers, he waves his hand. "Some people came by to look, but nobody signed up. These things take time. It's not like buying a bag of candy, you know?"

When we come to the Chinese medicine store, Mr. Yook is in front sweeping up the sidewalk.

"Good morning, Mr. Yook."

He points at a pile of debris on the ground. "Careful, don't kick that!" We skirt around a heap of dust and food packaging. The Chinese medicine store was close to the stage, and it looks like a lot of trash blew into their corner. Clementine picks up an empty cup near a retaining wall and tosses it in the trash. I do the same with a doughnut bag. In a few minutes, we've gotten the big pieces of litter and Mr. Yook has swept up the rest. Clementine magically produces a bottle of hand sanitizer and offers some to me and Mr. Yook.

"Thank you," says Mr. Yook. He looks around and shakes his head. "Such a mess!"

Clementine and I exchange a glance. We did our best to clean up yesterday with the team, but we obviously missed quite a bit.

"Mr. Yook," Clementine says hesitantly, "we were wondering if you have any thoughts about yesterday. Did you see an increase in sales?"

He shrugs. "Maybe, maybe not." He leans his broom against the wall. "I have a customer at the register. We'll talk later."

We stare at his back as he disappears inside.

"I feel bad about the litter," I say.

"Yeah," says Clementine. "I wonder if we can make it up to him somehow." It starts to feel a little obnoxious to keep staring into the medicine shop, so we turn back toward Fragrant Leaves. "On the bright side, we heard from happy people too."

I intend to reply with something vaguely intelligent, but my mind goes blank because Clementine threads her fingers through mine. It sends a tingling warmth up my arm, which goes straight to my brain and wraps it in a deactivating force field.

"Hmm?" I say. I think she just said something else, but I'm not sure.

"You look distracted," she says, and the expression on her face is far more devilish than usual.

"Sorry, what were you saying?"

She points toward a corner. "Let's go check out that store over there."

"Clementine, that's a vending machine."

She shrugs. "You never know."

Seems like I'm not the only person whose brain circuits are malfunctioning. But before I can finish that thought, she's pulled me around to the other side of the vending machine. Now that we're up against the wall, I realize that it blocks our view of most of the parking lot.

Which also means we're out of their view.

"Oh."

Clementine chuckles low in her throat, guiding my hands to her waist as I lean down to kiss her. I decide her lip gloss is cherry flavored, not strawberry. As I tighten my arms around her waist, she reaches up and combs her fingers through my hair. It makes me shiver, which is a strange sensation because the rest of her is so warm. She traces lines down my shoulders with her fingertips, then slips a hand up the sleeve of my T-shirt at the same time our kiss deepens. . . .

Clem's eyes sparkle when we finally come up for air. She gives me a playful smack on the shoulder. "Okay, back to work!"

"You are so strange," I say, which she seems to take as a compliment. From the sly look on her face, she's clearly aware of how maddening I'm finding her habit of switching from kissing to business and back again.

"What?" she asks innocently.

I give her a mock disapproving shake of my head. "You're gonna pay for this."

She smirks. "I certainly hope so."

By unspoken consensus, we don't hold hands when we walk into Fragrant Leaves. I guess we're both a bit self-conscious, although we're probably deluding ourselves if we think we can get past the aunties when their antennae are up. The mahjong crowd seems to be having an intense morning, though, and no one gives us a glance.

"Hi, Mrs. Mok," says Clementine brightly as we pass the register. I let her chat Mom up as I start one of the hot-water pots boiling. At least my parents can't yell at me for sleeping in if Clementine's here. Mom seems in good spirits as she answers Clementine's questions about rally day. Finally, Clem takes out her laptop and we settle ourselves in a corner booth.

"All right, should we just go through the stores one by one?" she asks. "Your mom says they had an uptick in business yesterday. Maybe about a thirty-three percent increase."

Well, that's good.

Clementine does the typing, saying what she's writing out loud so I can chime in with anything extra. We're mostly on the same page with our impressions. After we type notes for the first two stores, I go into the kitchen and come back out with a pot of oolong steeped in freshly boiled water.

Clementine sniffs in appreciation as I pour her a cup. She takes a slow sip and hums her approval. "Mmm, thank you. Fragrant Leaves knows how to do tea."

I chuckle. "Well, we are a tea shop."

"No, really," she says. She closes her eyes, her expression blissful as she inhales the steam from her cup. "The temperature's perfect, the scent is open. The bouquet moves smoothly up into my nose and down. I can never get this kind of complexity when I make tea at home. I took a workshop on gongfu cha a while back and I've been hoping to up my brewing game, but I haven't had the equipment or the time to practice."

I stare at her.

She pushes her tea to the side and starts typing again. "Okay, what should we say for Master Zhuang? Seems optimistic?"

We keep working, but I'm stuck on the comments she just made about our tea. Clementine's mentioned being a customer here in the past, but she's apparently much more of a tea connoisseur than she's let on. And that comment about wanting to learn gongfu cha but not having the equipment or time? I've heard that before.

Or, more accurately, I've read that before.

Clementine lifts her fingers with a flourish. "So I think that's all of them. Did we miss anyone?"

Somehow, I still have the presence of mind to answer. "I don't think so."

What are the odds that two different teenage girls I know would have taken a gongfu cha workshop recently and had the same reaction?

"Fantastic." Clementine pushes her laptop toward me. "Why don't you take a look? I'll be right back. Feel free to make any changes."

She runs off toward the restroom, leaving me with her open laptop.

I scan over the words on the page, but they might as well be gibberish for all the sense they're making in my brain. Clementine can't possibly be Hibiscus. Hibiscus is superficial, obsessed with gimmicks, and has horrible taste in everything. Clementine is the complete opposite of that in every way.

I look down at the task bar to see that Clementine has a browser open. There's one easy way to put this question to rest, but I shouldn't. She's trusting me with her computer. It would be wrong to violate that trust.

Feeling like a creep, I click on her browser, open another tab, and navigate over to *Babble Tea*. When the obnoxiously dreamy header image appears, I click the log-on link. It takes a few seconds to load, during which I tap my fingers on the table, stare at the bathroom door, and wish we had faster Wi-Fi. Then the log-on page appears. There it is, plain as day—Hibiscus auto-filled in the log-on space along with a password.

My stomach drops through the floor, leaving a gaping hole in its wake. I stare at the computer screen for an amount of time that's somewhere between three seconds and eternity. Then the bathroom door opens and shuts across the room. I jump high enough to announce my guilt to the entire restaurant. *Stay calm. Play it cool.* By the time Clementine sits down, I've minimized the browser and brought our report back up on the screen.

"What you think?" she says.

"Um, looks great." Did I remember to close the tab with her blog? My heart is beating wildly enough to injure itself against my rib cage.

She gives me that sunny smile again. "Fantastic, I'll send it off to Rui and Silas and see what they think. Are you free tomorrow? Maybe we can drop by headquarters and touch base with them in person."

"Yeah," I say. My voice sounds like it's coming from very far away. "Yeah, that sounds great."

Hibiscus.

Clementine.

Hibiscus is Clementine.

Clementine is Hibiscus.

I don't know how I managed to keep it together until after Clementine left. She's a journalist, right? Don't they have sixth senses like spiders? Or anti-spy software that records keystrokes and detects intruders through the laptop camera?

The enormity of what I've just done feels huge, like something that should send shock waves over a three-mile radius. Even if Clementine didn't notice, it seems unavoidable that someone else must have. Maybe someone at the tea shop was looking over my shoulder, or heck, some kind of snooping-jackass-detector-drone was taking pictures through the window.

But nobody noticed. Clementine took her computer back and dashed off a quick email. Then she closed up her laptop, kissed me goodbye, and left to catch her bus.

I watched her go. Like, that's how pathetic I am. It didn't even occur to me to walk her to her bus stop. I just watched the door shut behind her and made a beeline for my computer. I've been sitting here now for the better part of an hour, interrupted halfway through by some tourists wanting a pot of jasmine. It was not my finest brew.

On my screen is a Clementine/Hibiscus review of a boba place from last spring. I've been reading her posts in reverse chronological order, starting from the post she made yesterday. Now that I know who she is, it's hard to believe I didn't see it before. There are signatures of Clementine all over this blog—fake flowers and candles that appear both on her photos and in her real-life tabling setups, a yellow scarf I've seen her wear, references to being "on deadline," the ever-present commenting of Nikegirl—who I now know isn't actually a sneakerhead.

At one point, my mom asks me why I'm mumbling to myself, and I mumble an incoherent answer.

My phone buzzes. It's a text from Clementine.

I accidentally stole the pens from the petition desk yesterday lol.

I send back a laugh emoji. I feel like sinking into the floor.

The next day at school is the first time I've ever been grateful that Clementine and I don't have classes together. Still, we're supposed to meet up after school to go to Chinatown Cares. I'm so stressed about it that even Bryan comments.

"Dude, isn't having a girlfriend supposed to make you happy?"

I ignore him. Time marches inexorably on. Clementine shows up by my locker after last period.

"Hey!" She squeezes my arm.

It's like one of those sci-fi movies where someone keeps on flickering back and forth between two images. I see Clementine in front of me. She's beautiful, charming, fantastic all around. I'm happy to see her. But in the back of my mind is this nagging suspicion that maybe there's something else underneath.

"Hey," I say.

"How was class?"

"All right." I guess I should say more. "And you?"

"Not too bad." She frowns. "Is everything okay?"

So much for trying to pretend everything's normal. "I've been feeling a bit off. Maybe I'm coming down with something after the rally."

"Oh, that's too bad." She squeezes my hand. "Hope you feel better." She doesn't try to make conversation on the bus ride over, which makes me feel both glad and crummy.

Silas saunters out from behind his desk when we walk into Chinatown Cares. "My favorite high school activists! How are you two feeling?"

"Good!" says Clementine. "Danny might be getting sick, though."

"Bummer," says Silas. "We call that the rally plague."

Rui comes running and hugs us both. "Yup, it takes a few days to recover from these things! Come to the conference room. We have doughnuts."

"Left over from Saturday?" Clementine asks.

"Don't be ridiculous. Doughnuts don't survive for that long."

We pull up chairs around the table. I stuff two chocolate doughnut holes into my mouth. Doughnuts, at least, are always what they appear to be.

"I read through your report," says Rui. "Thank you so much for putting it together. Everybody on our side was happy with how the rally went. You should be proud of your part in this."

"We do have an update." Silas gives us a meaningful glance through his horn-rimmed glasses. "And it's a bit of a downer, but that's how things go. News came through today that the sale to Kale Corp has been finalized."

The chocolate lump in my esophagus stops moving. "Finalized? Like, they own the building now?"

"They closed on it today," says Silas gently.

I try to swallow the doughnut again, but the lump stays stubbornly in place. "What does that mean?" I ask. *Are we finished?*

"It means the timeline is more set now," says Silas. "The store owners will probably get a formal deadline for accepting Kale's buyout offer. It doesn't mean we have to stop fighting. It's not over until our stores move out and Kale moves in."

Next to me, Clementine is looking equally confused. "Is there anything we can do?"

"The exact same things we've been doing," says Rui, calm and deliberate. "Continuing to drum up community support and reach out to the press."

Clementine tugs on her braid. "Let me know if I can help in any way. I can free up time on my schedule if you need more feet on the ground."

It messes with my head how determined she looks. Would Hibiscus be willing to put in extra hours? Or would she just be excited about the new modern options at the Kale store?

Rui smiles. "That's why we love you, Clementine. Why don't you stay tuned?"

We don't stay at Chinatown Cares for long. After going over the rest of our report, Clementine and I head to separate bus stops for our trip home.

"Hope you feel better," she says. She looks extra sympathetic, which just makes me feel like more of a jerk. "Hey, I make a mean chicken broth. How about I drop some by your house tomorrow?"

"Oh, I wouldn't go to the trouble. . . ."

"No trouble at all. I'll just pop it in the Instant Pot. It's all about putting in the right herbs." She gives me a quick hug. "Catch you later!"

On the bus ride home, I pull out my phone and start scrolling through *Babble Tea* again. Here's what I don't understand. Clementine loves Chinatown. She loves these teahouses, and she's put so much work into saving what Chinatown is. Hibiscus, on the other hand, couldn't care less about saving Chinatown. She's always trying to make changes and switch things up. I mean, look at the crimes that she's committed against tea in pursuit of blog hits.

But the more I scroll through, the more I start to think that maybe I was being unfair. I always thought Hibiscus was trying to put Chinatown down, but she says a lot of good things about Chinatown too. There are descriptions of cute stores and kind notes about people. Her blog posts about community make many of the same points Clementine's told me in person. I guess I'd just assumed Hibiscus didn't really mean what she said, that it was just for show. The blog post equivalent of #blessed and overexposed photographs. Maybe I was so convinced she was a vapid blogger that I didn't think she could actually be sincere.

But what about the whitewashing? Okay, I still maintain that adding cream and sugar to jasmine tea should be a felony in any judicial system. But could it be possible that Clementine was just messing around? Maybe she was doing it for herself, instead of courting white readers for hits?

That leaves the question: If Hibiscus isn't a vapid poser, what does that make me, the guy who's been trolling her for years? An ass of the highest order. Each comment section gives me a front-row seat to how much of a tool I was. I wonder why she never banned me from her site.

I click the home button, and it takes me to the front page. Looks like Clementine's put up a new post about iced chrysanthemum tea with raspberry puree. It's ridiculous. It's gimmicky.

I have no desire to comment.

I think I'm going to be sick. I wonder what Clementine would think if Bobaboy just quietly disappeared. Maybe he could meet some untimely end. On a whim, I Google "how to fake the death of a screen handle," but I'm too distracted to scroll through the results.

Maybe I'm overthinking this. Maybe Clementine wouldn't think much of it if Bobaboy simply went away. Maybe she'd just figure that he's found someone else to terrorize instead.

By the time I get home, I've concocted several different scenarios for Bobaboy's demise. Maybe he should get hit by a giant boba truck. That'd be poetic, wouldn't it? Though, who am I kidding? I'm not actually going to carry through. I'm going to ghost, like the classy person I am. Let Bobaboy and Hibiscus's feud fade off into the past and never speak of it again.

My phone buzzes. It's from Bryan.

> Hey, our video's blowing up

What's he talking about? I text back.

> What?

My phone starts buzzing. The caller ID says it's Bryan. Weird; he never calls.

"Dude, you have to look at Linktropolis," he says as soon as I pick up. "Our video's gone viral."

"What?" He's way too excited for this hour of night, and I have way too many other things going on to deal with it.

"Our video! The one we made about tea culture versus influencer culture. It got voted to the top of Jasper City Chinatown."

Every single one of my internal organs shrivels up and disappears. I'm surprised that my phone doesn't dissolve in my hand.

"You posted our video?"

"Well, yeah." He sounds puzzled. "I figured we were done with it, right?"

I hang up and open Linktropolis so quickly it leaves skid marks on my CPU. There it is, a link from GrandRiceAzn to a video called "Traditional Tea Culture vs. Influencer Tea Culture." I have a full-on out-of-body experience as I press play. It looks like Bryan's done some more work on the video since I last saw it. He's added more sound effects, cool transitions, even a few emojis of puking teacups. The production quality is actually quite good.

It's a disaster.

I close the video and look at the comment thread. There are hundreds of comments. On a video about tea? I mean, authentic brewing is not exactly a mainstream concern. Our video's amusing, I guess, but is it really that good?

I start to understand as I scroll through the comments, and it's not good at all. Almost all the comments are negative, and they're not just criticizing Hibiscus's blog posts. Some people are calling her a traitor to the Asian race.

How can we be surprised that racism is real when our own people cater to whiteness like this? says one comment.

Yeah, it's just depressing, adds someone else.

It gets worse.

> This is everything that's wrong with Asian chicks. It's not enough for them to leave Asian men out to dry, they have to reject Asian tea too?

> You think she's Asian?

> Dude, she's named Hibiscus.

It looks like people from all the worst corners of the internet are here. I check the link history, and it looks like our video's been reposted on a bunch of other subcities.

And then I see this.

> I just left a comment on her blog.

> Me too.

> Yeah, me too.

Muttering a few choice words under my breath, I open a new tab and surf back to *Babble Tea.*

There's the familiar *Rabble Tea* header, with Clementine's scarf in the background. I scan to the comments. Usually there are forty or fifty on a post. I think I remember twelve or so replies on the iced chrysanthemum post the last time I checked. Now there are hundreds, and they're just as bad here as they were on the link aggregator.

My stomach churns. Has Clementine seen these yet? She must not have, or she would have deleted them, right? I imagine her picking up her laptop and reading these for the first time. Then I go to Twitter and search her screen name. Yup, they're piling on there as well.

I close it all and dial Bryan.

He picks up after the first ring. "Did you just hang up on me?"

"Take down the video!"

"What?"

"Take it down! Have you seen the comments?"

"Not recently." There's a silence and I hear some clicking in the background. "Dude, this is getting kind of messed up."

"Ya think?"

"All right. All right. I'll take it down. Just lemme finish my ice cream."

"No, do it right now!"

"All right, I will." There's another silence and I hear more mouse clicks. "It's down. You seem really stressed about this."

"That's because it's Clementine!"

Pause. A single clink of a spoon. "What?"

"Hibiscus is Clementine! And we just sent a whole bunch of trolls to her blog."

Now there's a long silence. No spoon noises at all. "You're kidding," he finally says.

"No. I'm not. I swear I'm not. I just found out today."

"Hibiscus can't be Clementine. Clementine is smart."

I'm not in the mood to watch Bryan go through the same process I went through a few hours ago.

"I swear it's her. I just . . ." It's like the entire day has coalesced into the form of a Mack truck and finally chosen this moment to drive over me. "I gotta go."

CHAPTER TWENTY-FOUR

CLEMENTINE

I'M IN MY ROOM, TRYING TO SORT OUT WHICH OF
my pens belong to me and which need to be returned to Chinatown Cares, when the first notification pops up. It's a blog
comment from a screen name I don't recognize, so I don't
bother to read it. A few moments later, my phone buzzes again.
And then again. This is a lot of comments, even for a day when
I've posted something new.

So I pick up my phone and scroll through the notifications.
The alerts themselves don't tell me much because they cut off
after the first few words. But I can see that quite a few of the
comments are left by anonymous or new accounts. Could this
be a spambot attack? They've been more common recently, but
these commenters don't look like bots with number string tails.
And though I can see only the first few words of each comment,
it's enough to give me a bad feeling.

Only when I go to my computer and open up my blog do I
see the full extent of it splattered all over my dashboard. This

isn't a spambot attack. It's a troll attack, and each comment is more hostile than the next. There are people accusing me of all kinds of horrible things, from being clueless and uselessly performative to being a traitor to my race. Some of the insults are sexist. A few people tell me they hope I die.

At first, I'm in shock. Where are these people coming from? Should I delete them? Do I need to document the messages first? My phone keeps buzzing and I break out in a cold sweat. Finally I regain my wits and turn on moderation for all comments.

My hands shake, and I fist them in my lap. What is going on? Did something go viral?

I sign on to Twitter, where my notifications are even worse than on my blog. Scanning through them is like sticking my hand in sewage, but I need to get to the bottom of this. What in the world are these people yelling about? There's someone saying that bloggers like me are all image and no substance. Someone else questions my IQ.

Finally, I catch a side conversation in one of the replies. Someone's asking for an explanation, and another person responds with a link. I click through to a video by some guy named GrandRiceAzn, and what follows is horrifying. Image after image of my blog comes up, coupled with ridiculous animated GIFs. There's something about traditional tea culture vs. influencer tea culture, and the whole thing is just vicious. The fact that they took all these images from my blog for the sake of publicly skewering it . . . I feel violated. By the time the movie finishes, I'm shaking.

And then I notice the video's caption.

Hey all. Bobaboy and I were bored so we made this.

Bobaboy? This is far worse than anything he's ever done before.

My blog notifications have stopped since I turned on comment moderation, but my Twitter notifications keep piling up. I turn off notifications there too.

I open up a text to Adenike.

> There's something wrong with my blog.

The reply comes a few minutes later.

> What's going on?

> Look on Twitter.

There's a pause, and then the three typing dots appear on the screen.

> Oh wow. Bobaboy's more of a scumbag than I thought.

I can't disagree there.

> I've turned on moderation, but they keep on coming.

My imagination's going wild. I blog anonymously as Hibiscus, but can I stay anonymous if the internet's really after me? What if they dox me?

Another text comes from Adenike.

> This is bad. Have you told your parents about this?

> They're out on a date night. I'll tell them when they get back.

> You shouldn't be reading any of this. Give me your password and I'll block the trolls for you.

She's right. I feel a rush of gratitude for her, and that she's here for me even after I've been a less than ideal friend these past weeks. I send over my password.

> Thank you for existing. 🖤 Should we keep a record of these messages?

> I'll take screenshots. Go do something else. I'll take care of this.

Easier said than done, but I dutifully turn off my phone.

CHAPTER TWENTY-FIVE
DANNY

I'M A HORRIBLE PERSON.

There's really no way around it. I'm a scumbag. The lowest of the low. Pretentious magazines write investigative think pieces about people like me when they need an article about how the internet is destroying humanity.

Bryan took down his original post, which deleted all the comments in that particular thread. But by the time we came in with our feeble attempts at damage control, the video had already been copied to mirror sites and remade into half a dozen memes. I tried to tell people to cut it out, but that just egged them on. People started making more memes, this time featuring me too.

This is messing with my head, because I've always thought of myself as someone who despises trolls. In fact, the one time I was nice to Hibiscus on her blog was when this super-racist guy left comments on her posts a couple years ago. I was all righteous indignation back then, dropping mics and shaking my head about the state of the world, and now I'm personally responsible for sending hundreds more guys like him to *Babble Tea*.

All next morning at school, I'm obsessively refreshing Twitter. There's a #influencerteaculture hashtag now, with people posting their own versions of outrageous tea creations. The top search result is currently a photoshopped tea fountain with dolphins spewing Earl Grey over a plate of scones. The initial pile-on slows by midmorning but by no means stops. I see that Clementine's shut down the comments on her blog.

What I really want to know is how she's doing. But how can I check in on her if I'm not supposed to know about her blog? Finally, I send her a text.

> Hey, how's it going?

No response. I go back to Twitter and refresh it.

"You don't look good, man," says Bryan from the seat next to me in English class.

"No shit."

I told him the whole story this morning, and he feels horrible about everything as well.

"You heard from her yet?" Bryan asks.

My phone buzzes. It's Clementine. My palms break into a cold sweat.

> Hey, I'm so sorry. Something came up. I don't think I can drop by your place today. Can we take a rain check?

I'll admit, I'm kinda hurt that she doesn't want to tell me what's really going on. At least, I feel that way for a full half second before realizing what a douchebag thought that is.

Maybe I should just tell her everything. *Hey, you know Bobaboy888? That guy who's been terrorizing your blog for the past two years and who's now brought an entire troll army to your doorstep? That was actually me. MY BAD. So, how about that second date?*

I pick up my phone.

> No prob. Hope it works out.

There's a special circle of hell reserved for me.

I go back to the tea shop after school and make a few more futile efforts to put out the fire. But it's no use. The genie's out of the bottle. I've created a monster, and Clementine's going to have to live with it.

I rage-close my browser and bury my head in my hands. There's no easy way out of this. The dishwasher thrums in the background, judging me with its three-toned clanging. I'm just going to have to bite the bullet. Tell her everything, and if she hates me, she hates me.

I sit up and text Bryan.

> I'm gonna tell her I'm Bobaboy.

A few seconds later: *Good luck man.*

You can practically hear the funeral dirge playing.

Should I text her? Email her? No, I think I have to do this in person. I open up a message.

> Hey, how are you feeling? Still feeling stressed out?

I spend the next five minutes staring at my phone until the typing dots show up.

> I'm all right. A project I was working on kind of blew up in a bad way. Taking some time to recover.

I wonder why she doesn't just come out and tell me about *Babble Tea*. Is she that dedicated to being anonymous?

I type out and delete the next sentence several times before forcing myself to press the send button.

> Sorry to pile more stuff on you now, but do you think you could come over to the shop later? There's something that I wanted to talk about in person, but I don't think I can get away long enough today to go to your place.

> Well, that sounds ominous ☺

> Ha. It's kind of complicated.

More waiting.

Sure, I can come over. Maybe around six?

Yeah, that's good.

I look at the clock. I've got forty-five minutes before she shows up, maybe an hour. That's forty-five minutes to figure out how to confess everything. How do I even start?

Hey Clem, I was curious. How do you feel about trolls? Say, on a scale of one to ten?

Charming.

Maybe I could try a different approach. Fall on the ground, beg for forgiveness? Offer her a knife from the kitchen to symbolically behead me? Though, at this point, I wonder if she'd forget about the symbolic part.

Thing is, I really like her. And I think she likes me too, but I don't know if that's enough to get over all this. I mean, what's a few weeks of getting to know each other in real life compared to years of snark and generally hating each other's virtual guts? Then bring in Bryan's and my spectacular screwup on top of that . . .

The clock's moved fifteen minutes. I have thirty minutes left.

Where do we even have this conversation? Do we really want to hash this out in the kitchen or some corner of the customer area? Maybe we can take a walk around the mall so we don't have my parents walking in.

As if summoned by the thought, my parents walk in. I ignore

them until I realize that they've stopped a few feet away and that their eyes are shooting tractor beams at me. I glance up to confirm. Yep, definitely an ominous parental pose. Like the point in a zombie film where you look up to find that you're surrounded by decaying corpses, and they start clamoring for your brain.

"Danny," said Dad, "we wanted to talk to you." From his tone of voice, I can tell he wants to have a *talk*. At the most inconvenient time possible. Do difficult conversations attract each other or something?

I cringe. "Can we talk later? Clementine's about to come over."

Mom looks at Dad in that way she does when they're telepathically making decisions in front of me.

"We're taking the buyout," Dad says.

The words don't make sense. "The buyout?"

Dad touches the mole under his ear. "We're going to take Kale Corp's offer of money and move out."

I'm still thinking about Clementine—what I'm going to say to her, how she's going to react. So it takes a long time for Dad's words to take shape in my brain. And when they finally do . . . "You're closing the store?"

Dad and Mom exchange a glance again, and Dad sighs. "Maybe you heard already. Kale Corp owns the shopping mall now. They can evict us if they decide to. And right now they're offering us a lot of money to go voluntarily. If we fight this for months, they might not." He gives a matter-of-fact shrug.

"With the money Kale gives us, we can pay off some things we need to. We can take some time off and decide what to do next."

Mom's clutching Dad's arm, though I can't tell if she's supporting him or receiving support. "The business at the store hasn't been good," she says gently. Carefully, as if this is news that she expects to shock me. "This might be our chance to try something new."

You know, I've long wondered when Mom and Dad would finally acknowledge in front of me that the store wasn't doing well. I never thought it'd be in the same conversation where they told me the store was closing.

"But—" I'm stuttering. "But the other stores are counting on us."

"We talked to Mrs. Lau and Master Zhuang," says Dad. "They're both considering the same thing."

Mrs. Lau? Master Zhuang? The two of them had seemed the most sure of the bunch. I'm sliding down a cliff now, and I grasp for anything I can. "But what about our regulars? What would they do?"

"They understand," Mom says. "They know how hard we work."

She didn't really answer my question.

"There are other places for them to go," says Dad.

Maybe, but none of them are our shop. "It just . . . it just feels like we're taking the easy way out."

Mom's lips tighten at that, and Dad stiffens. I can almost

feel the air around us grow cold.

"Danny." Dad's voice cracks the air like a fissure through ice. "Just because a choice gives us more money doesn't mean it's the easier choice. Don't you ever confuse those two things."

"We poured our lives into this restaurant," says Mom. "Our customers have become our family. Don't you think we want it to go on?" She lets out a long, thin sigh. "Yes, we are tired. The money will give us a chance to rest. But do not think for a moment this is easy."

It's not her words that get me but what I hear under them. Mom's always been the strong one, the one who gets up in the morning and gets everything done, even when Dad couldn't seem to move. But now, the space behind her words feels shaky. Hollow. Like if I pushed too hard, something would break.

There's silence after that. I don't know what to say.

Dad clears his throat. "You're still young, and you've been raised in America. You think you can save the world, but that's not always true. Sometimes you have to bend with the circumstances."

Save the world? That's Clementine, not me. I've never thought of myself as a world saver. But over the past few weeks, I'd at least started to believe that maybe we could save this strip mall.

I think about my parents, coming over with so little money to a land that spoke a different language, pouring so much of themselves into a restaurant that slowly faded away. And I think about the aunties and the uncles who lived through poverty, war, and famine. Am I just a spoiled brat to them, crying about this shop?

Dad speaks again. "You can keep working with the Chinatown Cares organization if you want. You seem to enjoy it, and they do good things."

I don't answer, and they both walk away.

CHAPTER TWENTY-SIX

CLEMENTINE

THE TROLLS DON'T STOP. I FEEL BAD ABOUT TELL-ing my parents right after their date, but it just keeps piling up. So I bring it to my mom, who jumps into mama bear mode. She asks her journalist friends for advice, and she takes over the moderating of my blog.

"Send Adenike a huge hug from both of us," my mom says, looking over the logs my friend had put together. "She's done a great job, but you girls should not be dealing with this by yourselves."

It's draining. Even though I'm no longer seeing those attacks coming in, it's stressful just knowing that they're there.

I also feel bad blowing off Danny. It feels weird to be going through this massive disaster and not share anything about it, especially since the main reason I never told him about my blog is just because I wrote that review about his teahouse. All that worry about awkwardness pales in comparison to everything that's happened in the past twenty-four hours, but now I just don't have the energy to tell him.

Later that evening, Danny messages me and asks if I can come over. He wants to "talk." I admit it's kind of ominous. At this point in our relationship, could any "talk" be a good thing? Maybe he wants to tell me that he isn't ready for a girlfriend, or that he's dying of cancer, or something. The one silver lining is that I'm too exhausted from everything else to obsess over the possibilities.

The sky's already dark when I take the bus to Fragrant Leaves. Danny's mom waves to me from behind the counter.

"Clementine!" she says, carefully taking an empty pastry tray out of the display case. "Danny's in back."

I've been in Fragrant Leaves' kitchen several times now, but I still get nervous around all the equipment. While I'm sure this kitchen is simple by restaurant standards, I always feel like I'm a step away from getting pulled into a stand mixer.

Danny's at his corner desk. His computer's on, but he's just staring at the wall behind it. Something about his body language doesn't look right.

"Danny?"

He doesn't move. Suddenly, I feel cold.

"Danny?"

He turns and stares at me, clearly confused to see me here.

I glance at my phone. "Did I come at the wrong time?"

He finally snaps back into himself. "Oh, sorry, no. This is the right time. I just . . ." He shakes his head. "Sorry, I'm kind of in shock."

"In shock?" I take a step closer. "Is everything okay?"

He rubs his temples, squeezing his eyes closed like he's trying to get rid of a headache. "My parents just told me they're taking the buyout. They're closing the store."

I have a hard time making out his words because he's talking so softly. "Wait, did you say they're closing down Fragrant Leaves?"

He nods miserably, shoulders stooped.

"They're not going to fight anymore?" I ask.

He doesn't reply, but defeat is etched all through his posture. It's hard to process. After all this, the late nights and long days spent pounding the pavement. The schoolwork I cut corners on, the newspaper responsibilities I blew off in order to give these stores a chance . . . I always knew there was a possibility we might fail, but I never thought it could end like this, with Danny's parents closing the store less than a week after our rally.

"But they can't," I blurt out. "Not after all we've done."

Danny's expression goes from misery to something stonier. "They can't, because of all *we've* done?"

I kick myself. "I'm sorry. That's not what I meant. Of course it's not about what we've done. It's your parents' shop and your family's lives that you've poured into this. But we've come so far with the fight, and there's so much at stake here. The community stands to lose so much if Fragrant Leaves closes. If any of these stores close."

Danny sighs. "I told them that, but they're too tired, and they're worried Kale Corp will lower their buyout offer if they fight longer."

"I understand," I say. And I really do. I've been around long enough to know how much this restaurant takes out of Danny's parents. I've seen how busy they are, day to day, and how they're there from morning to close. But I also remember how well the rally went on Saturday—all the people who showed up in support, all the hope we felt. "It just seems we're so close," I say. "Our support is growing. More news media is catching on. It'd be such a pity to take the easy money now and give up. You can't always expect things to work out right away. These fights take effort."

At the words "easy money," Danny flinches. For a moment he looks confused, and then his expression hardens. His eyes get fiery, and not in a good way.

"You think this is the easy way out? That's rich, coming from you, living in your luxury apartment with your journalist parents. It's easy to say that when you're not the one pouring everything into keeping the restaurant running. My family's not here to go through crap just so you can feel like you're making a difference with your posters and activism."

I was starting to feel bad about what I'd said, but then he had to throw in that last zinger. The trolls commenting these past few days said similar things about Hibiscus, that she was more preoccupied with her image than actually helping the Chinatown community. When I saw those comments, I knew in my gut that they were false. I could prove it by pointing to my work with Chinatown Cares, tell myself that I really was making a difference. But now here's Danny, my partner through it all, the one person best situated to back me up on this . . . saying the exact same thing as those trolls.

"That's not fair." I hate how my voice quavers.

He glares at me. "Isn't it?"

My pulse speeds up as heat flushes through my chest. "Look, it hasn't been all rainbows and sunshine for my family either. It's not like journalism is a booming industry right now. My parents have dealt with their share of layoffs and closures, but they made changes to survive. They moved on from what the industry was like twenty years ago. They still have jobs because they've adapted with the times."

I regret my words the moment they come out of my mouth, but it's too late. Danny's mouth drops open, and he gapes at me.

"There you are, Hibiscus," he whispers.

What did he just say?

He's shaking his head, blinking like he just stepped out of a darkened movie theater. "You almost had me fooled. I thought I'd misjudged Hibiscus, because you seemed more in touch with reality than she ever was. But you're not, are you?" His voice hardens. "Life isn't as easy for the rest of us as it is for you, Clementine. Not all of us can put up a blog post with over-exposed pictures and come away thinking we've changed the world. Real life is different."

The sheer vitriol in his voice is bad enough. And then, there are his words, some of which don't make any sense at all. "Hibiscus. How'd you know I was Hibiscus?"

Danny snaps his mouth shut. Now he's the one who looks stunned.

"You said Hibiscus," I press on, my urgency growing. "Didn't you?"

"I didn't mean to say that," he says, almost to himself.

There's a rushing in my ears as I struggle to think straight. "Nobody knows I'm Hibiscus. No one but my parents and Adenike. Did she tell you?" Even as I ask, though, I know she wouldn't.

Danny tries a few times to form words. "I saw your log-in on your computer," he says.

But that makes no sense. I'd never leave that blog open in front of him. "You were snooping around on my computer?"

He puts up his hands. "I didn't mean to snoop."

"Then what happened, then?" My voice rises. "Did my laptop happen to fall open in front of you and load itself to that page?"

He doesn't answer. And in that long stretch of silence, other pieces fall into place. *Dreamy overexposed pictures. Out of touch.* I've read those insults many times on my blog, especially from one specific person.

"Are you Bobaboy?"

The look in his eyes tells me everything.

"Oh my God." There's a boulder on my chest. "That was you. You made the video."

Sheer panic crosses his face. "No, that wasn't me. I didn't make the video."

"You're not Bobaboy?"

"No." He shakes himself. "I mean, yes, I'm Bobaboy, but we

didn't mean to send all those trolls over. That's why I asked you to come here. I was going to tell you about what happened, and then my parents—"

I grab on to the center table for balance. "You made that video. And you posted it."

"Not on purpose. Clementine, I can explain. . . ."

I back away. Really, what I want to do is run, but the kitchen's starting to spin and I don't want to knock anything over. How in the world did I end up in a situation like this?

"Clementine, please."

I can't even look at him. Instead, I turn tail and flee, nearly colliding with Mrs. Mok as I barrel through the doorway toward the cash register.

"Clementine!" Danny's shouting now.

I mumble an apology to Mrs. Mok, then tear out of the restaurant as fast as I possibly can. The hard concrete of the sidewalk slams against my feet, and I almost run right past the bus stop. Mercifully, the bus arrives quickly. The ride itself is a blur, but I manage to pull the bell at the correct stop. When I return to our apartment, Mom and Dad are both in their office. I'm glad, because I'm in no state to talk with anyone right now.

Danny is Bobaboy.

Danny's the resident troll on my blog who's been there for who knows how many years. All those things he said, all those insults . . . And to upload a video like that the same day we had our first kiss? What kind of sick person does that?

I go straight to my room, toss my bag into the corner, and sink down in front of my laptop. The keystrokes to get to my blog are automatic—a few clicks and I'm on the dashboard. My eye goes first to the comment moderation queue. It's not nearly as long as before, but there're a few troll posts that haven't yet been dealt with. Another reminder of what Bobaboy put me through. I click past those to the posted comments and type "Bobaboy888" into the search bar. The cursor spins, and then on my screen I have the entire record of everything Bobaboy's ever said to me.

Over the next hours, I read through each comment—every snarky barb, every insult he's ever hurled my way. Each one feels like a shard of glass. But there were some fun moments too, weren't there? A few joking exchanges here and there where the snark took a back burner. Was I wrong to take them as signs that he wasn't so bad after all? To use them as reasons not to block him?

After I wade through it all, I close the window and go to Linktropolis. The original video posted by GrandRiceAzn is down, but it's not hard to find a copy. I watch it again. Every single snarky GIF, every sarcastic caption.

Danny made this. He thought it was funny.

I don't know how I could have been so wrong about a fellow human being.

CHAPTER TWENTY-SEVEN

DANNY

THAT WAS NOT HOW IT WAS SUPPOSED TO GO.

I stare at the empty doorway through which Clementine just disappeared. In the dining room, the bell rings as the front door opens and shuts.

This was not how I'd planned to tell her.

Mom comes into the kitchen, weighing a dishrag in her hand, brow wrinkled. "Everything okay?"

"It's fine, Mom."

She casts a doubtful glance toward the door and then back at me, but she leaves me alone. I'm not sure if it's because I actually pulled off looking okay or because I look like hell warmed over, but she does.

I'd had it all planned. I was going to lay it out and be perfectly transparent, beg Clementine's forgiveness. I definitely wasn't going to blurt out in the middle of a fight that her blog alter ego was everything that I hated about humanity.

But she'd said those things about my parents, about how

they needed to change with the times, insinuating that our business was going downhill because Mom and Dad weren't being smart enough about it. All the privileged, clueless rhetoric that I hated on Hibiscus's blog had come out of Clementine's mouth, in Clementine's voice, with Clementine's words. Maybe I wasn't wrong about her after all.

Do I even want her forgiveness anymore?

My phone buzzes. It's from Bryan.

How'd it go?

My first reaction is to toss my phone in the trash, but I don't think I could afford a new one. Finally, I unlock the screen, download a picture of a dumpster on fire, and send it over.

That bad, huh?

The landline in the office rings. It's one of those old-school phones, with a ringer that sounds like a fire station bell. Dad answers it. His voice goes loud, then soft. Mom runs over.

My cell phone keeps buzzing.

What happened?

Want to talk about it?

No, I don't. A few more texts come through, but I ignore

them. Yesterday I had a girlfriend, a cause I believed in, and a family tea shop.

And now?

Mom's tearing around the kitchen and the office. I make myself smaller, hoping she doesn't try to talk to me again.

Her footsteps came closer.

"Danny?"

I scowl.

"Danny Mok." Her voice is sharp. "Are you listening to me?"

It's not a good idea to ignore Mom when she uses that voice. I turn toward her, not bothering to wipe my mood from my face. But it's her expression that scares me. Mom doesn't look angry. Mom looks crestfallen.

"Danny," she says. Her voice shakes. "I need you and Dad to watch the store. I have to go to the hospital."

The word takes a moment to register. "Hospital?"

She nods, and she grips her purse as if it might keep her from flying away. "Auntie Lin just had a heart attack."

CHAPTER TWENTY-EIGHT
CLEMENTINE

I'M A SHELL OF A PERSON OVER THE NEXT DAYS.
The troll attack was bad enough, and adding the news of Danny on top of it . . . I'm barely able to function.

Mom spoils me with hot chocolate in bed. She thinks I'm still down from the blog disaster and keeps asking if I want to talk.

"I'm all right, Mom. I just need some time to recover."

I take a step back from Chinatown Cares, telling them I'm busy with newspaper stuff. I also take it easy with the newspaper, telling them I'm busy with Chinatown Cares. I do fill Adenike in on everything that's happened, and she offers to hire a hit man on my behalf. I tell her I'll think about it.

A few days after the big fight, I get a text from a number I don't recognize.

> Hey Clementine, this is Bryan. I got your number from Wei on the newspaper staff. Sorry for texting out of the blue. Can I talk to you sometime?

I leave that message on my phone for half a day. I'm tempted not to reply at all, but my curiosity gets the best of me.

> Did Danny send you?

> No way. Danny would kill me if he knew I was doing this.

I ignore him, and he texts back a few moments later.

> I know this is probably the last thing that you want, but I really think we should talk. I'm not going to play matchmaker or anything. I just think there's some stuff you should know.

I show the text to Adenike over copy edits. "What do you think?"

"Ugh." She fiddles with her pen. "You could go either way. Bryan seemed like a decent guy the few times I met him. Kinda weird, but decent. But then, so did Danny."

"Ugh, indeed."

There's a big part of me that wants to cut off anything remotely related to Danny and never think about him again. But then there's that niggling curiosity again. I never could let an unanswered question go.

"Well, I don't see how things can possibly get any worse." I toss the comment out carefully, like a fisherman casting a line.

"Famous last words," says Adenike.

I open up my phone.

> Okay, how about the boba place down the street after school tomorrow?

> See you there. Thanks.

I get there early the next day. I'm sitting at a table, waiting for my drink, when Bryan comes rushing in, his perfect hair tilted more to one side than usual. He's looking left and right, and he's kind of at a loss. I know I should wave him toward me, but I can't quite gather up the goodwill. So I just wait until he sees me.

"Are you going to get an order?" I ask as he sheepishly comes to sit at my table.

"Nah. Cuz if you hate me and decide to run me out of here, I'd have to abandon my half-finished cup of tea." He tilts his head, and then he adds under his breath, "I guess I could get my order to go." But he doesn't move.

Finally, he shakes out of his thoughts and leans over the table. He seriously looks like he's about to face a firing squad. I'd almost feel bad for him, except for the fact that I don't at all.

"For starters," he says, "I'm really sorry for what happened. Posting it online was completely on me."

I tilt my head. "Posting what?"

"The video," he says, as if it's the most obvious thing.

"Why is it 'on you'?"

As Bryan screws up his face in confusion, the rest comes together for me. Bryan is GrandRiceAzn, the guy who actually posted that disastrous video. I don't know why I didn't catch on to that earlier.

"But GrandRiceAzn said he made the video with Bobaboy," I say.

"Yeah, I made it with Bobaboy." He shrugs. "We were just messing around."

My hackles rise, and he puts up both hands. "I don't mean that as an excuse. Because now it's clear to all of us that this was much more than just a harmless joke." He shakes his head. "Man, those comments on your blog were wrong in so many ways. Nobody should have to be on the receiving end of that." He looks at me, his expression surprisingly earnest. "You should know, though, that I don't think Danny was planning to post the video. It was just this thing we were passing back and forth because we didn't want to do real work. Danny went to the rally the next day, and I thought, 'Hey, this is pretty good editing, why not just upload it?'"

He wipes his palms on his jeans. "When Danny found out the video went viral, he freaked out and made me take it down right away. He spent all night trying to get people to take down their copies too. Danny was a total zombie the next day because he only got, like, an hour of sleep."

I press my lips together. "I didn't sleep that night either."

Bryan gives me a painfully apologetic smile. "Well, yeah, I

guess you wouldn't have."

Bryan's trying so hard to be smooth, and I'm not buying it. "Even if Danny didn't post the video, he still made it, didn't he? Am I supposed to feel better because he only wanted to say nasty things about me in private?"

He absentmindedly pats his hair spikes with his palm. "You're right. We were jackasses. Whether or not we did it in public or private doesn't change things. I guess it was easier when we didn't think of Hibiscus as a real person. She was just this blog personality we made fun of."

"Wait." I put up a hand. "Danny didn't know I was Hibiscus?"

He shrugs. "He didn't when we made the video. Somehow between that time and the time I posted it, he found out. You didn't tell him?"

"No."

I think back to the day after the rally. There was a moment when I came out of the bathroom, and Danny seemed jumpy. He'd pushed my computer away as if he didn't want anything to do with it. Or didn't want to be caught with it. . . .

The barista calls out a name for pickup. She gives Bryan a suspicious glance.

Bryan cringes under her gaze. "But yeah, I'm definitely not saying we were saints or anything. I just didn't want to leave you thinking that Danny orchestrated it all, like Dr. Evil or something. He felt terrible about everything. I think he would've felt terrible even if it had happened to some girl who wasn't you. And he was going to confess it all. That was why he called you to come over Tuesday night, but I guess it didn't really go as planned?"

This stops me. The revelations just keep coming. "That was why he wanted to talk to me? I thought he wanted to tell me that his parents were closing the restaurant."

Bryan frowns, taking out his phone and scrolling through his chat history. "See here? This was right before you went over to his place, right?" He hands me the phone.

I'm gonna tell her I'm Bobaboy.

Good luck man.

The next texts are from a few hours later, when Bryan asked how it went and Danny sent a picture of a dumpster fire.

It's weird to be looking at this conversation, a window into my life from another angle. But Bryan's right. It does look like Danny invited me over so he could confess to his role in the troll attack. But then, how did everything go south?

Bryan clears his throat. "Anyways, if you still decide you hate him, I totally understand. I mean, he gets on my nerves sometimes too, and I'm sure he'd say the feeling's mutual. . . ." He drifts off as he realizes he's rambling. "I just wanted to make sure you knew everything."

I wordlessly hand over his phone. Bryan flips it around and puts it in his pocket.

"So, uh, I guess I'll catch you later?"

He lets himself out when I don't answer.

I sit at that table for a long time afterward. The condensation gathers on my boba cup as I try to gather my thoughts. Was this really all some epic misunderstanding? But no, it's not that simple. No matter what happened with the fight, and whether or not he knew I was Hibiscus, Danny's still Bobaboy, and we've still been fighting online for years. And he still made the video. What difference does it make that he didn't post it?

I pull out my phone and text Adenike.

> Can I come over?

> Sure. Everything go okay with Bryan?

> There's been some new developments.

> I'm all ears.

Adenike lives in a high-rise not too far from my building. Her parents are surgeons at the medical center a block away, so it's an easy commute for them. The doorman knows me on sight and waves me in.

When I get off the elevator on Adenike's floor, she's already waiting barefoot in the hallway. She looks me up and down as if she's checking for missing limbs.

"So . . . on a scale of one to ten, how much of a jerk was Bryan?"

"I can't do math right now," I say.

"Want some comfort food?"

"Yes, please."

She steers me through the door into her dining room and sits me at the table. Peppa Pig's voice drifts over from their living room, where Adenike's younger sister and brother lie sprawled in front of the TV. Nike puts a bowl in front of me that's filled with what I can only describe as fried rice, but more tomatoey. It's steaming hot and definitely fits the comfort food bill.

"This is good. Did you make this?"

Adenike smiles. "My grandmother took it on herself to make a decent cook of me this summer. She didn't succeed, but at least I've got jollof rice down. Just don't tell her I made it vegan."

Adenike's told me plenty of stories from her Nigeria trip this summer—going to museums and clubs with other IJGBs (I Just Got Backs) from overseas, hanging out with aunties who sounded remarkably like the ones at Fragrant Leaves, throwing money at her cousin's wedding, and lugging a suitcase full of dried fish and Indomie noodles through customs.

Mrs. Olowe passes through the kitchen. She's always either impeccably dressed or in her scrubs, and this time it's the latter.

"Hi, Mrs. Olowe."

"Hello, Clementine. Eat up. You're too skinny!"

"Oh, I will. It's delicious."

We wish her a good shift at the hospital. After she leaves, I fill Adenike in on the whole story.

She tents her fingers. "So we're trying to figure out where

Danny stands on the asshat scale, given this new information?"

"Yeah, I guess you could say that. I mean, he didn't post the video, but he still made it."

"True." Adenike taps glossy purple fingernails on the dining table. "Though I give him props for deciding to confess everything so soon."

I scoop up the last of the rice. "But does that make up for everything he's said as Bobaboy over the years? I mean, does not knowing that Hibiscus was me make it any better?"

"That's true. He's said some pretty nasty things."

Danny's words echo in my head. *My family's not here to go through crap just so you can feel like you're making a difference with your posters and activism.* Could Danny be right? Am I so in love with the idea of helping people that I've put my own satisfaction ahead of the actual individuals I'm trying to help?

An annoying part of my mind is also bringing up some comments I made to Danny during our fight, things I said about his parents. I don't feel good about them.

I suck in a deep breath. "The last time I talked to Danny, I said some things I probably shouldn't have. About his parents."

Adenike nods. I'm kinda relieved she doesn't ask for specifics. Though she hasn't expressed a strong opinion either way, I'm finding it helpful just to talk things through with her. My mind's starting to organize itself.

"I think I need to speak with Danny again," I say, "if only to sort out exactly what happened with the blog and the video and all that. I want to hear his version of the story." Maybe it's my reporter instincts. Secondhand information just doesn't seem as good. Plus, a corner of my conscience is nagging at me. Regardless of whether Danny was in the wrong, I should have been more careful about bringing his parents into our argument.

I stay a little longer at Adenike's, filling up on jollof rice and talking about random things. She's been looking at journalism programs to apply to, though she hasn't spoken to her parents about it.

"They're under the impression that I want to be premed," she says, twisting her mouth to one side.

"You're going to have to talk to them eventually," I say. "They're proud of the awards you've won with your articles, right?"

She gives a noncommittal shrug. "Yeah, they think it's a great hobby."

By the time I leave that evening, it's too late to think about tracking Danny down, but I promise myself that I'll go to Fragrant Leaves tomorrow.

I make it through the next school day without any major disasters. I don't see Danny, which I'm grateful for, since I don't really want to have this conversation at school. I do head to Fragrant Leaves right after our newspaper meeting, because I know I'd lose my nerve about talking to him if I went home.

I'm a little worried about seeing Danny's parents, since I don't know what they might have heard from our fight. But Mrs. Mok's face lights up with the same friendly smile when she sees me. "Clementine! Looking for Danny?"

I go up to the counter. "Hi, Mrs. Mok. Yes, is Danny here?"

"Ah, he's not here today." Mrs. Mok puts a receipt onto a spike next to the cash register. "He went to pay his respects to a family friend."

Pay his respects? "Is everything okay?"

Mrs. Mok sighs. "A longtime customer passed away. She was a good friend. Danny called her Auntie Lin."

I freeze at the name. "The same Auntie Lin who's here playing mahjong all the time?" But she had seemed so healthy the last time I saw her.

Mrs. Mok straightens a napkin holder on the counter. "Heart attack," she says, her voice somber. "Very sad. You know her? The family will have a memorial service this Saturday at ten, at the funeral home down the street."

"I only met her a few times, but she was wonderful. I'm very sorry for your loss." I pause. Suddenly the drama between me and Danny feels much less significant. "I guess I'll see if I can catch Danny later."

"You want me to tell him you came?" Mrs. Mok calls after me.

"No, that's okay. I'm sure he has plenty to worry about right now."

The news about Auntie Lin puts some things into perspective. Yes, the past week was horrible. And yes, I'm upset that the Moks are closing their store, and I'm unmoored by everything that's happened with Danny. But at least I'm still alive.

I don't mean that in a glib way. Being alive means there's hope for making things better.

I decide to wait before getting in touch with Danny again. He's lost someone close to his family. He needs time to grieve.

Over the next days, I think a lot about Auntie Lin. It's remarkable how much of an impression she left on me in just those few times I was there. I think about her loud voice, her infectious personality, the no-nonsense way she had of talking about things. She had no filter, which made for some awkward moments, but because of that you really couldn't doubt her heart.

After a few days, I start thinking that I want to go to her memorial service. By all accounts, she was an incredible woman, and I want to know more about her. I go back and forth about whether I should go. Danny will be there, and I don't want him to think that I'm stalking him. Plus Auntie Lin must have many close friends and family. I don't want to intrude.

But the thought doesn't leave me. So on Saturday morning, I find myself putting on dark slacks and a blouse and taking the bus to the funeral home. I wait until just after the starting time to enter, so that the people who knew her better have a chance to get seats. It's probably a good thing I did, because it's standing room only by the time I come through the door.

I find an unobtrusive place to stand by the back. There's a picture of Auntie Lin up front, surrounded by flowers. Soon, a man comes to the podium and starts talking. He's Auntie Lin's son, and he gives a moving tribute about her as a mother. It doesn't take me long to realize that this is a trilingual funeral. The son speaks in English, and someone stands next to him, translating his words phrase by phrase into Cantonese. In the audience, I catch a few attendees whispering Mandarin translations to their companions.

After the son finishes, Auntie Esther from the tea shop talks about her long friendship with Auntie Lin. In her soft, cultured voice, she recounts Auntie Lin's decision to start a flower shop back in the day and how she prevailed despite discrimination. Someone from Auntie Lin's apartment complex follows with stories of the dinners she cooked and hosted for her neighbors. A friend from the park speaks of the way Auntie Lin was a second grandmother to all the kids at the playground.

The stories keep coming, painting a picture of this incredibly full, interconnected life. I have an urge to take out my notebook, and for a while I resist. But I can't help it. Soon, I'm madly scribbling notes. I'm not sure why. I just have this sense that something beautiful's in the air, and I have to preserve it as best I can. Thankfully, nobody around me seems to mind or even notice.

The service ends with a slideshow, and then people line up to pay their respects to the family. I catch a glimpse of Danny in line with his parents right before I slip out the door.

Snippets of the memorial service stay with me the entire bus ride home. Like all memorial services, it was tinged with sadness, but I was also struck by the outpouring of love. I don't know if I've ever seen such clear evidence of people who've cared for and supported each other over decades. Auntie Lin's funeral illuminated a living and thriving community in every sense of the word.

My fingers are twitching by the time I get home. As soon as I get in the door, I make a beeline for my computer and start typing.

I just came back from a memorial service celebrating an amazing woman. She was not someone I knew very well, but even in the few hours I spent with her, I got a sense of her energy and love for everyone. I would like to share with you now about the life of Auntie Lin.

It's one of those times when the words just come pouring out. I type the essay in one long sprint—no snack breaks, no distractions. I hardly notice the time passing by. When I finish, I'm completely drained, but in a nice way. It's that feeling you get when everything inside you has been emptied onto the page, and you know that it's good.

I stare at my screen. I wrote this piece like a woman possessed, but now that it's finished, I'm not sure what to do with it. I want people to see what I experienced, to know this version of Auntie Lin, but I also want to respect the wishes of her family.

I grab my purse and pull out the program from the funeral. The names of her relatives are listed there, as well as contact information for flowers, cards, and tributes. I take a deep breath and compose an email.

Dear Mr. Lin,

My name is Clementine. I'm a high school student who met your mother a few times during her morning mahjong games at Fragrant Leaves tea shop. I attended her memorial service and was incredibly touched by the stories I heard. It inspired me to write this tribute to her, and I thought you might like to have it as a keepsake. Please do not feel obligated to read it if this is not the right time.

Sincerely,

Clementine Chan

CHAPTER TWENTY-NINE

DANNY

THE TEA SHOP IS QUIETER WITHOUT AUNTIE LIN. The mahjong games still happen, with the regulars pulling an assortment of new people to play. We serve tea.

Life goes on, but in the back of my head, I know this won't last much longer either. Because the tea shop will soon be gone.

It's hard figuring out what to do with my time these days. I haven't seen Clementine since the big fight. Part of me wishes I could have that conversation again, the way I'd planned this time, but Clementine's made it pretty clear that she doesn't want to have anything to do with me. And even if she did, would I want to talk to her? The whole Hibiscus thing has really messed with my mind.

Since Clementine was my liaison to Chinatown Cares, I'm in limbo with them too. I suppose I could call them up directly, but again, it'd be too much weirdness. Way too many questions I don't want to answer. As for my other time-wasting activities, I've lost my taste for many of them too. Even thinking about

Linktropolis makes me queasy, and it's not like I want to get into any more fights on *Babble Tea*.

Maybe it's a good thing, because college applications are just around the corner, and I'd been diligently ignoring them up until now. One afternoon, I finally sit down and make a list of local colleges—the UCs and Cal States close by, the private colleges . . . And then it hits me. I don't have to stay around here anymore. There will no longer be a tea shop that needs my help.

The thought sets my heart pounding.

I remember watching this PBS documentary on something called learned helplessness. These scientists kept a dog in a cage and shocked it all the time without giving it a chance to escape. (I mean, who does that?) After a while, the scientists changed the cage so the dog could jump out, but the dog had given up by then. It just sat there and continued to get shocked.

My cage is opening, and I don't know where to go. Even the act of clicking over to NYU's application feels like diving off a cliff. But I do it. I create an account and start filling out the application.

Once or twice, I wonder what Clementine might think.

CHAPTER THIRTY

CLEMENTINE

A FEW DAYS LATER, I GET AN EMAIL.

Dear Clementine,

Thank you for writing such a beautiful tribute to my mother. Are you going to publish this somewhere? We would like to share this with our family and friends.

Jonah Lin

I'm surprised to hear from him. I guess I'd assumed that he would be too preoccupied with family matters to get back to some random high schooler. It feels good to know that the profile struck a chord with him, though I'm not sure how to respond to his question about publishing it. In the past, I would have loved to post the article on *Babble Tea*, but after the troll fiasco, I'm not sure if that'd be a good idea.

Dear Mr. Lin,

Thank you so much. I'm glad that you liked the article.
I do write a blog about tea and local Chinatown issues,
and I'd usually post something like this on there, but the
blog has been the target of troll attacks lately. I would
hate to put something up about your mother and have
it treated disrespectfully. You are welcome to post it
on your own social media or forward it directly to your
friends and family.

Clementine

His reply comes a few hours later.

Dear Clementine,

You are a wonderful writer, and this is a wonderful
article. If people on the internet decide to disrespect it,
it is a reflection on them, and not on you or my mother.
I would be honored if you would publish it on your blog.

Jonah

A spark of excitement hits me as I read his response. I was
prepared to let this profile sit on my hard drive, but the truth
is, I do want people to see it, and I'm glad that Auntie Lin's son
feels the same way. So I double-check that the comments are
moderated, and I turn on phone notifications so I'll know when
something comes in.

And then I post. In the minutes that follow, I have plenty of time to second-guess myself. Then the responses start rolling in.

This is beautiful. She sounds like a wonderful woman.

Such a great tribute.

I love this. I feel like this is Chinatown, if you know what I mean. Like, we talk about community and culture. This is it, right here.

That last comment gets me thinking, because it puts into words what I've been feeling for the past days. In a way, this post about Auntie Lin is similar to what I've been trying to accomplish with my blog all along. Yes, *Babble Tea* is a tea blog, but it's also my love letter to Chinatown. The community that's sprung up around my tea reviews is in some ways a miniature version of the Chinatown community, albeit an imperfect one, as Bobaboy loved to point out. While my profile on Auntie Lin isn't about tea, it celebrates Chinatown in the same way.

I think back to the Chinatown spread in our paper, the one that seemed so great while I was planning it but now reads so obviously shallow and superficial in comparison. I don't get a chance to redo that one, but perhaps I can try again here.

CHAPTER THIRTY-ONE

DANNY

I'VE BEEN MUCH BETTER ABOUT WORKING ON MY
college applications these days. Still, I'm not a complete saint. I
still waste time on TikTok once in a while, and there are plenty
of internet rabbit holes to fall down even if you never log on to
Linktropolis. As I find myself knee-deep in short-answer questions about items I'd take to a desert island (a brick of Pu'er and
a Wi-Fi router, obviously), the Web's siren call gets stronger.

One day, I log on to TikTok to find all the Asian influencers
freaking out over this one blog post. It's weird, 'cause who reads
blogs these days? But everybody's just going on and on about
how touching and inspiring it is. Right before I click on the
link, I glimpse the actual URL. It's a *Babble Tea* link.

Cue blog PTSD. Clementine's gone viral again? At least it
doesn't seem like it's in a bad way this time.

I try to resist going there. I really do. It's too much of a land
mine. But people just keep talking about it. Video after video,
commentary after commentary.

Finally I take the bait.

Clicking through to Clementine's blog feels like voluntarily stepping into a live volcano. I brace myself as the familiar header loads, waiting for the lava to come spewing out. The new post pops up. "A Memorial Service, a Life, a Community." Huh. Funerals aren't exactly *Babble Tea*'s usual . . . well, cup of tea.

I just attended a memorial service celebrating an amazing woman.

It doesn't take me long to realize that this is about Auntie Lin. I'm shocked at first, but I keep reading. The post is good. Really good. It's Clementine at her best, the blog equivalent of how she was when she spoke at the rally—powerful and poignant, beautiful and self-assured. I didn't even know she was at the funeral.

The comments on the post have already blown up. People who knew Auntie Lin are responding with their own memories of her, and those who didn't are sharing about how Clementine's article resonates with their own Chinatown experiences. People are engaging in a way I haven't seen in a long time. It's refreshing, after the toxicity of the past weeks, to see something so uplifting.

I read for a while, and then I close my browser. The article and the responses to it are a lot to take in after all that's happened. Talk about emotional whiplash. I'm glad to see all the positive stuff on that page, but I don't completely trust it.

Footsteps sound behind me. I turn around to see my dad walking through the kitchen to the back door.

He catches me looking and absentmindedly scratches his ear. "Not too many customers right now. I'm going for a walk."

Then he leaves, as if nothing is out of the ordinary. As if it's perfectly normal for a slow afternoon to send him on a relaxing stroll instead of deeper into his spreadsheet cave. I peek into the office. His computer isn't even on.

I put my phone away and go up front to wipe the tables. Some customers I don't recognize are scattered around the dining room. Uncle Tony's pacing the space between two rows of tables, tapping pressure points on his forehead.

He pauses when he catches sight of me. "Danny! You're graduating this year, right? Where are you going for college?"

"Hi, Uncle Tony. I'm applying to some places around here, and also in New York City."

He nods approvingly. "What do you want to study?"

"I'm not sure. Maybe physics." But the answer feels glib. I think of the past days. "I might want to work with Asian communities after I graduate. Maybe with Chinatown citizens or something." I simply fished those words out of thin air, but now that I've said them, I kind of like the idea. It's even something I could do in New York, if I could hook up with a Chinatown organization over there.

Uncle Tony's face lights up. "Oh, that's good, Danny. Yes, get back to your roots. Make changes in Chinatown, and then go larger." He raises a finger. "You can be the first Chinese

American president. Much better than being a doctor."

I grin. "Thanks, Uncle."

Mom comes out and plops into a chair, taking advantage of a quiet moment to rest her feet. I walk behind the counter and throw my rag into the dirty bucket. After seeing my dad go outside, I kinda want to take a stroll too.

"I'll be right back," I tell Mom. "Just going to walk around a bit."

It's a sunny day, not too hot, not too cold. The parking lot is about half-full. I pass by the gift shop and the Chinese medicine store. Master Zhuang is at the door of the kung fu studio, seeing off some students after class.

"Danny!" he booms. "I just saw your father walk by."

"It's a nice day for walking," I say. "How are you?"

He shrugs good-naturedly. "The sun's out. Had a good class. Can't complain."

I don't hear much of the gossip between the store owners, but I know that they've all discussed their choices with each other. Master Zhuang wasn't one of the first to want to stop fighting, but he wasn't one of the last holdouts either.

"Have you found another place to rent yet?" I ask.

"Not yet, but a friend told me about some places that might be good. I'm going to talk with the landlords there. Wish me luck?" He raises his hand for a high five, and I oblige.

I end up in front of the grocery store, which makes me think about octopuses. If I want to see them again, I guess I'd better do it while I have the chance. My feet know the way: past the bags of rice in front, through the cash registers, down aisle twelve so I can check out the Asian snacks, then hang a right at the back wall to get to the seafood section.

A big tank up top has tilapia swimming in circles. Another has crabs piled on top of each other, looking like they're playing some fight-to-the-death version of King of the Hill. In front of the tanks are basins full of clams and a green mesh bag of live frogs. No octopus. After one last look around, I double back to aisle twelve to pick up some shrimp chips on my way out. I find Mrs. Lau in front of aisle five, next to a blue plastic barrel filled with salted duck eggs.

"Danny!" She offers me a cube of yolk the size of my pinkie nail. "Want some salted duck egg? This batch is good."

"Thank you." I pop it in my mouth and let the saltiness melt on my tongue.

Mrs. Lau hands me a plastic cup full of rice porridge, plus a spoon. "You have to eat it with congee. Otherwise too salty."

"Thank you, Mrs. Lau." I take it by the edges so I don't burn my fingers. "How have you been?"

She sighs, indicating the store. "Busy. Packing up, lots to take care of. Making sure all my employees have somewhere to go."

"How are Henry and Mary?" I ask about her son and daughter-in-law.

She shrugs. "They'll start looking for jobs after we get everything closed down. We will see." She sounds very pragmatic about it all, but I catch a shadow in her eye.

"And what about you?"

"Me?" She seems surprised at the question. "I spend more time with my grandchildren. My son might need me to watch them if they get a new job. If you have your own store, your kids can run around all day. As long as they don't knock over too many things, it's okay. But if you're working at someone else's store, then you need a babysitter."

"You're a good grandmother," I say.

"Ah, well, family is everything, isn't it? When you grow old, that is what you realize."

She takes a spoonful of pork sung and dumps it on my congee. "Try this. Very fresh." Then she steps back and looks around the store. She sighs, and her shoulders fall. "We have many good memories from this store. Many memories."

CHAPTER THIRTY-TWO

CLEMENTINE

THE BUZZ AROUND AUNTIE LIN'S PROFILE CONTIN-
ues for days before it dies down. And it gets me wondering. If
I were to write more posts like the one I wrote about Auntie
Lin, what would they be like? Would I write profiles of other
Chinatown citizens? Maybe I don't have to wait for someone to
die before mapping out the ripple effects of their lives.

The next afternoon, I visit my favorite old-school café, the
one where Racist Adam's Apple Guy hit on me weeks ago.
Auntie Chen greets me like a long-lost daughter, and I guess
it has been a while since I've come here. She's a bit confused
at first when I ask whether I can write an article about her. It
takes a bit of explaining and clarifying, especially since I'm trying to communicate in English. But as she starts to understand
what I'm proposing, I can tell the idea intrigues her. Her eyes
brighten, and she even suggests bringing in her sister to help
with any translation snags.

A few afternoons later, we all sit down together, and Auntie

Chen tells me her life story. I'm a little worried at first that the article might end up too similar to my post about Auntie Lin, but this auntie's story is vastly different. She talks about living through the Cultural Revolution in China before moving here. Like Auntie Lin, Auntie Chen faced discrimination and challenges when starting her business, but despite all that, she's successfully kept her restaurant open for decades. Auntie Chen tells of how she never married and how because of that, she's incredibly close to her two sisters. She regales me with tale after tale of the three helping each other through different seasons of life.

I end up interviewing all three sisters, plus some of their friends. Just like at Auntie Lin's funeral, these different points of view come together to form a complete picture. When I finish writing, I visit the tea shop again and take some photos of Auntie Chen with my phone, and then I beg our paper's photo editor for tips on editing them.

When this article goes up on my blog, the comments roll in again, just as warm and enthusiastic as the first time. People start emailing with suggestions of other people to profile, and I file them away. The thought of doing more interviews makes me nervous, because each interview would make Hibiscus less anonymous. But on the other hand, there's a lot of good that can be done here.

CHAPTER THIRTY-THREE
DANNY

A WEEK LATER, CLEMENTINE POSTS ANOTHER PRO-
file. This one's well done too, and the internet seems to agree.
The week after, there's another one. I start getting into the habit
of checking every Thursday.

I keep waiting for the other shoe to drop, for a fight to break
out in the comments and for everyone to split into factions and
eat each other alive. But it doesn't happen. I also expect the
overall enthusiasm to die down, but the reaction to this series
continues to grow.

I feel kind of conflicted about it. Don't get me wrong—I'm
glad to see this happening. But part of me wonders where all
this love for Chinatown was when we were taking petitions
door-to-door or when we were inviting people to our rally. I'm a
little bitter, to be honest, but when I finally get over myself, an
idea forms at the back of my mind.

I push the idea away at first, because doing anything about it
would require talking to Clementine, and we're not exactly on

speaking terms right now. But after a while, I realize that this is bigger than the two of us.

How do I get in touch with her, though? I haven't spoken to her in weeks, and texting her feels too intrusive at this point. After going back and forth on it, I finally open up the comment form on her website and type out a message there. Is that better than texting, or does it just make me seem more stalkery? Eventually, I get tired of second-guessing myself and hit submit. A blue line of text comes up.

Thank you for getting in touch. Your form has been submitted.

I stare at my computer until my vision blurs.

CHAPTER THIRTY-FOUR

CLEMENTINE

THE NEW PROFILES ARE A LOT OF WORK, BUT I find them rewarding. I've never had this much genuine engagement. I do worry about the trolls coming back, and we do get a few snarky or nasty comments, but the community's quick to shut them down, and I moderate as necessary. The overall tone stays positive.

Blog fame plays games with your mind. I spent years building up *Babble Tea*, and though we had a nice community, nothing had nearly as much impact as this random post I wrote on a whim. On the one hand, it's great that people are celebrating Chinatown. At the same time, I'm keenly aware that we recently failed in a big way to help the real-life corner of Chinatown we'd tried so hard to save.

As the days pass, Kale Corp's plans move along quickly. I keep tabs on them through the news. There's even an article that mentions local protesters staging a rally. It's strange to see all our work boiled down to one paragraph in a news article.

One evening, the local news station does a feature on the restaurant that's taking over Danny's tea shop. Apparently, Kale's starting up a chain of ethnic fusion restaurants, and they interview the head chef, an up-and-coming young Chinese American woman who's really into modernizing Asian cuisine. She's wearing a chic black suit for her interview and her hair is pulled back in a sleek bun. Everything about her radiates competence.

"I have great respect for tradition," she says, "but I also want to modernize. We live in a multicultural world, and I think we should take advantage of it. I love combining what I've learned from other cultures with what I've inherited from my own Chinese heritage."

The chef's words sound disorientingly similar to things I've said in my fusion tea series. What's more, she sounds like she genuinely believes what she says. It's much harder to hate her when she's no longer a faceless entity under the Kale banner. Still, it doesn't change the fact that Danny's family's teahouse has been there for years, as steeped in Chinese culture as you can get. And soon it won't be there anymore.

I'm somber as I turn off the TV. Reflexively, I bring out my phone, scrolling through my email on my way back to my room. A form submission from my blog catches my eye.

It's from Bobaboy888.

I freeze in the middle of the hallway as my fight-or-flight instinct revs up. One thing hasn't changed after all this: Danny's screen name still sets my heart pounding. But why would he send a message through my blog?

After a few moments' hesitation, I click.

Hi Clementine,

I hope it's not too weird for me to message you. You did
a great job on your recent posts. They're really touching
and spot-on. I was just thinking the other day—a lot of
people on your blog seem to care about Chinatown.
Maybe you can tell them about some of the current
Chinatown Cares initiatives. Did Silas or Rui ever tell you
about the community land trust? Might be worth asking
about if they haven't.

Danny

The message leaves me bewildered and, to be honest, a little
hurt. There's no mention of anything that's happened between
the two of us at all. We might as well have been casual acquain-
tances. Then I see an addendum at the bottom.

P.S. I decided to apply to NYU. I'm almost done with
my application. Thank you for putting the thought in my
mind.

It seems like a peace offering. And though it's not nearly
enough to smooth over all that's happened, it's enough for me to

consider his suggestion. I do remember hearing Silas mention a community land trust, but I'd never asked after it in more detail.

The next day, I finally get my act together and call Chinatown Cares. Silas picks up the phone.

"Clementine! So great to hear from you. How've you been?"

"I'm sorry it's been so quiet on my end," I tell him. "I had several projects go haywire, but things are better now. How are you?"

"Well." In my mind's eye, I see him leaning back in his chair. "You've probably heard by now that most of the Hudson Street tenants have decided to stop fighting. They're going to take the buyout money and look for other options, so we're trying to support them however we can. We're helping some of the owners find new storefronts, and we're advising them in their negotiations with Kale."

"Yeah, I heard." I bat at the tassels on my window shades. The news hurts more when it's said out loud.

"It's unfortunate," said Silas. "Only Mike Mao, the gift shop owner, is still holding out, but it's much harder for one store owner to fight on his own."

"How's he doing?"

"He knows what he's up against," says Silas. "I think he's just going to try his best. Anyways, how does the news hit you, Clementine?"

I wasn't planning on saying anything, since it felt selfish to complain when it wasn't my store being lost. But as soon as Silas asks, the answer comes pouring out. "To be honest, it's frustrating to do so much work and just stop, you know? Especially since it seemed like we were finally getting traction at the rally. I would've liked to keep fighting."

"Yeah." Silas's voice is mellow, smooth like the custard of Danny's mom's egg tarts and just as soothing. "I hear ya. We get emotionally involved in these fights, and it hurts to fail. It hurts to see people move out and lose what they've built. I find it helpful to remind myself of our main purpose, which is to aid the people of Chinatown. That means supporting them in whatever choice they make. Because in the end, it's their lives. But supporting individual store owners in these situations doesn't mean that we have to stop fighting the forces that make those tough choices necessary. Building community is a marathon."

He's right, of course. I'm far enough removed from things now that I can see that. It still sucks.

"There was something I wanted to ask you about," I say. "You've mentioned that Chinatown Cares is working toward starting a community land trust, is that right?"

"Yeah." He sounds surprised that I brought it up, but pleased. "It's a perfect example of a marathon approach toward bettering our community."

"I see," I say. "I'd love to hear more about it."

CHAPTER THIRTY-FIVE

DANNY

NOT THAT I CHECK MY IN-BOX OBSESSIVELY IN THE days after I message Clementine, but . . . I kind of check it obsessively.

When there's no response that day or the next, I start to wonder. Did the form submission go through? Did she even get it? Maybe it went through but she deleted it after seeing it was from me. Or maybe she read it but found it so offensive that she deleted it afterward.

After refreshing my email for two days, I give up any pretense of not being pathetic and start checking her blog too. That's how I know, two days and sixteen hours later, when she posts something new. The post is called "A Chinatown for Chinatown Residents."

I'm so happy that people are seeing the spirit and beauty of Chinatown. At the same time, all this love gives me mixed feelings. Our community is changing. The very people who give our community its flavor are being forced out to make room for wealthier inhabitants and more lucrative businesses.

I saw this firsthand in the recent Kale Corp takeover of the Hudson Street Mall, a development that will displace all the businesses currently there, including mom-and-pops that are decades old. Though community organizations worked tirelessly with the businesses to fight the move, they ultimately did not succeed. This breaks my heart. But instead of sitting here and feeling sad, what if we rallied together to make a difference in other ways?

I want to bring your attention to a current project being pursued by the community group Chinatown Cares. Many of you are familiar with the abandoned boarding school near the old bank. It's up for sale, and Chinatown Cares would like to purchase it.

Why should you care about this? Because Chinatown Cares has an innovative plan for managing the property. Instead of selling off apartments and commercial spaces to the highest bidder, they want to form a community land trust. A board consisting of actual Chinatown residents would make decisions about how best to use the space. This means keeping residential units at an affordable price for local families. It might also mean renting commercial space to the same mom-and-pop shops that are being squeezed out of other places, or opening up a community center.

Imagine community spaces that are planned with the input of Chinatown residents. Would that be playgrounds or parks? Teahouses for afternoon mahjong or dim sum restaurants with karaoke nights? An office of multilingual resources to fully educate citizens on how to navigate our civic society?

All this is doable, but it takes money. Government assistance can get us partway there, if we can convince the right authorities to support us. Beyond that, we will need to raise substantial funds from other sources. This is where you come in. If you agree that this land trust is a fantastic idea, please consider signing our petition and contributing to the linked fundraiser.

Again, thank you for everything.

Love, Hibiscus

After watching the comments pile up on the post, it occurs to me to go check the fundraiser. That's when my jaw drops. There's already a long list of donors, and more appear when I refresh. People are putting their money where their mouth is.

That's when an email pops up from Clementine. I hesitate only a moment before opening it up.

Hey Danny,

That was a great idea. I just posted on my blog, and the response seems to be strong so far. Thank you.

Clementine

It's the first communication I've gotten from Clementine since our big fight, and I read every word several times. It's strange to be talking about *Babble Tea* with Clementine and not Hibiscus. Theoretically, I know they're the same person, but I don't think it's quite sunk in.

For the longest time, I thought Hibiscus was clueless and out of touch. Then I met her in real life and thought she was the most amazing person ever—until I didn't anymore. I suppose it's possible that Clementine really was clueless Hibiscus the whole time and I just hadn't seen it. But those new blog posts don't read like they were written by someone so out of touch.

Or maybe I've been thinking about things all wrong. Maybe my mistake was trying to put Clementine/Hibiscus in a bucket—either clueless or perfect. Maybe Clementine's just a person like anyone else, who gets some things and needs help gaining perspective on others. And maybe it was unfair of me to always be laser focused on those times she *didn't* get it. It certainly was unfair for me to punish her for them like I did.

I hit reply.

Hey,

Thanks for writing that post. You explained the land trust idea really well. I think the article's going to make a big impact.

Danny

Fifteen refreshes later:

Well, it was your idea. I just executed it.

Clementine

I could let the conversation end like this. That would be the path of least resistance. No need to risk more drama.

And yet, it doesn't feel right. I hit reply again.

Hey, I never got a chance to apo—

Too casual? I delete it and start again.

I'm sorry for . . .

Too abrupt. Delete delete delete.

I stare at my phone. *Grow a spine, Danny.*

Before I can change my mind, I dial Clementine's number and press call.

I have a full-on out-of-body experience as the phone rings. Fifteen seconds? Fifteen hours? I have no idea. I think about putting my phone down and hanging up, but I'm not sure my arm is still connected to my brain.

The phone stops ringing, and the silence that follows also has that timeless quality, like I'm suspended in some alternate reality.

Clementine's voice sounds on the other end. She sounds hesitant. Surprised.

"Danny?" I still get a thrill at the sound of her saying my name.

"Hey." This is the point where I realize I didn't exactly think this through. "Um, is this a good time?"

Another pause. "No."

My skin melts off.

She rushes on. "Sorry, I meant, 'No, I'm not busy right now.' It's a good time."

"Oh, okay." My heart gamely attempts to start beating again. It stutters a few times. I don't die. "Sorry to call you. I guess it's kind of unexpected."

"It's all right. I'm glad you called."

It's amazing how much one sentence can do to melt the tension away. My entire body relaxes. It's easier now to find the words I need.

"So I, uh . . . I never got a chance to apologize for what

happened with the trolls. For snooping around on your computer. For being Bobaboy in general. I was a jerk. I was angry about a bunch of things, and I was convinced that there was this specific type of person who was killing Chinatown. Which is silly when I think about it. But silly or not, I projected all my issues onto you. I must've made your life pretty miserable over the years."

There's another silence. My words hang there like specks of dust.

When she finally speaks again, her voice is thoughtful and subdued. "Thank you. To be fair, I could have blocked you if I'd wanted, but I never could bring myself to do it."

Now that she's mentioned it, I *have* wondered why she never blocked me. "Why not?"

She chuckles softly. The sound feels warm, as if she'd reached out and taken my hand. "Well, you earned some brownie points when you shut down that racist guy back in the day. But honestly? Part of me enjoyed our bickering. I liked the back-and-forth, and I'll hand it to you that you made some good points once in a while." She pauses. "Every once in a *long* while."

"A long while?" I muster up as much faux outrage as I'm able, though I'm smiling. "I don't think you're giving me enough credit here."

Clementine laughs full-on now, and my chest opens up at the sound.

"Fair enough, fair enough." Her voice drops. "Seriously, though, you were right. I was kind of clueless sometimes. There were many things I was ignorant about, and you helped me see them, even if it annoyed me." She pauses a moment. "So you're applying to NYU. Are you excited?"

I don't think anyone's asked me that yet, and I don't have an answer. "I guess?"

"Hmm. That eager, huh?"

I chuckle sheepishly. "I don't know. I guess I'm glad it's an option, and I mean, I *am* excited. But I also feel bad that it's the teahouse closing that finally makes me think I can do this. And when I think that Fragrant Leaves wouldn't be here when I come home for vacations, it's depressing. Maybe that doesn't make sense."

"No, it makes complete sense." She says it with such confidence that I feel it too. "You love the tea shop, but at the same time, it's totally natural to want to try something new. It's unfortunate that you were in a situation where you felt you had to choose between the restaurant and the East Coast, but it's not your fault. You don't have to feel guilty about finding a silver lining in the loss of Fragrant Leaves. It doesn't mean that you love the restaurant any less."

It's striking how she managed to put her finger on everything I was thinking, when I couldn't even untangle it myself.

"Thank you," I say.

My mom's voice drifts in from the counter area. "Danny, can you wipe down the tables?"

Her voice sends shards of reality into our little bubble. And it's ironic, because even though we were just talking about how much I love Fragrant Leaves, I suddenly wish more than any-thing that I were having this conversation somewhere else, where there are no customers and dishes clamoring for atten-tion. But if Mom is calling me from the front, it means she's pretty busy at the cashier.

"Hey, I gotta go. My mom's calling me," I say. I wonder if Clementine can hear how bummed I am about it.

"No worries," she says. She pauses again. "It's good to hear your voice."

"Good to hear yours too."

It takes me a while after hanging up to realize that I'm smil-ing at my phone.

CHAPTER THIRTY-SIX

CLEMENTINE

WHEN IT RAINS, IT POURS. SURE, I EXPECTED TO
get some signatures and a few donations, but what actually happens is beyond my wildest dreams. The donations go up and up. People share the fundraiser left and right.

A local news station contacts Hibiscus through the blog and asks for an interview. I refer them to Chinatown Cares, and Rui (who I told about my secret identity after the fundraiser went viral) tells them to interview this great student volunteer of theirs named Clementine.

A lady with a giant foam microphone and a guy with an even larger camera show up at my house and ask me questions about our work with the Hudson Street Mall. A few hours later, my parents and I gather excitedly in front of the evening news. Mom whoops as the anchor introduces our segment, and Dad cringes at the obnoxious transition music. A voice-over describes Hibiscus's viral fundraiser before cutting to an interview with Rui. Then I'm up. Mom squeezes my shoulders as I spend my entire thirty seconds of fame obsessing over how my right cheek twitches when I talk. At the very end, the newscaster plugs our fundraiser and shares the website's address.

The segment's barely ended when my phone starts buzzing.

Adenike says, *Go get 'em, girl!*

From Nadia: *Clementiiiiine. I saw you!!!!!*

Felicia simply says: *Hey, nice interview!*

And Bhramara sends: *Beautiful and eloquent as always!*

I reply quickly to each of them with thanks and heart emojis. It *is* kind of a rush to see yourself on TV.

My phone rings. It's Rui.

"Clementine!" I can imagine her wide-eyed over the phone. "Have you looked at the donations page? An anonymous donor just left a donation for ten thousand dollars."

"Wow."

"I've never seen anything like it. You're a rock star. You really are."

Rui's super nice, as always. And I know she's genuinely thrilled, but something about the conversation makes me restless. "Well, it's more the news station's doing than mine. They're the one who broadcast the details about the fundraiser."

"But it was your blog post that set it all off in the first place! Anyways, I know you want to be a journalist, but if you ever decide to pursue a future with social change organizations, I think you could really go in that direction too."

"Thanks, Rui. That's really nice of you to say."

"Well, it's true! How have you been doing, by the way? How's Danny?"

And now I feel bad. Amid all this attention, I haven't thought once about Danny.

"Danny's doing well." I remember our recent phone call and smile a little. "He's been working on college applications, I think. It was actually his idea to mention the community land trust on the blog."

"Well, you two make a great team. Say hi to him for me."

"Will do."

After we hang up, I sit silently for a while, feeling ill at ease despite a phone call that was pretty much positive in every way. I love Rui. We raised a lot of money. The land trust might indeed be a go. But everyone's focused on me and Hibiscus, when I'm not sure they should be.

I'm good at writing, and I'm good at getting ideas out there. But I'm not connected with Chinatown's citizens the way Danny is. I can't fall into easy Mandarin or Cantonese conversation with the aunties or sub for them at the mahjong table.

What I did for the community was flashy. My actions looked good on paper, and to be fair, we needed the money that it brought in. But I can't shake the feeling that it's the actions Danny and countless others take on a daily basis that keep a community going in the long run, even if it doesn't make the evening news.

My phone buzzes. It's a text from Danny.

Hey, I saw the spot on the news. That's awesome!

Speak of the devil, if the devil gave you butterflies in your stomach.

> Thanks. I think I looked kind of twitchy.

> Haha. FWIW I didn't notice any twitches.

> I should have given them your info too.

> Well, you know how devastated I am when I don't get a chance to say my piece in front of millions of people. ☺

I grin despite myself. It's nice to be joking with him again, and I appreciate him being a good sport about all this. I know him well enough now to see beyond his supposed stage fright to the selflessness underneath, his willingness to quietly help behind the scenes without seeking recognition for himself.

> Hey, don't write off a public speaking career yet. You were GOOD at that rally!

> Only cuz I had an excellent speechwriting coach.

I almost send a heart emoji in reply but scale it back to a happy face. The thread goes silent, but I'm still thinking about unsung heroes—those who don't have the microphone but put in the work day in and day out to build up the community. On a whim, I bring out my phone and open up to our newspaper's social media posts about Chinatown Cares. There's Bryan's video of Danny and me tabling in the cafeteria, a few selfies I took while canvassing door-to-door, and tons of videos and posts from rally day itself. I can't help but notice, though, that a good number of the photos are of me, Danny, or other students from our school. There are some images of store owners, but they make up about half the total, if that. It makes me wonder—what kind of message were we sending about who was important? What did it say about what we really valued? The more I think about it, the clearer it becomes what my next profile needs to be.

And so I gather my courage, pick up my phone, and make a call.

CHAPTER THIRTY-SEVEN
DANNY

OUR REGULARS HAVE SEVERAL WELL-WORN HOB-
bies: mahjong, morning tai chi, gossip . . . For a brief period of
time, they add a fourth: watching the Chinatown Cares fundraiser numbers. Every morning, aunties and uncles look up the
latest total on their phones. It becomes their preferred method
of greeting when someone walks in the door.

"Did you see, one thousand more this morning!"

"Wah! Let me look it up."

It's like they're talking about last night's football game.

At this point, it seems like the land trust acquisition is gonna
happen. They've raised enough money, and all the media attention made it a popular cause for politicians to jump on. A city
council member posted a message of support on his social media
the other day, and it racked up a whole bunch of likes.

It's great to see so many people invested in our community.
At the same time, I still wonder where all this enthusiasm was
when we were trying to get support for the mall. And I don't

think I'm the only person who thinks this. When the other store owners come by, I hear snippets of the same complaints. It's hard not to feel like a neglected stepchild.

One afternoon Mrs. Lau drops by with a flyer about a business owner meeting.

"Another one?" asks my mom.

"Because of the fundraiser," says Mrs. Lau.

I'm wiping tables nearby, and I move myself closer to eavesdrop.

". . . developing the boarding school into commercial buildings . . . ," Mrs. Lau is saying. It takes me a while to decipher the Cantonese terms for "boarding school" and "commercial buildings," and I lose track of the next few sentences. ". . . affordable rent . . . Silas says we can apply to move in."

"But when would they get it done?" asks Mom.

"Maybe Kale might delay moving in. All this publicity is bad for them."

Mom looks thoughtful. "Do you think you might try to apply?"

"Maybe."

They move on to other topics, and I sneak away to the back room. Will the land trust let Hudson Street Mall businesses have first crack at the new commercial spaces? That'd be huge. Still, the thought of the tea shop staying open doesn't make me as ecstatic as it should. Next to my computer is my pile of printed-out college application instructions. NYU is on top.

If the restaurant stays open, what would that mean for me?

I stare at the application pile for a while, but I can't space out for too long, since I have a huge physics test the next day. In a move so responsible that I surprise myself, I clear my table of everything except my physics book and my list of practice problems. No Googling, no signing on to TikTok or obsessing about the restaurant.

Naturally, my phone buzzes in my pocket. It's a text from Bryan.

> Hey, did you see the new Babble Tea post?

I guess it's Thursday, time for a new post. I type back.

> Not yet. Physics test tomorrow.

My phone gets the three typing dots.

> So . . . you probably want to read this.

I didn't realize Bryan was such a *Babble Tea* fan these days. Go figure. I guess Hibiscus has won us all over. I do plan to read the new profile, but I'm kind of in a circuit diagram zone right now, and I want to get through these practice problems before my mom calls me into the dining room.

I turn my phone over and push it to the other side of my desk. Two minutes later, it buzzes again.

And again two minutes after that.

Two minutes later, there it goes.

I growl and flip my phone over on the table. My notification screen is plastered with updates from Bryan.

> Have you read it yet?

> Really, dude, the test can wait. Trust me.

> Danny Mokkkksfdajif

Good grief. I pick up my phone.

> What are you, some 12 year old fanboy?

> When have I ever led you wrong?

> I'm running out of fingers to count with, and I haven't gotten past first grade.

> Okay okay fine. But you really want to read this.

> Fine.

I open up my phone and surf to *Babble Tea*. Just like Bryan said, there's a new post. And featured in the photo are . . . my parents.

TOBY AND POLLY MOK:
FRAGRANT LEAVES TEAHOUSE

Toby and Polly Mok met over a pot of tea.

"We were at a dim sum restaurant in Hong Kong," says Polly. "Each of us came separately with other friends, but our friends knew each other, so we all sat together at a big table."

"The friends left after a while, but Polly and I stayed all afternoon," says Toby. "Even now, when I smell chrysanthemum tea, I think of her on that day, smiling in a pretty blue dress."

This is wild, reading about my parents like this. I knew that they met at dim sum, but Dad's never told me that bit about the chrysanthemum. I keep reading.

Toby and Polly were married a year later and soon decided to try their luck in the United States. After a few years working at local restaurants, they decided to open their own teahouse.

"Tea is friendship to us," says Polly. "We wanted to make a place where people could spend time together."

Fragrant Leaves teahouse's doors officially opened 25
years ago. Despite challenges, it's become every bit the
community that Polly and Toby dreamed of. A steady
group of regulars come in every day to play mahjong
and chat.

What follows is a long list of quotes from the aunties and
uncles. There are some great descriptions of the quirkier regulars, and Clementine also touches on how much we as a
restaurant have gotten back from our customers. She even tells
the story of Uncle Tony fixing the air conditioner. I wonder why
I never saw her interview our customers, or my parents for that
matter.

After the bit about the regulars, Clementine explains the
Kale Corp takeover and protests. The following line catches
my eye.

The Moks are not sure what lies in store for them.
"Maybe we'll open the shop somewhere else. Or maybe
not," says Toby. "We're considering several options."

I'm annoyed not to know what those options are. Dad seemed
serious the night after the rally about being more open with
me, but they certainly haven't confided in me about their future
plans. But before I can wallow in grumpiness for too long, my
eye falls on the next line.

Fragrant Leaves is a big part of Toby's and Polly's lives, but it's by no means the only thing they hold dear. A few years after the Moks opened their shop, their lives changed once more when they had their son, Danny.

"We are very fortunate to have a son like Danny," says Toby. "Maybe we don't tell him that enough. He grew up in this restaurant. Even after he was old enough to spend time at home by himself, we made him stay here, because we wanted to be with him. Family is important to us, far more important than any restaurant. If we let Danny go home, we knew we would never see him. This way, we live our lives together."

The Moks are brimming with stories about Danny's childhood. Polly's face lights up as she recounts him toddling under tables and begging the waiters to give him piggyback rides. And though the restaurant was the family's home base, they did occasionally find opportunity to range farther.

Polly looks back particularly fondly on a trip to New York City. "We were there for a cousin's wedding. You know, most kids don't like the noise and pollution when they visit, but Danny was so happy. He stared wide-eyed at everything. He was obsessed with the subway and didn't want to get off! He loved the stores, the food stands. I can see him living there one day, when he's older."

Danny is now a high school senior, and the thought of him going to college leaves them a bit misty-eyed.

"It's always hard, thinking about your children growing up and starting lives of their own," says Toby. "But all parents want to see their children get their wings."

I read the profile over and over.

Growing up, being raised by your parents, you kind of assume that you're the expert on them. At least, you'd definitely know more about them than some person writing an article. But there were things in Clementine's post that I never knew before. And, I dunno, seeing Mom and Dad through someone else's eyes was . . . strange.

But most of all, I'm obsessing over that section about me. Did Mom just happen to start talking about New York, or was Clementine asking leading questions? I need to know.

We close up the restaurant on the earlier side tonight and drive home together. Dad settles onto the couch with a newspaper as Mom flips through our mail. My legs take me automatically to my room, where I take off my backpack. But I can't bring myself to close the door, and I don't want to sit down.

I know what I would usually do. Usually, I'd keep my questions to myself. I'd try to puzzle out my parents' inner thought lives—by myself. I'd convince myself that I know what they're thinking, and then I'd move on with my day. But all that no longer feels like the rock-solid life strategy it used to be.

So I turn around. Those ten steps back to the living room are the hardest ten steps I've ever taken.

Mom looks up from a grocery mailer. Next to her is a slowly growing pile of coupons she wants to keep.

"I saw the article about you guys on *Babble Tea*," I say.

Mom's eyes brighten. "Ah yes! Clementine, such good writer! Did she interview you too?"

"No, just you." I don't want to talk about Clementine's interview process, though, so I keep going. "There was something I was wondering."

Dad puts down his newspaper and peers at me over his reading glasses. "What do you want to know?"

I take a deep breath. "So that part about . . ."

The New York trip. I should just ask about the New York trip.

The grocery mailer bounces in Mom's hand. "The part about what?"

"The part about your future plans for Fragrant Leaves. I was wondering what you were planning."

Well, I did want to know about that too.

"Ah yes." Dad seems to take my question in stride. I sense no caginess or disapproval. "We've been thinking about it. Maybe you heard that there will be new commercial spaces opening up in the land trust purchase. We could try to open up there."

The way Dad says it, though—he doesn't sound very serious about that possibility.

"Do you think you will?" I ask.

Dad brushes back a lock of his salt-and-pepper hair. "I don't know." His voice is thoughtful, sober but not necessarily unhappy. "We've been doing the teahouse for a long time. It's taken a lot of our lives and our energy, and sometimes we think we might want to try something new. I have a friend in Taiwan. He runs tours of tea plantations, and he wants me to partner with him to bring in tourists from the United States."

There's excitement in his voice when he says the last part, and I totally get it, because the idea excites me too. Those trips that Dad used to take, the ones that we loved so much . . . I feel a buzz at the thought of them happening again.

I look at Mom. "Would you do it too?"

She shakes her head. "No, just Dad, but I'm also thinking about other things. Silas called me the other day. They're talking about turning part of that boarding school into a community center. He knew we weren't sure about opening the teahouse again, and he wanted to know if I want to be involved with the center instead."

"But none of this is for sure," Dad adds. "Maybe we might still reopen the restaurant."

"I see." I'm surprised at how easy it was to get information out of them. Maybe they're serious about being more up-front with me from now on. "It . . . helps me to know these things. I know you don't like to share this stuff with me sometimes, but it really does make me feel better to know what you're planning. Even if the plans aren't concrete yet, or if they might not turn out well."

Mom and Dad share a look. It's a long one, and I feel like they're having a whole conversation with their eyes. Finally, Mom draws a deep breath. "You're right, Danny. We haven't shared much with you in the past. We had many reasons we didn't, and not all of them were good ones. Part of it was that we wanted to protect you." Mom pauses here, and Dad gives her an encouraging nod. She smiles wistfully. "But to be honest, part of it was also that it's hard to talk to your child about times when you're failing. Your dad and I need to remind ourselves that we can't shield you from the world's disappointments. We need to remember that you're growing up now. Growing up very nicely."

I blink at the prickling behind my eyelids. "I don't think you failed. I think you built something wonderful."

And now Mom's wiping at the corners of her eyes. She crosses the room and wraps me in a tight hug. "Someday," she whispers, "you will have kids of your own, and you will understand how much it means to hear words like that from your son."

I squeeze her tight, breathing in her familiar smell, the residue of flour and sugar and tea that I've always associated with her. I hear footsteps on the carpet, and Dad rubs my back, his callused fingers catching every so often on my T-shirt.

After a long moment, we let go. Dad gives me one last pat. "We will try to be more open with you, Danny," he says gently.

"But under one condition."

I clear the roughness from my throat. "What's that?"

His eyes sparkle. "You need to be more open with us too," he says. "You've been standing there this whole time, looking like you want to say something big. But you haven't said it yet, have you?"

Now I feel kind of sheepish. I guess I'm not as much of a mystery as I thought. But I find now that I'm ready to ask. "I saw that you mentioned our New York trip in the article."

Mom claps her hands together. "Yes! Fun memories, right?"

"I was surprised you remembered that I liked it."

Mom laughs. "Of course I did. Your eyes were so big! Like cookies!" She holds her thumbs and index fingers apart to indicate just how big and then mimes begging with her palms together. "And after we came back home, you begged us every day for a month, 'Can we pleeeaase move to New York?'"

Dad nods in amusement. "We're your parents. Of course we notice."

The way they're acting now, the fact that they've noticed . . . Even so, the next words take all the courage I can muster.

"So it's funny that you guys mentioned New York, because I'm thinking about applying to colleges there."

Mom nods encouragingly. "That's a good idea. Uncle Charlie can help you get settled there if you go."

She's so matter-of-fact about it that it kind of stops me. "Are— are you sure? 'Cause if you start up the teahouse again . . ."

Dad holds up his hand. "Danny, you carry too much worry

on yourself. It's like I said in the article. We keep you in the restaurant because we want to see you every day, not because we need you to work there."

"Of course," says Mom, "if you're around, you might as well help out." Her shrug is peak Asian mom, but then she turns serious. "But I know at times, when things have been very busy, we've put more on you than we should, and I am sorry for that. You are a very good son, Danny, and it was too easy to just let you help."

Dad lays a hand on my shoulder. "But that doesn't mean it's what we want for you," he says. "Don't worry about us. We have a lot of choices. Remember, we got along fine for many years before you were born."

Mom finger brushes my hair. And though it falls out of place the moment she takes her hand away, she still looks at me like I'm the best thing she's ever seen.

"You are our son," she says. "It is our joy and our responsibility to see you successfully out into the world. We want you to become the person you're meant to be."

CHAPTER THIRTY-EIGHT

CLEMENTINE

I FEEL A LOT MORE VISIBLE AROUND SCHOOL IN
the days following the TV interview. People stop me in the halls
to say they saw me on the news. *Babble Tea*'s readership goes
up too, and I recognize several new commenters from school.
Hopefully they don't recognize me as Hibiscus, though.

The day after the Fragrant Leaves profile goes live is a prime
reminder of why I prefer to blog anonymously. I have no idea
how Danny will react to the post, and I'm absolutely terrified
about running into him at school. Back when I was writing the
article, it somehow made sense not to let Danny know I was
interviewing his parents and his customers. It was no small
feat conducting all the interviews in times and places where he
wasn't around. Of course, I overlooked the key weakness to that
plan, which was that Danny would eventually see the article no
matter what.

"Well, it's too late for regrets," I tell Adenike as we walk
down the hall between classes. "I'm here. He's presumably also

here. If we see each other, we see each other."

Adenike hands me another Starburst. Maybe she's being supportive, but mostly I think she's just trying to shut me up. She's been on the receiving end of my anxious babble all morning.

"You know you'll have to face him eventually, right?" she says. "It probably won't be that bad. I mean, it was a nice article."

"You seem more optimistic about Danny these days. Weren't you offering to take out a hit on him a few weeks back?"

"Well, I only have what you say to go on, but Danny doesn't seem to be quite as evil recently, and hit men are expensive. I guess it feels like you two still have some issues to iron out."

We round the corner. "Speak of the devil," I mutter.

There he is, in that corner locker bay with Bryan. He's usually not there at this time of day, or I would have taken the long way to history class instead. Along with a full-body adrenaline rush at the sight of Danny, I feel a wistful twinge in my chest. I've missed him.

Next to me, Adenike slows.

"Why are you slowing down?" I mutter.

"Oh, am I slowing?" she asks amiably as she lags farther.

I tilt forward, trying to get her to speed up by sheer force of will. But then Danny looks in my direction, and our eyes meet. This time, the jolt that hits me stops me in my tracks. He looks good. His shoulders fill out his dark-gray T-shirt, and his hair is slightly messy but still cute. There's a lightness to him that's new since the last time I saw him. Danny's lips twitch a bit—the hint of a smile.

"Hey Clementine." Bryan says my name at least twice as loudly as he needs to. "And Adenike."

Well, I can't exactly walk on by now. Adenike trails behind me as I approach the locker bay. Danny straightens as I get closer. He's holding a book in his hand, which adds some distracting definition to his biceps.

"Hey," I say to him.

"Hey." He pushes his hair back from his forehead, where it reluctantly stays put.

It takes me a moment to come up with my next words. "How are you?"

"All right."

Belatedly, I realize I'm not including Bryan in this conversation at all, or Adenike for that matter. But it seems impossible to bring them in right now. For all intents and purposes, Danny and I are in a bubble. Everything else is fuzzy.

"I saw your newest blog post," Danny says.

"Oh yeah," I say in a rush. "I hope it was okay. I'm sorry I never—"

"No, it was great," he says. "Thank you." His face softens. "After reading it, I ended up talking to my parents about colleges on the East Coast. They're excited about me going out there."

"Really?" A genuine smile wells up. "That's amazing."

He smiles back. The mirth in his eyes warms me. "Yeah, it really is."

For a moment, nobody says anything. And then I remember Bryan and Adenike watching us. Once again, I'm aware of all the kids streaming down the hall to their next class.

Danny blinks too, as if suddenly remembering where he is. "So I guess I'll see you around?" he asks.

I deflate at his words, which is silly. It's not as if I thought he'd sweep me up and ride off into the sunset. "Yeah, definitely," I say, putting on my most agreeable face. "I'll see you around."

I'm in a trance as we walk off. Adenike waits until we're out of earshot before speaking. "You all right? Should I check your vitals? I knew I should have paid more attention when my parents did these kinds of things." She reaches for my wrist and feels for my pulse.

I shake her away. "I'm okay! That went better than expected."

"Yeah," she agrees. "It was actually quite benign."

"I dunno." I wipe my sweaty palms on my jeans. My hands feel empty without a Starburst wrapper to torture, but she's not offering any more. "Maybe Danny and I can be friends again after a while." Even as I say that, my heart sinks a little bit.

Adenike gives me a sidelong glance. "Are you having any second thoughts about writing that profile of his parents?"

"Second thoughts?" I look at her. "Not at all. I'm glad I did."

"Good." She gets a sly expression on her face. "Speaking of articles, I finally talked to my parents about applying to journalism programs."

I clap my hands, simultaneously thrilled and feeling like the worst friend ever for not asking about it sooner. "That's great! What did they think?"

Adenike twirls one of her braids around her finger. "They

were nervous about my job prospects, but they were a lot more receptive to it than I expected. It helped my case that your blog has been getting all this news coverage these days. So I could make a point about how words can make a difference."

I bear-hug tackle her from the side. Luckily for both of us, she manages to regain her balance before we both plow into a thumbtack-studded bulletin board.

"Oh, Nike," I say. "The only thing that boosted your case was your long list of awards and the actual journalism professors knocking down your door to study at their programs. That said, I would gladly write a hundred blog posts if it helped you become the investigative journalist I know you can be."

She laughs. "Would they all be as anxiety inducing as the last one?"

I grimace. "That might be a bit much, huh?"

She nudges me with her hip. "Probably. I'm running out of Starbursts."

CHAPTER THIRTY-NINE
DANNY

BRYAN LOOKS AT ME LIKE I'VE LOST MY MIND.
"'I'll see you around'??"

"What?" I'm the picture of nonchalance as I go back to my locker and eye the books on the shelf. My English book is sandwiched between the taller math and physics textbooks. That won't do at all. I switch their position so they're ordered by height. Or maybe I should sort them by color. . . .

Bryan's footsteps stop right behind me. "Did you seriously just say, 'I'll see you around'?"

"What's wrong with that?" Yup, color's the way to go. Maybe light to dark. . . .

"Nothing. Nothing at all, if you're trying to get through life as lonely and companionless as possible." He pushes his way into my line of sight. I frown. Bryan's not a bad-looking dude, but there are other faces I'd prefer to look at up close and personal. "You liked the article, right?" he asks.

I give up and look him in the eye. "Yeah. It was really good."

"So . . ." Bryan drags out that syllable so long, I worry he'll keel over. "You're going to do something, right? 'Cause it'd be pretty pathetic if you don't."

"Thanks, bro. Really tactful there."

"I'm serious. They give prizes from obscure European academies for bad judgment of that caliber."

He shakes his head and starts pacing the locker bay, making a big show of peering underneath all the lockers.

"What are you doing now?"

"Looking for your stones, in case they fell off somewhere close by."

"Good grief. I'm gonna do something. I just— It's complicated. Give me some time to figure it out."

He kicks a dust bunny into the corner. "Just buy her a box of chocolates or something."

"I don't think she's into chocolates."

Suddenly, he stops. When he turns around, Bryan's face has an expression of sympathy usually reserved for lost puppies or overly tight jockstraps. "Well, that's a bummer. If only there was some way to figure out what she's into. Like, if only she'd spent the last few years of her life writing blog article after blog article about her obsessions. . . ."

I stare at him. "I can't tell if you're a genius, or if I'm just exceptionally clueless."

"Don't think too much about that question, man. You wouldn't like the answer."

CHAPTER FORTY

CLEMENTINE

I HAVE GRAND PLANS FOR THIS SATURDAY, AND they all involve doing absolutely nothing. Comments are still trickling in on the Fragrant Leaves profile, along with the occasional reshare. Even though they're overwhelmingly positive, I'm still feeling the need to step away from the internet for a while. I want to go an entire morning in a quiet room without anyone looking at me or expecting a response from me, in person or online. I want to spend the entire day in my room with a sheet mask between me and the world.

I stretch the sheet mask routine for as long as I can. I even do cucumbers over my eyes and play some New Agey music. After a while, though, I get restless and opt for some nutrition-free television. There's this K-drama my mom's been obsessed with about a boy band that gets lost in a time warp. I load it up and settle in with three scoops of ice cream. The boy band members are cute in that K-pop way, and their personalities appear to ping-pong between supermodel and tortured soul.

The earnest yet conflicted lead singer with the golden voice is stepping up for his big concert moment when our phone rings. It's the apartment landline that nobody calls except for the front desk downstairs. My parents aren't picking up, so I pause the show and run to answer.

It's Luke, the security guard. His voice sounds distant through the receiver. "Delivery for Clementine Chan."

I rack my brain, trying to remember what I might have ordered. I'm tempted to head downstairs in my pajamas but decide that my standards haven't sunk quite that low. Instead, I throw on some yoga pants and a tank top. At least my face is silky smooth from that sheet mask.

Luke's leaning back in his chair with a John Grisham paperback in one hand and his feet propped up on the security desk. He waves me over and gestures at the delivery in front of him. It's the bottom half of a box, like something you might get from a takeout line at a burger place. There's no logo, though. In the middle stands a plain paper cup overflowing with a frothy drink.

"Are you sure it's for me?" I ask. "I didn't order any food."

"Clementine Chan," says Luke. "The young man said it loud and clear."

Do I have a fast-food stalker? "Did he look like a serial killer, by any chance?"

"He looked normal enough to me, but you never know with serial killers. They really run the gamut." Right. I forgot that Luke is big into true crime and will talk your ear off about cold cases with any provocation.

The drink itself is like nothing I've seen before. The top is piled with whipped cream and sprinkles, and there's a maraschino cherry on top. It looks almost like a Frappuccino, but it doesn't smell like coffee. There's a hint of cinnamon, but it's not a pumpkin spice drink.

That's when I see the card tucked inside the box. It's homemade and not incredibly artistic, with words written out in plain block letters. A smile tugs at my lips.

"You gonna drink it?" Luke looks pretty invested in my answer. His book is now propped open, facedown, on his desk.

"Yeah, I think so."

It really should come with a straw. I get whipped cream on my nose and both cheeks. And that's when I see Danny come around the corner. I jump at the sight of him, which results in more whipped topping on my face Danny's eyes flicker from the drink to the cream on my nose. His grin is just the slightest bit evil. "Hey," he says.

I try to play it cool. "Hey yourself."

There's really no way to surreptitiously wipe whipped cream off your face, so I don't even attempt to be discreet. The cream leaves my skin sticky, and for a moment I consider licking my hand like a cat and giving my cheek a good scrubbing.

"How does it taste?" Danny asks.

I hadn't much registered the taste, honestly. But I do have a lingering impression of clashing flavors that should never exist in the same place at the same time. I lick what's left of the whipped cream off my lips and shrug apologetically. "Maybe not my favorite?"

Danny's eyes linger just the slightest bit on my lips before he turns to the drink box. He picks up the card inside and runs his fingers over the words: *Mocha Iced Oolong Cinnamon Latte.*

"I kinda like it," he says with the air of someone admitting an addiction to daytime soaps or chia pets.

I screw up my face. "Really?"

That crooked smile can still make my stomach do a flip-flop. "Maybe a tad less cinnamon," he says.

Luke clears his throat. "I'm gonna head out for a cigarette break."

He winks quite obviously as he leaves. The elevator across the lobby dings and a distracted woman in a suit strides out, eyes fixed on her phone. She goes out the front door, and then the lobby's empty.

For a moment, neither of us says anything. Danny runs his fingers through his hair, causing it to stick up like a bird's nest. My fingers itch to smooth it down.

He chuckles, which makes that dimple on the bottom left corner of his mouth appear. My heart squeezes. "You know, when I saw your flyer up on the bulletin board all those months ago," he says, "I don't know what I expected, but I'm pretty sure I didn't expect to end up here."

I laugh. "Well, when Bobaboy left his first annoying comment, I didn't expect things to end up this way either."

"Oh . . . speaking of Bobaboy . . ." Danny grimaces. "I heard that he met an untimely demise. Run over by a truck."

I raise an eyebrow. "A truck?"

"A boba truck. It was an ugly sight. Milk tea everywhere. Boba pearls clogging the sewage drains. Streets flooded with tea."

"Oh, well . . ." I bite the inside of my cheek to keep from smiling. "That does sound pretty bad. Should I send flowers?"

He nods toward the drink in my hand. "Send one of these."

I take another sip, then make a face. "I think I'm done with this."

He shoots a glance at the cup. "I'm tempted to finish it up for you."

"Be my guest."

Danny shuffles his feet. "But . . ." He glances up at me in a way that manages to be both sheepish and debonair at the same time. "I do want to kiss you too, and drinking that might decrease the chances of that happening."

That's all the reason I need to put my monstrosity of a drink on the security desk. From there, it's only a couple steps to wrap my arms tightly around Danny's waist. He smells like newly roasted oolong. His lips, when they meet mine, are like warm milk tea.

"You smell like nutmeg," he says after a while.

"Well, that's your own fault."

Danny lets out a tragic sigh. "Well, as much as I love that drink I invented, I'm kind of in the mood for something else. Care to join me for a pot of some *good* tea?"

I purse my lips. "I do know this one tea shop. Fantastic traditional tea. Great place for old-people watching. They're closing
soon, though, so we better get our fill while we can."

Danny tilts his head, mulling it over. "Sounds like a nice
place. Lead the way."

And so we clasp hands and step out into Chinatown.

Acknowledgments

Clementine and Danny was a new genre for me and very creatively refreshing. I learned a great deal while writing it, both in terms of craft and real-world insight.

First of all, shout-out and gratitude to my agent, Jim McCarthy, who was the first person to think that maybe I could write a contemporary rom-com.

Huge thanks to Jennifer Ung, editor extraordinaire, whose vision, insight, and positivity carried this project to its full potential. And whose smiley animal photos always gave her editorial letters that extra sparkle.

Publishing takes a village these days, and I'm grateful to the entire HarperCollins team, including but not limited to: Rosemary Brosnan, Suzanne Murphy, and Jean McGinley for their leadership. Celina Sun for her behind-the-scenes help as Jen's assistant. Designer Kathy Lam and cover artist Peijin Yang for making this book so visually stunning. Caitlin Lonning and Sona Vogel for painstakingly checking all my timeline, grammar, and consistency details. James Neel for production. Lisa Calcasola, Patty Rosati, Andrea Pappenheimer, and the Harper sales team for connecting this book with readers. And last but not least, Tara Feehan and Laura Raps for handling contracts and finances.

There is much in this story that was outside of my personal life experience. Thankfully, many generous people were willing to take the time to help me learn. I'm incredibly grateful to Chinatown Community for Equitable Development (CCED) in Los Angeles, who welcomed me as a volunteer and answered my questions about community organizing. Special thanks to Patrick Chen and Sophat Phea for their kindness and generosity.

Michelle Yip-Yang graciously took the time to talk to me about her experience growing up in a family-owned restaurant and provided many useful insights into Danny's psyche. Many thanks as well to Kunle Adeyemo for sharing about Nigerian and Nigerian American culture.

Writing is a solitary process, and I'm grateful to many writing groups for friendship and emotional support, especially the ladies of Courtyard Critiques, Fantasy on Friday, and The Trifecta.

As always, I'm thankful to my family. My ever-supportive and long-suffering husband, Jeff, for weathering the pandemic with me. My daughter, who's slowly giving me more time to write these days. My parents for their constant support (and willingness to babysit). And my in-laws for their never-ending enthusiasm.